/

To
my dear
friend Karen

Thank you for your support
over the years!
I hope your enjoy
the read.

Irresistible Impulse

Irresistible Impulse

A Novel By
Joe Lester

Joewolf Publishers
Editorial and Sales Office
Joewolf Publishers
P.O. Box 80127
Conyers GA 30013
jjoewolf@aol.com
770-922-6655

Cover design by Camille Garick
www.cordovafineart.com

Editing and interior layout by Arlene Robinson
BettyBoopWrites@aol.com

Prologue

New York City

Where the hell is he? Stephanie tapped her Blahnik pump against the table leg and glanced around the crowded club again. Still no Klaxton. When he telephoned her, he was near tears. "Angie's freaking out again," he'd whispered. "I just told her I got a page to go to the hospital. I have to talk to somebody. Please?"

There was no way she'd say no. Three years before, Dr. Klaxton Staples was convicted of killing her best friend. Stephanie believed in his innocence, and said so. Yet she had paid a price. Forced to testify at the trial, Stephanie's name and face were all over the papers, and every TV broadcast, too. After that, there was no way she could keep the same lifestyle she and Cheryl were used to. In their business, a woman might be the hottest thing on two heels, but if word got out that she was bad news, no man wanted to be seen with her. So it had been tough since Cheryl died. Very tough.

But now, things were about to change. She just knew it. At least Klaxton didn't judge her for what she did to make money. Every time she visited him in jail, he told her how grateful he was. When she heard that he won his appeal, she knew he'd come around at some point. When he called, all upset, she was glad to meet him at the Blue Note in an hour. But that was at six o'clock. She got here at seven, and now it was nearly eight.

She took another sip of Crown Royal and reflected on her options ... which were somewhere between none and none. She still had some of the things the last brother gave her. Nice things. *Sparkly* things. But lately, she had more stuff at the pawnshop than in her jewelry box. Tonight, she needed cash. Cash for rent. Her car note was due. And these Blahniks, fine as they were, weren't going to last much longer.

Before he went to jail, Klaxton always seemed to have plenty of money. And Klaxton owed her, big-time. Not so much for what she'd said in his defense, but what she didn't say. If he didn't have money tonight, Stephanie would just make a little investment in her near future. It was the least he could do. And she shouldn't have to sleep with him to get it. Uh, uh. She'd already done enough to get a nice paycheck.

"Sorry!"

She whirled around to see a breathless Klaxton fly around her table. He pulled out the chair opposite hers.

"*Really* sorry I'm late," he gasped. Klaxton's handsome chocolate forehead glistened with sweat, and he reached up to wipe it away as he lowered himself into the chair. A worried frown creased his face and stayed there. "Angie didn't believe me about the page. I didn't even dare to call you on your cell. I *swear* I think she's got mine bugged."

Stephanie signaled the server and gave Klaxton a smile. "Well, you're here now. What do you want to drink?"

"Riesling," He pulled his flip phone from his jacket and turned it off. Stephanie noticed that, as he did, his hand shook.

The instant the server left, she gave him another bright smile and reached up to smooth the bodice of the low-cut, midnight blue dress. Knowing his favorite color was blue, she'd chosen it just for him. "So, what's going on with you?" she said. "I was glad to hear you got out last week. And ... this might sound crazy," another smile, this one come-hither, "but it sure looks like prison life agreed with you."

"Yeah, maybe," Klaxton said, and his chuckle sounded empty. "But it sure does feel good to be a free man. It was great my first few days out. Got a decent haircut, some new threads. And Angie and I made love nonstop for the first two days! But now I can't leave her sight without getting the third degree."

He stopped and leaned back in the chair, looking beaten. "My practice is dead and buried. Been in a coma since the trial, and it's still got 'Do Not Resuscitate' written all over it. My patients went to the other partners in the practice, and hardly any of them are coming back.... I checked. That's why Angie didn't believe me when I told her I had an emergency. She knows I don't have any patients. It's ... It's like I was always guilty, and I'm *still* guilty."

"You've been exonerated in a court of *law*," Stephanie said, her brown eyes clouding with empathy. No matter how much his admission about his failed practice disappointed her, no matter how desperate she was for money right now, she knew he'd gotten a bad rap from the justice system.

He took a deep, ragged breath, blew it out. "Makes no difference. I'm telling you, there's no future here for me. That's why we're heading south. Atlanta's supposed to be the mecca for black people anyway. Angie's always wanted to move there 'cause she hates the cold weather. I didn't want to leave New York. Still don't. But it looks like that's our best shot—go down there and start clean."

Stephanie jerked her eyes away from his and fought the sudden lump in her throat. "Oh? I love Atlanta. Great party town. Had a couple of gigs when they had the Super Bowl there. Could've had a full-time situation, too. But ... Cheryl didn't want to go with me."

Klaxton's wine came, and he drank most of it down in one long swig. "How have *you* been?"

She shrugged. "Good, I guess. Been through a couple more guys. Same-old, same-old. They love you, then they leave you, or vice versa. Then you move on."

Then she looked at him, and saw tears. Her voice soft, she said, "Ah, speaking of Cheryl—"

His eyes hardened. "Let's not. How about I buy you a nice steak? You like it still bleedin', right? And we need another drink, too. Waiter!"

∞

Several drinks later, Stephanie vaguely remembered them staggering into a taxi. It was daylight now, and the morning sun slithered in through the Roman shades across from her bed. Klaxton snored gently beside her, curled into a ball with the top sheet wrapped around him.

Her aching head dropped back onto the pillow. *Oh, hell. What have I gotten myself into? And what's the use? He's leaving anyway!*

One

Fighting to catch her breath, Stephanie pulled the gold satin sheet over the soft curves of her body, glad once more that she had followed Klaxton to Atlanta. It wasn't so much the steady flow of cash he provided her, but the things he did for her that money couldn't buy.

Klaxton wasn't a murderer, like that first jury had said. Stephanie never doubted his innocence. Yet her attraction for him was much more than what he wasn't. Klaxton Staples was a passionate lover with a wild, confident energy. When he and Cheryl were together, Stephanie forced herself not to notice his sexual charisma. But now, she understood why Cheryl found him so irresistible ... and so hard to let go.

On the other hand, he was a hard catch. But that didn't matter, not now. Sure, he was married. But in the past few months, she realized that her relationship with Klaxton was more than a business investment. Much more. She'd never known love, never wanted to. Until now.

She allowed her mind to roll over the idea of feeling this way forever.

After a moment, Klaxton leaned over and whispered in her ear, "Baby, as hard as it is for me to leave you lying here looking so sexy, I gotta get going."

Stephanie's smile collapsed. "I ... I thought you didn't have to go into the office today. That's why I changed my schedule. For *you*." She sighed. "Sometimes I wonder if you appreciate what I go through to be with you."

Scowling, Klaxton rose from the king-sized bed, retrieved his pager from the dresser and sat back down, buying time to think. After three years in a New York prison, his conviction was overturned. Cheryl's family put up a squawk when they learned of it, but he was free ... and intended to stay that way. Now, nearly a thousand miles away, it was like he wandered around in a dream, and when he woke up, he'd find out that it really *had* been a dream. And from the signs Stephanie was giving him lately, he was locked into another deadly nightmare—one where he could lose his wife and his career again. He couldn't risk that. If Angie found out that Stephanie had followed them to Atlanta, every good thing in his new life would be ruined.

He wasn't really worried that Stephanie would tell Angie about them. Toward the end, Cheryl had threatened, but Stephanie actually helped him talk her out of it. Yet as long as he and Stephanie kept seeing each other, there was always a risk she could turn stupid, too.

It has to end. And it has to end today. If things went well today, he and Angie would have their own medical practice again—their second opportunity to become entrepreneurs, experience the American dream. No more working for the temp service or HMO. No more listening to a medical administrator reminding him how grateful he should be to even *have* a job. No more being afraid that someone would find out about Stephanie. With his incarceration fully behind him and self-employed again, he would truly be free.

The relationship with Stephanie had been a risky mistake. But he could fix it. He *would* fix it.

"Look, Stephanie," he said, pulling away from her warmth, "I told you from the beginning, I got one wife at home already. Don't ruin a good day with some crazy-ass talk, all right?"

"Baby, you know I'm not trying to do that," she said, her voice rising. "I … I just don't want you to go yet."

When he turned away from her, Stephanie knew she'd crossed a line. She moved closer, allowing her breast to brush against the small of his back while she stroked his hair. "I, of all people, know how seriously you take your work. Kiss and make up?"

Klaxton wanted to smile but his muscles wouldn't cooperate. He really didn't have time for an argument, but he had to do something. She'd been Cheryl's friend, and after Cheryl's death, their attraction was more sentimental than physical. But it hadn't taken long for their shared memories to evolve into something more. For Stephanie, at least. Even so, his urgency to end things wasn't from any one thing Stephanie had said or done. Just little things, like the way she was acting this morning. But Klaxton knew in his gut that this was heading in the wrong direction.

This has to be the last time. He tried to force himself to believe it. But again, he couldn't find the will. With a rueful half-smile, he leaned back and softly kissed her earlobe. "Yeah, kiss and make up. Who could stay mad at a woman like you?" Klaxton had to admit that if he had one weakness, it was his inability to resist attractive women. It was never about love; he just needed them. Just needed them somehow.

∞

While Klaxton showered, Stephanie lay back on the bed, covered herself with the satin sheet and decided to leave well enough alone.

They'd been brought together by Cheryl's murder. In her mind, that set their bond apart. She still remembered the chill of excitement the first time she spotted him at the Blue Note—not on the prowl, just unwinding after a hard night. The downtown Manhattan nightspot was a favorite of black professionals—the type of place where everyone wore a suit and carried a business card regardless of the need for either. The dance floor was usually empty; most patrons spent their time sipping expensive drinks rather than partying. In that, Klaxton Staples was the typical regular, sitting alone at a tiny two-top, a chocolate-brown man with warm, sparkling black eyes, low-cropped hair, Armani blazer and gold cufflinks. Stephanie had watched him strumming his fingers in time to the music as he nursed his drink.

As it turned out, Cheryl saw him first, and had already staked out her claim. Stephanie teased the lily-white Cheryl about her attraction to men of color, but her friend laughed it off, saying, "Handsome men are a dime a dozen. But there's something about that one. Has nothing to do with the color of his skin." Later, Stephanie agreed with her.

It was Cheryl who had loved Klaxton first. With Cheryl dead, only his wife stood in Stephanie's way now.

Stephanie considered herself an independent woman, a free spirit, but when Klaxton and Angie moved to Atlanta, she followed. Klaxton hadn't been exactly happy when she arranged to bump into him outside the clinic where he'd been assigned. But when she started working her sensual allure on him, he'd been unable to break away. When money started rolling in from his new job, he made good on his promise to take care of her. Now, his sudden ambivalence worried her.

Klaxton reentered the room, the water droplets he'd missed while drying off still clinging to his muscular thighs. As he pulled his slacks on and fastened them, she drew herself to a sitting position. "Klaxton, can I ask you something?"

"Baby, can it wait 'til later? I really have to go." His pager beeped and he grabbed it off the bed.

"It's just that ... I thought it would be different for us when we got away from New York."

Us? Stunned, Klaxton let out an I'm-not-in-the-mood-for-this-right-now sigh, eased his feet into the Italian kid loafers he'd left near the side of the bed, then moved to the mirror to straighten his tie. "Different? How did you think it would be different? You knew I was a married man." He reached for his coat, hung neatly over the Cardio Glide next to the dresser.

Stephanie pulled in a long breath. "Klaxton, I'm always here for you. Whether it's for a midday quickie or a midnight rendezvous after you take care of an emergency at the hospital. My world *revolves* around you. Yes, I know you're married, but it doesn't mean I have to like it. Am I just supposed to just sit back and—"

He'd thought reason would work, but her tone of voice told him otherwise. And he *had* to make that meeting. "Don't take it there," he said. "I appreciate what you've done for me, but ... *we* didn't come here. There is no *us!* You followed me here on your own. You're a grown-assed woman who made her own choices."

She didn't reply.

A moment later, he picked up his briefcase, put his hand on the doorknob and turned to face her. "I'll make this one real easy for you. You're not the only one who's been thinking around here. And what I've been thinking is ... why don't I just take care of your rent for the next few months, and after that, you're on your own. Consider the car and the clothes a consolation prize." He put the briefcase down, reached in his jacket pocket and pulled out his checkbook.

"Why would you *say* something like that?" Her eyes darted from the checkbook to his face. "Tell me you didn't mean it."

Klaxton remained stone-faced as he withdrew a pen and began writing.

"All I did was ask you one simple little question," she said, "and you and your selfish ego took and blew it all out of context." Still clutching the gold sheet to her chest, she sat up straighter. "Have I ever asked you to get a divorce? Have I *ever* asked you to stop seeing other women? No. Why? Because we have an understanding, and I *thought* we cared about each other."

No answer came from him, and her desperation grew. "When you were in jail," she said, "you told me the loyalty I showed you, you could never repay. You promised me you'd always be there for me. And I trusted you. I *trusted* you!"

He stopped writing and glared at her, hoping she couldn't see his terror at what she'd just said. "You've lost your ever-loving mind. Sure, I was thankful for what you did for me. Still am. But ... promising to take care of you *forever*? No way, no how!"

He finished writing the check and tossed it on the table next to the bed, then reached down for his briefcase. "I'll leave this money right here, since that's where you're used to getting it."

"You bastard! You *bastard!*"

Klaxton got through the door just seconds before the heavy crystal vase shattered on the other side. He could still hear her calling him every name under the sun as he strode to the apartment's front door.

∞

Stephanie wanted to race after him, beg him to come back. Instead, she forced herself to calm down. She couldn't let the unknown—her future with Klaxton Staples—overwhelm her.

He didn't mean it, she thought as she dabbed at her eyes with the soft sheet. *I know he loves me. It's just a matter of time.* Her beautiful brown eyes narrowed. *He can't dump me. I won't let him.*

∞

Klaxton parked the black SL500 Mercedes convertible in the parking lot of the medical complex just minutes before his scheduled appointment. The fall morning was crisp and clear, he was on time, and his shoulders felt lighter than they'd felt in months.

The drive had helped clear his thoughts. Allowing Stephanie to move to Atlanta had been a mistake. Lately, all they'd done was fight. The lovemaking afterward was great. But now it was clear that she had developed visions of marriage, complete with two kids and dog. Well, he wasn't available for that. The only common interest they shared was the bedroom. If she didn't want to accept that, that was her problem.

He entered the building and was immediately ushered into a richly furnished office. "Dr. Fry?" he asked.

The smiling man behind the desk shook Klaxton's hand. "The one and only. And you must be Dr. Staples."

"Call me Klaxton."

"I'm Joe. Please, have a seat."

Nodding, Klaxton slipped easily into one of two wine-red leather visitor's chairs; Joe moved from behind his desk and settled into the other one. Only slightly shorter than Klaxton's six feet, and with flecks of gray just beginning to show in his goatee, it was clear to Klaxton that the older man held authority wherever he went.

Klaxton cast an appreciative glance around the office. "This is nice. I haven't seen African art of this quality since New York."

Joe nodded as he followed Klaxton's gaze. "Unfortunately, I don't get a chance to spend as much time here as I thought I would. The ladies up front stack my appointment book like pancakes at IHOP on a Sunday morning."

Klaxton grinned. "I hear what you're saying, but it sounds good to me. As I'm sure the leasing agent told you, my wife and I are leaving the HMO. Definitely ready to get our own practices up and running."

"I hope I can help you out," Joe replied. In his eagerness to buy the two-story building in Atlanta's tony Buckhead community, he'd underestimated the difficulty of attracting enough tenants to cover the hefty mortgage payment. At first, things seemed to go well. Joe's first tenant, a young pharmacist from Texas, was a fortuitous find. But Joe still needed to fill the two vacant spaces upstairs, and quickly. And the current prospect called out "success" in every sense of the word.

"I really understand what it's like to make the jump you're about to make," Joe said conversationally. "I worked as the medical director of a minimum-security prison for six years, but after a while—"

The intercom on his desk buzzed, and Joe reached out to answer it.

"Dr. Fry. You forgot to sign off on Mrs. Stilwell's record."

"I'll take care of it as soon as Dr. Staples and I are finished, Vickie," he replied. "In the meantime, please hold any calls that aren't urgent." He clicked off the intercom and smiled at Klaxton. "That's Vickie Renfroe. Excellent receptionist, but impatient at times. She's still young."

As Klaxton and he continued chatting, Joe observed him more closely, seeing in better detail his neutral-color Armani suit. Joe's much less expensive wardrobe, including the dark gray suit he wore today, suffered from the typical neglect of an older bachelor who dressed himself. Fortunately, the white jacket of the working physician covered most inadequacies.

Klaxton cleared his throat and said, "As you know, the leasing agent showed the office suite to Angie and me last week. I can go ahead and tell you that it's our first choice."

The realtor had called the previous day with the good news, but Joe still had to hold back his sigh of relief. "I'm glad you were pleased," he said. "So, you think it will do for both your practices?"

Klaxton nodded. "The location is excellent. The size is just right, too. I'm a family practitioner, Angie's an ob-gyn. I think the space will work for us."

"Sounds like you two make an excellent team."

Klaxton accepted the compliment with a smile. "I like to think so. Angie was a little concerned about her pregnant patients. But once she saw the elevator, it was a go. That will make it easier on my pediatric patients too. The in-house pharmacy's a nice extra. So, if all is well with you, I think we can draw up the papers."

"That we can do, my man," Joe said, fighting to keep the exultation out of his voice as he extended his hand. "I'll have my attorney deliver the lease for your signatures tomorrow. By the way," he asked on impulse, "do you golf?"

Klaxton smiled and glanced at Joe's putter in the corner. "I took it up last year so I wouldn't get drummed out of the profession. But I don't get out as often as I'd like."

"Maybe I can treat you to a round at my club this weekend."

"Can't this weekend," Klaxton said, annoyance shadowing his face. "Angie and I are having a party Saturday night, and she's got me running around all day tomorrow to get it together." His face brightened. "Hey, why don't you come over Saturday, help us break in the new house *and* celebrate our new partnership at the same time? I'm sure Angie would love to meet you and your wife."

Joe nodded. "I just might take you up on that. But ... I'm a single man these days. Okay if I come alone?"

"Why not invite your staff?" Klaxton offered. "And if you decide to come alone, that's okay too." He rose from the chair. "I'll leave the directions with your receptionist."

"Hang on a second. I'll get Vickie to show you out by the private entrance." To Klaxton's confused look, Joe explained, "That's the way most of us come in and out of the building."

∞

In the reception area, Joe greeted Vickie, then formally introduced her to Klaxton. "Well, Klaxton," he finished, "welcome aboard. And convey my regards to your wife, too. I'm looking forward to meeting her. Oh, and, what's the dress code for Saturday?"

"Man, just come casual. We're just going to lay out a nice spread, put on a little '70s music, throw some bones down and probably play some bid whist. Nothing fancy."

Vickie rose from her chair and waved her hand toward the back of the office. "Down this hall, Dr. Staples."

With a final nod and smile at Joe, Klaxton followed her.

He stepped in front of her and Vickie smiled, noting that the view from the rear was every bit as nice as from the front.

They reached the back entrance, but when Klaxton tried the door, it wouldn't open. "Sorry, Dr. Staples," Vickie said. "I have to deactivate the alarm to let you out. Just a little security measure ... sometimes we work late. The cleaning lady's here at night, too."

"Oh," Klaxton said. "Thanks. And oh, I need to leave directions to our house for Dr. Fry."

While Vickie fumbled at the keypad inputting the code, Klaxton used the nearby counter to write directions to his house. He slid the piece of paper along to her, unable to help noticing the way her dress hugged her curves. "You and the rest of the staff are invited, too."

"That's very kind of you," she said, holding the door open to let him through. "And I think you and your wife will like this area. The patients are great, and there are plenty of nice places for lunch around here." She smiled, letting her eyes linger on his. "I'm not sure if I can make it Saturday, but I'll try."

Klaxton stepped out of the door, calling, "Thanks for seeing me out. I'll see you soon." *And I sure am looking forward to seeing more of you.*

The unbidden thought made him scowl as he made his way to the parking lot.

∞

Whew! Vickie's knees had almost buckled at the thought of seeing that fine broth'a on a daily basis. But his wife was probably a real looker, too; that's the way it usually worked. If she saw a good-looking man, she believed it was okay to let him know. But when the wife was involved ... *and* in the workplace ... it was a bad idea to let nature take its course.

It's not gonna be easy, though, she thought. Still, maybe she *would* stop by the party Saturday night on the way to her weekend job at the club. *No harm in paying a courtesy call at the invitation of the newest tenant, is there?* The thought made her smile.

Trying to regain her professional demeanor, Vickie straightened her uniform and headed back to her desk.

Two

Klaxton shook his head and smiled as he pressed the button to unlock the Mercedes. The woman who just flirted with him was beautiful. And he got a nice little vibe back from her, too. But he'd been down that path before—in fact, had taken the off-ramp from that road this very morning. He'd be a fool to travel it again, especially with someone who'd be working in the same building with him and Angie.

On the other hand, he mused, adjusting the rearview mirror and snapping the seatbelt closed, *she sure is fine. And there's no harm in looking, is there?*

He started the car and backed out of the parking space. Smiling, he recalled his father joking, "Women are like streetcars, son. Another one comes along every five minutes." Klaxton was only a little kid then. Now, all grown-up, he understood just what his father was talking about.

Even so, he would never consider leaving his wife. He loved her. And Angie not only loved him, but *needed* him. She was vulnerable in a way Klaxton still didn't understand after all their years together. She was a strong woman, but submissive about certain things: where to live, how to manage their finances, which side of town to locate their medical practice. These were all Klaxton's decisions by default, and Angie assented without complaint. She didn't have to. Angie was an educated woman who could pay her own way. But she always deferred to him in these traditionally male bailiwicks. That—Angie's reliance on him—was the real reason he'd finally summoned the courage to break it off with Stephanie that morning.

It was heartening to see Angie so happy these days. He'd fought against the move from New York, but for once, Angie had held her ground, and with good reason. Even if he didn't want to admit it, his Big Apple lifestyle before Cheryl's murder put a strain on their marriage. The fast-paced life of the city—especially those high-rolling midday stock-trading parties that took him away from his medical practice far too often—precipitated the need for a major realignment in Klaxton's priorities. On some level, perhaps more than one, maybe Angie knew it, too.

The move to Atlanta was Angie's attempt to get him away from the intoxicating drama of a city where people never slept. He understood that. Yet he'd fought it because he didn't want to give up that rush. Even two years after the move, he still missed it. Missed it bad.

The light at the corner changed, creating an opening ahead of him, and he jumped on it, pulling smoothly into the heavy flow of traffic on Peachtree Street.

He and Angie had met as residents fresh out of medical school. Their paths crossed after they returned to their native New York, at the dinner her father's cardiology practice threw to court some of the highest-achieving residents in the city. From that moment, there was electricity between them. Two and a half years later, Angie became Angela Bowen-Staples.

Not without conflict, though. Her upbringing had been nothing like his. *Her* parents had wanted a child, and planned accordingly. And Angie's wealthy parents provided her with the best of everything. Klaxton envied that. After his parents, then his grandmother died, he'd grown up in a series of foster homes, and rarely knew what it was like to feel cared for and wanted. But somehow, he'd managed to get into college, and then medical school.

And then, there was Angie's father to deal with. When Klaxton appeared, fresh out of medical school without a dime to his name, Klaxton quickly figured out that Dr. Bowen had groomed his only child to take over his prestigious cardiology practice and the family's wealth someday. Dr. Bowen looked at his future son-in-law as a threat to that plan, and reacted accordingly.

By the time Dr. Bowen retired, it had all come to a head. Normally a people-pleaser, Angie's decision to specialize in women's health was a blow to the well-known cardiologist. Their battle raged fiercely … further aggravated when she brought Klaxton home, and later announced their intent to marry. Yet after Dr. Bowen saw that Angie was determined to follow through on the marriage, he grudgingly accepted Klaxton.

Klaxton swerved to avoid a pothole, bringing him in direct line with the blaze of the afternoon sun. "Damn!" he said, screwing his eyes almost shut. "Where'd *that* come from?" Though only a weak October sun, nothing like the overpowering radiance of an August sun in New York, the glare was still enough to give him the beginnings of a headache. He was glad he was almost home.

No matter how much charm he possessed, Klaxton still had to work hard to impress Dr. Bowen. He got points by refusing to take money from the old man to help them start their private practices. Klaxton knew they could make a good living on their own. Until Cheryl Jaworski died, they had.

His pager beeped, and he drew it out of his jacket pocket, glanced at the readout and pressed the button for OnStar, his newest toy. The volume on the CD player immediately went down as he commanded, "Dial hospital." The page was about a young asthma patient he was treating through the temp service; the boy was back in the emergency room. He punched in the code for the charge nurse at the ER. After hearing the boy's vital signs, Klaxton barked, "Run a blood gas and get him on oxygen. I'll be there in ten minutes."

Watching for potholes, Klaxton made a U-turn and pushed the Mercedes toward Crawford Long Hospital just a few blocks away.

Three

Like many beautiful women, Angie Bowen-Staples took her looks for granted. Even at thirty-six, the mirror showed the taut body of a dancer or model. She took good care of it. Her skin, the color of a paper sack, glistened with the expensive moisturizer she had applied after her shower. In the flickering light of the scented candle on the table by the mirror, she could see that everything was still right where it was supposed to be. If only she could appraise her marriage with such ease, and with such encouraging results, she thought with a sigh.

Angie was never sure why she and Klaxton had so much trouble talking about the big issues in their lives. If they disagreed, he'd go silent, and if she asked him what was wrong, he'd just shrug his shoulders and say, "I'm straight." Maybe it was because of his rough childhood. She couldn't imagine growing up in foster care. The very thought made her shiver.

She wasn't blameless, either. Why did she hide her emotions from him? Why did she stay in a marriage that was broken by infidelity? Why did she tolerate a man who controlled her the way her father had? Her mother had put up with that, and Angie hated seeing her mom suffer. Angie blamed that stress on her mother's early death from a stroke. So why was she accepting the same terms in her own marriage?

Angie had prayed that their move to Atlanta would be a fresh start, but more and more, it looked like the only thing different was the scenery.

After a moment, she jerked herself out of that mindset. *Enough navel-gazing, girl. You better at least be dressed by the time the caterer arrives. And the flowers and candles aren't going to place themselves!*

She walked over to her country French lingerie chest to pick out color-coordinated lingerie for the Thai silk, cobalt-blue sari wrap she was wearing tonight. And earrings—maybe the sapphire and diamond studs. She fit them onto her earlobes, then inspected her party up-do in the hand mirror. With rare luck for a Saturday, Angie had finished her work at the OB clinic shortly after noon, said goodbye to her coworkers, and even had time to grab lunch before her two o'clock appointment at Montrease's World of Curls and Books.

This is my last time working on a Saturday, she thought, and smiled. Now, except for emergencies or deliveries, her weekends would belong to her again, to spend with her husband.

The thought made her smile—and then, her pager went off.

She sighed again, wondering if she'd forgotten to sign off on a chart in her hurry to finish her last day with the HMO.

But the number on the display was good news. Holding an ice-blue lace camisole in one hand, she grabbed the cordless phone and punched in a number. When she heard the click and "Hello," she said, "Hey, girl, what's up?"

Laughter greeted her, followed by, "Hey, Angie, where've you been? I've been trying to chase you down for the past two hours!"

"Girl, trying to see patients, make my hair appointment on time, pick out an outfit for tonight and figure what I'm going to eat to hold me over has taken a *toll* on me. You?"

Angie listened to the good-natured ribbing on the other end, reflecting on her first meeting with Ashley Heath, soon after she and Klaxton moved to Atlanta. She and Ashley were under adjacent hairdryers at Montrease's the first time Angie went there. Although Angie was a transplanted New Yorker, Ashley an Atlanta native, and one married and one single, they took to one another instantly. Angie's introverted style meshed well with Ashley's outgoing, almost brash demeanor. If Ashley didn't hear from her for a couple of days, she didn't hesitate to track Angie down. And Angie was pleasantly surprised to find that she liked being sought out that way.

"I actually just called to see what time the party starts," Ashley finished, "and if you need me to come early to help out."

"Thanks for the offer, but I think we're in good shape," Angie replied. "Klaxton hired a caterer, and he's going to do the grilling himself. All I have to do is the little fun last-minute stuff. Anyway, girl," Angie added, teasing, "I already told you three times that it starts at nine o'clock. I swear, you'd forget your head if it wasn't attached to your neck. How do you remember all those precedents from law school?"

Ashley's specialty was entertainment law, and she was proud of it. "That's where the money is in Atlanta," she confided to Angie once. "All those big-time athletes, singers and actors living here don't want to have to fly to California every time they sign a contract."

"Well, why don't you snag one a' them big-time celebs for yourself?" Angie had asked.

Remembering that, Angie felt a surge of anxiety. "Ashley ... Ash, I *do* need you to come over early tonight."

"You just said you had a fancy caterer," Ashley reminded her.

"Yes we *do* have a caterer, but I ... I need someone to help me get *myself* together. Klaxton invited some people he just met—from the Atlanta City Council, I think. And I want to look good. I ... I just need someone here to help me make sure everything goes just right. You know ... cross the t's and dot the i's?"

"Okay, woman, I got your back," Ashley said. "I'll be there at eight. By the way, did I tell you I was bringing a friend? He's playing tonight, but the game will be over before the party starts."

"Playing? Playing what?" Angie asked.

"Hockey. He's with the Thrashers." The answer dribbled out like cold molasses.

"Well, I guess there's no need in asking if he's black or white," Angie teased.

"Whatever. Look, I don't tell you what's best for you in your relationship ... *not that you'd listen anyway* ... so do me a favor and return that courtesy. It's not like you haven't known, *since you met me*, that that I don't waste my time with brothers. All black men are good for is heartache and headache."

"Ashley," Angie said patiently, "I was only kidding. And stop generalizing. All black men aren't dogs. There are plenty of successful black men out there."

"Success is *not* the issue. Dependability and trustworthiness are. Anyway, I *said* he's just a friend."

Angie knew this wasn't like Ashley. Ashley Heath, attorney at law, didn't sweat the small stuff. But trying to change Ashley's mind about something was like trying to move a mountain with a shovel and a wheelbarrow, and Angie wasn't about to try that right now.

"Calm down. You win!" Angie said. "Besides, it ain't that big a deal. Tell your *friend* I'm looking forward to meeting him."

Angie's pager buzzed again, and this time the number on the display caused her light mood to evaporate. "Let me run. My pager's going off and it's the hospital."

"Okay, Angie. See you at eight. Call me if anything changes, okay?"

The second Ashley disconnected, Angie hit the automatic dial on her phone for the hospital maternity ward. "This is Dr. Bowen-Staples, returning a page."

"Yes, Dr. Staples," said Myra Anderson, the chief OB nurse at St. Joseph's Hospital. "We have one of your patients, Gwen Johnson, and she's dilated."

"Gwen Johnson's not due for weeks," Angie replied. "How many centimeters?"

"She's at two, but this one's moving fast."

Angie knew she could rely on the nurse's assessment, and the patient did have a history of quick labors. But not early ones. Grimacing, she said, "I hate to tell you this, Myra, but as of one o'clock today, I'm no longer with the HMO. And," Angie sighed, "the InstaCare corporate office was supposed to have notified you *weeks* ago that Dr. Jeffries is taking over my patients."

"Jeffries?" She heard Myra groan. "He's on vacation until Monday. I can't believe this! We've got a woman who could deliver a preemie any minute, and she doesn't have a doctor! What's wrong with the HMOs?"

Angie felt as panicked as Myra sounded, but replied calmly. "Myra, that's one reason I'm not with them anymore."

"Please don't hang up! I've got to check with them to find out what to do."

Angie waited for Myra to return, staring at the burning candle, trying to center her thoughts.

But it wasn't Myra's voice that came back. "Sorry to keep you waiting, Dr. Staples," the smooth voice said. "Apparently there was a glitch in the processing of your termination. According to our Atlanta database, you're on call through the weekend. Your replacement isn't scheduled to start until Monday. Sorry, Doctor, but this baby is all yours—literally!"

Fighting to keep her voice even, Angie said, "You know, in just about any other situation, I'd tell you to stuff it. But unlike *your organization*, I put the needs of patients first."

She pressed the button to cut the voice off before it could start dribbling any bureaucratic nonsense at her, then threw on a pair of jeans and a t-shirt, praying for a quick and easy delivery. With another sigh, she grabbed up her medical bag, blew out the candle, and raced out of the bedroom.

Four

"Damn, she's always late," Klaxton grumbled. He checked his watch. Angie's message had said she would be back in time for the party. But here it was, 9:36, and no sign of her—not even another phone call with a new ETA.

He couldn't help grinning, though, when he passed through the dining room and saw the golden-brown barbecued chicken and ribs in the middle of the sumptuous buffet of salads, appetizers and gourmet desserts. The catering company provided the chicken and ribs, but Klaxton used his own special marinade and indirect-heat barbecuing technique to bring them to bronzed perfection. It took a little longer, but it was worth the wait.

He was glad for the mild weather, too. In Georgia, October could be warm or cold, depending on the unpredictable climate's mood. But even if there'd been a snowstorm, he would have still been outside, giving the grill its first trial.

He still wasn't happy with the way the evening was going. Around six, when he'd just laid the first batch of ribs on the cooker, the phone rang in the kitchen. He didn't make it in time, though, and had to hear the bad news via voice mail: "Sweetheart, the patient's labor is going fast. I'll be there by eight, I promise." Now, it was almost ten o'clock. What could have happened?

"Klaxton, it's about time you made your way down here!"

Wincing at the brassy voice he recognized, Klaxton stepped through the door and headed toward Ashley. As he walked, he glanced down toward the patio's lower level, where the music and dancing were getting started. When he reached her, Ashley grimaced and rolled her eyes. He attempted to match her coldness with a frown; even so, he couldn't resist giving her the once-over. Ashley Heath got on his nerves with her tough-girl attitude, but she was easy on the eyes, no doubt about it.

He forced himself to admit that part of his frustration with Ashley was really with himself. Given all the time she and Angie spent gabbing, he figured Ashley knew about the affair with Cheryl. Sure, Klaxton had been more discreet in Atlanta, and he'd been extra-careful not to look too long at Ashley, given she was Angie's best friend. But her frosty demeanor told him that she likely knew about New York.

"What are you frowning about?" Ashley asked.

"Just about my wife, who's gonna miss her own party," he replied.

"Look, she *said* she'd be here as soon as she could," Ashley scolded him. "So get off her back."

"Whatever. But she should have made sure she was covered. This is the first party in our new home. But I guess all I can do is wait." He gave her a mean smile. "Hey, who's that guy you came stepping in here with? He's a little *pale*, ain't he?"

His attempt to distract Ashley failed, just as he knew it would. "Don't go there, Klaxton! Don't take your problems with Angie out in attitude with me."

"Sorry," he mumbled.

"And—not that it's any of your business," she hissed, "but Richard's *not* my date. He's a client. Even if he wasn't, it's still none of your damn business." Only her love for Angie made her say the next words: "I'll take Angie's place till she gets here. I'm sure I can keep this party jumping 'til then."

"Thanks, Ashley," he muttered, and made a beeline for the lower patio before she could respond.

Despite appearances, Klaxton was happy at that moment. This was part of the life he missed so much. The house and patio were packed with happy people, and the night would only get better—with or without his wife. The catering staff was placing shrimp cocktails on the upper patio table, and the show on the lower patio was just beginning.

Klaxton watched as the disc jockey stopped the music blaring from the two huge speakers and announced, "Ladies and gentlemen, put your hands together for the good doctors for inviting us all out to their lovely home to show us how they do it in The Big Apple." Applause erupted as the distinguished voice of George Clinton chimed in with "The Atomic Dog."

Klaxton followed the music for a while, but his reverie was interrupted by a voice behind him—a voice he recognized.

"Hello, Vickie," he said, turning, trying not to gasp at the nearly frontless black silk number she wore. She'd obviously already been to the bar—maybe two or three times. "My wife's been detained on an emergency call," he added. "She'll be here shortly. Glad you could make it." He stuck his hand out to shake hers, but she grabbed it and put it around her waist.

"So you gonna dance with a sister, or just stand there with your mouth open?"

Watchful for a sign of Ashley, Klaxton led Vickie to the dance area, hoping his moves appeared more innocent than his thoughts.

"Nice house you have here, Dr. Staples," Vickie said over the music. "This place is big enough to put my apartment in umpteen times!"

"Thanks," Klaxton replied, trying to sound neutral while he and Vickie exchanged a few more pleasantries. The second the music stopped, he disengaged himself, said, "Thanks for the dance," and headed back up to the patio outside the kitchen. But he didn't quite make it there. By the French doors, a commotion was beginning to attract a crowd.

Straining to see over people's heads, he saw a furious Ashley, holding the kitchen phone's receiver in one hand and using the other hand to shake her finger at someone standing just outside the doors.

"You got a lot of nerve, slut!" Ashley was yelling. "I heard everything you just said. How you got the nerve to come in another woman's house, pick up her phone, and say some mess like that to her about her man? Get your sorry ass out of here!"

The object of the tongue-lashing backed away from Ashley. In doing so, she turned toward where Klaxton was standing.

"Stephanie?" Klaxton muttered. "What the hell?"

But before he could move, or even think, she was gone.

Dreading it, Klaxton walked over to where Ashley stood, breathing raggedly. "What's going on?"

"You tell me, Klaxton," she demanded, but waved him off before he could answer. "Your *wife* just called. She'll be here any minute. And I can't wait! You ain't about shit ... just another educated thug in a high-priced suit!"

"I—"

She waggled a red-tipped finger in his face. "I suggest you and that ... that Miz *Thang* you were sniffing behind clean up y'all's act, *joker*. You're already in enough trouble."

She stomped off, and Klaxton knew she was right. He was in trouble, and had no idea how to get out of it.

∞

About the time Vickie was grabbing Klaxton's hand for a spin to the music, her boss was maneuvering his SUV down the street of stately homes, squinting at house numbers. While Ashley was expelling the interloper inside, he was squeezing into a small space in a line of cars extending several blocks from the Staples' home. Joe Fry was also running late because of a patient emergency, but one that had only required him to examine the patient, then refer him to the on-call surgeon.

Clearly, Joe hadn't missed the party, he decided as he ran his eyes up and down the street jammed with cars. *Nice cars,* he noted. Mercedes, Beamers and an occasional Jaguar flanked the Staples' house like loyal servants paying obeisance to their sovereign. The brightly lit circular driveway stood out from the houses around it. Something else set it apart, too. The architect must have liked medieval England, because he had surely designed a castle. The tall, gray stucco walls were a series of massive, well-balanced cylinders topped with turrets. As he walked toward it, Joe almost expected to see a moat with a drawbridge. Instead, he saw a predictable set of double doors with a lighted doorbell.

But before he could ring the bell, the door flew open and a tall, tawny-skinned woman reeking of alcohol barreled out, almost knocking him down. She paused for an instant, turned and incongruously said, "Fine, thanks," as if responding to an old friend who had inquired after her health.

After watching her scratch off in a dented silver Honda, Joe stepped through the door and joined the party.

∞

Stephanie put the Accord into gear and eased out of the tight parking space. Coming to the house had been risky, but what did she have to lose? She had no idea who that man had been, but he looked important. A sudden chuckle escaped her lips. *I should'a offered to go down on him. If he was someone close to Klaxton, that would'a been perfect!* But she was angry, and drunk, and starting to feel woozy, and she needed to get herself home.

The fear on Klaxton's face when he recognized her was more than she hoped for. And she hoped he was getting hell right now. Regardless, her mission was complete. She had revealed herself on the phone to Angie as Klaxton's mistress, and let Klaxton know about it too. Her work was done. All she had to do was sit back and wait for him to come crawling after Angie threw him out. And if he didn't, she still had a card left to play.

Five

The atmosphere inside the house was charged, and the energy came from both the thumping, screaming music and the din of conversations among guests in various states of intoxication. It took Joe a while to get to the kitchen, but he eventually found it by following one of the catering staff's pointing fingers. Klaxton wasn't in there, so Joe made his way to the lower patio, where he saw his host standing alone. When he got within earshot, Joe said, "Nice party, Doc. Sorry I'm late."

Klaxton whirled around, grabbed Joe's shoulder with one hand and shook his hand with the other. "Oh, the party's just getting started," he replied. "Glad you could make it."

"Did any of my staff make it over?" Joe asked, wondering why Klaxton seemed so tense. "I shared your invitation with them."

"Yes, as a matter of fact, I did see your receptionist. Vickie made her entrance about an hour ago. She's, ah ... quite a girl."

Hoping it wasn't Vickie who'd caused Klaxton's uneasiness, Joe gave him a quick smile. "We had a really crazy week. I'm glad you gave us this opportunity to come over and blow off some steam."

Over the crowd noises and bass beats, he heard a woman squeal, "Girl, where have you *been?*"

Joe looked up to see two women embracing. One of them, looking exhausted and wearing hospital scrubs, smiled as she answered the other's question, speaking loud enough for those nearby to hear. "Long night at the baby-factory. An emergency C-section, and a preemie to boot. What a night!"

Klaxton looked at Joe. "Like I said, my wife's a workaholic."

Joe smiled in commiseration, and Klaxton led him over to introduce them.

Klaxton kissed Angie's cheek and asked, "I thought you were all wrapped up at InstaCare, baby. What happened?"

"Three letters ... H– M– O." As she spoke, she took Ashley's arm and drew both of them nearer to the two men. "Their records got messed up, which means I'm on call until tomorrow night at midnight."

The two men nodded sympathetically, and Angie gave Klaxton a pointed look.

"Excuse me," Klaxton said, turning to Joe. "Dr. Fry, I'd like you to meet my better half, Dr. Angie Bowen-Staples."

Extending her arm gracefully, Angie smiled. "Nice to meet you, Dr. Fry. My husband and I are looking forward to working with you. Thanks for coming tonight."

Joe shook her hand. "It's a pleasure, and please, call me Joe. I'm really happy you and Klaxton decided to lease the space."

Klaxton turned to Angie. "Come on, let me fix you a plate. You must be starved."

"Just give me a minute to change and I'll be right there."

"I'll help you," Ashley piped up, narrowing her eyes at Klaxton.

Angie glanced into the dining room, then peered down at the lower patio. "Klaxton, you forgot the candles! You knew I wanted them out!"

Klaxton winced. In his zeal to fire up the new grill, he'd forgotten to put candles on the tables. "Sorry honey, I know how special they are to you. Go on and get changed. I'll take care of it."

She gave him a forgiving smile and kissed his cheek. "I'll be right back."

∞

While Ashley helped Angie get dressed, she filled her in on Stephanie's intrusion. "I can't believe that bitch had the nerve to say all that stuff to you on *your own phone!*"

Tired as she was, Angie felt a violent wrenching in the pit of her stomach—an all-too-familiar sensation. "Hey, it's okay, Ashley," she managed. "I know you took care of it ... probably better than I could have."

Ashley finished fastening the peacock-blue sari over her friend's shoulder. "How can you be so casual about another woman claiming she's slept with your husband? I heard what that bitch said to you on the phone—and if I hadn't paid a fortune for the dress I'm wearing tonight, I would have kicked that heifer's ass."

Now, Angie was glad she'd never told Ashley about New York. If she had, her friend's rage might have spilled over into far worse. Unable to look directly at Ashley, Angie did a final check in the mirror, then took a step toward the bedroom door. "Ashley, can you just let it go? I don't know what that woman's reasons were, but she was lying. I'm sure of it. And I don't want some lying, jealous whore ruining our party. I ... I'll handle it later, okay?"

When Ashley didn't reply, she stopped turned around, a plea in her tired eyes. "I need you to do this for me. *Please.*"

Ashley didn't want to let it drop. But a house full of strangers waited downstairs. She sighed. "Damn, Angie, I can't believe the stuff you take off that niggah."

Arms linked, they headed downstairs, each lost in thought.

∞

When Ashley and Angie reemerged, they found Joe and Klaxton sitting on the patio.

"Klaxton, I thought you'd be dancing," Angie said, giving his shoulder an affectionate squeeze. "I hope you aren't boring our new landlord with all that Dow Jones/NASDAQ garbage."

"Actually," he said, grinning, "I was just telling the good doctor here what a lucky man I am."

Klaxton's comment put a scowl on Ashley's face, but she forced herself to be nice. "I guess it's time to slow the music and turn up the lights, huh?" she said in a friendly tone she didn't feel. "Gotta be able to see all that good food you cooked, eh, Klaxton?"

Joe watched Ashley as the women talked. Ashley Heath had the looks, the chic and the saucy attitude that likely made her irresistible to every man she met. The shimmering midnight blue dress she wore hugged her curves just right, and her short, tapered hairstyle with burnished highlights gave her a young, yet sophisticated and professional look. She was gorgeous, he decided. A little sassy. But she intrigued him. And he felt drawn to her in a way he hadn't been drawn to a woman in a long time.

Not entirely comfortable with the feeling, he excused himself and headed toward the bar for a refill. His ploy didn't work; Angie and Ashley followed, and he heard Angie telling the object of his interest, "Let's get this party started."

Ashley giggled and gave Angie a high five in the self-assured way beautiful women have, then turned to the bar. "Bartender, could you please get us something good to drink?"

"Certainly. What can I get for the pretty ladies?"

Ashley ordered coconut rum with pineapple juice; Angie went for a glass of Riesling.

"And for you, sir?" the bartender asked Joe.

"Molson Ice, my good man," Joe replied, still gazing at Ashley, who was now talking to a tall, athletic-looking white man who'd just staggered up to the bar.

While not a hockey fan, Joe made an effort to follow the local teams, so he recognized Ashley's companion, who was towering above him. Richard Perry was one of the best goalies in the National Hockey League, and his acquisition by the Atlanta Thrashers several years ago had been major sports news. Pricey, too, from what Joe could recall. Afterward, Perry had also made his share of news, both on and off the court.

Joe introduced himself, then added, "Enjoyed that game against Hartford last week. You sure got some attention in the third period, didn't you?"

"True," Perry replied, slurring the word a little. "Unfortunately, it's what happens *after* the game that usually gets the most attention." He let go of the bar to shake Joe's proffered hand, but lost his balance and had to quickly replace his hand on the bar to keep from falling against it.

Joe made no reply. On the ice, Richard Perry was poetry in motion, and Joe supposed that was more important anyway.

Perry accepted a drink from the bartender and began lapping it down with exaggerated concentration. Seeing his chance, Joe made a courteous withdrawal to a corner near the dance area.

The DJ's voice boomed over the microphone. "Let's keep this party going! Set it off on the left, y'all. Set it off on the right, y'all. Set it off!"

People began to clap and chant along. Angie waved at Klaxton and said seductively, "Whatcha gonna do?"

He slid off his brown cashmere blazer and tossed the jacket on a chair, strutted behind Angie to the middle of the floor and yelled, "It's our party, let's turn this motha' out!"

Joe turned to Ashley, but before he could ask her to dance, he heard a voice say, "Let's go, Boss!" Vickie grabbed his arm and began dragging him toward the floor.

Joe was stunned at the change in Vickie's appearance. In street clothes, she looked a lot different from the demure young receptionist he saw at work every day.

"Come on, Dr. Fry, show me some of them old-man moves you got," she challenged.

"Who you calling an old man?" he shot back, grinning. "Look out."

He noticed Klaxton and Angie on the dance floor, leading the rest of the dancers in the Bus Stop. His grin widened. "Are you too young to remember this?" he asked Vickie as he dipped, made a half-turn, and bounced three steps backward in time with the other dancers.

"Ha! I was *born* at a bus stop," she replied. "Let me see you get down like this." Like a ballerina, she bent over, whirled around and swung so close to his crotch that he instinctively pulled back, looking like a kid learning to roller-skate.

He managed to keep up with her, but when the music changed to slow, he took it as his cue to escape. "Thanks, Vickie. I had no idea you were such a dancer. Old man that I am, I'm going to sit this one out."

"Dancing's in my blood, Dr. Fry, just like my singing." She tossed her hair and rolled her shoulder to the beat of the music. "But for a dude in his 50s, you're not so bad yourself."

Joe's laugh was easy. "Hey, watch out, young lady. I may look old to you, but I'm still way under half a century ... forty-three and holding."

When he reached his observation post, listening to the slow groove and still catching his breath, he felt a presence beside him and looked over. Ashley Heath was standing next to him, smiling.

"Dr. Fry, I know we haven't been formally introduced, but I was hoping you wouldn't mind giving me a hand with some house-keeping." She held out a garbage bag half filled with beer bottles.

This was the opportunity Joe had been waiting for. He checked on Vickie's twenty; she'd drifted off and was talking to man across the dance floor. With Vickie at a safe distance, he turned back to Ashley. "I'd be pleased to help. Let me take that, Ashley. It's Ashley, right?"

"It is, Dr. Fry, and thanks," Ashley said. "Klaxton and Angie will bless us in the morning."

"Please, call me Joe. And I should be thanking *you*. It's a pleasure just to be in the presence of such a beautiful lady."

Ashley smiled. "Are you enjoying yourself?"

"Yeah, it ... it's a nice party."

While Joe was trying to think of another comment to keep the conversation going, Ashley looked over at Vickie, in motion on the dance floor again, and said, "You need to put a short chain on that receptionist of yours. That girl is hotter than a red chili pepper."

"She's young," he answered quickly. "And people can be as different as night and day when they're drinking."

Ashley gave a snuffling laugh. "She seemed sober enough earlier tonight when she was pawing Klaxton." She stopped herself and took a deep breath. "Well, maybe she *was* a little tipsy. I'm just protective of Angie. You're right, though. Alcohol seems to give people the courage to do what they're too smart to do without it." Her gaze went to the other side of the room, where her date was leaning drunkenly over another female who looked equally intoxicated.

Joe followed her gaze with sympathy. "Yes, people do seem to get courageous when they're drinking. But I've probably known Vickie for about as long as you've known Klaxton and Angie, and I really don't think she meant any harm."

Ashley shrugged. "Maybe so." She pulled another trash bag from a box under her arm. "Let's go and grab some more bottles. Maybe we'll even put 'em down long enough to do a little dancing."

"I'd like that," Joe said, and followed her, marveling at how much fun a party could be. He had almost forgotten.

Six

Joe's SUV was packed into the long line of luxury vehicles on the street like the biggest sardine in the can. Being careful not to collide with the $60,000 Jaguar hugging his back bumper, he eased the big Cadillac forward and backward, turning the wheel a hair each time, until he was able to break clear of the Porsche Boxster in front of him and headed to Atlanta's West End. "Okay for you," he muttered to the Porsche's unseen owner, "but hey, mine's paid for at least."

Light traffic and pleasant thoughts of Ashley made for a quick ride home, yet other, older memories still clung like dark clouds in his consciousness. In less time than it had taken him to escape the crush of parked cars at the Staples' Northside home, Joe pulled into his driveway.

He climbed the porch stairs in darkness, and chided himself for continually forgetting to replace the blown bulb in the porch's light fixture. "That's what bachelor life will do to you," he groused, and resolved to take care of the chore the very next day. He was always careful, but he worried about his live-in housekeeper losing her footing in the dark. At Mrs. Caldwell's age, a fall could be serious.

Bachelor life did other things, too. Inside the house, he could find his way around even if every light bulb was blown. There was no danger of stubbing a toe on shifted-around furniture, either. Without a wife or children, there was no one to move anything around. And Mrs. Caldwell was obsessive about putting things back where they belonged. No matter how often he left things awry, he could count on them being straightened out right away.

He asked her about it one day not long after she'd come to work for him, when he saw her dusting a vase. She had just dusted the table it normally sat on, and he noticed she placed the vase on the table, peered at it with grave concern, then shifted it slightly. It looked fine to Joe, but apparently not to her; she repeated the same procedure. After the fourth or fifth cycle of that, he had to know what was going on.

"When the spirits of the dead come to visit," she had said, "it upsets them to find things different from when they left. That, Dr. Fry, is when they start to cause trouble."

"Well, I'll never have to worry about angry spirits as long as you clean my house," he'd joked.

But in spite of his teasing, he and she were more alike than he wanted to admit. Joe had seen some things in his house that he hadn't been able to explain. Not by conventional reasoning, anyway. Occasionally, he found some things moved in his bedroom—sometimes a book, sometimes his robe. But a couple of times, something happened that would probably have scared even the most entrenched sinner straight.

It was before Mrs. Caldwell came to work for him, and after a hard day of rounds at the hospital. He had discarded his jacket on the bedroom chair, then went into the bathroom to run water for a long soak. He turned on both of the huge antique bathtub's taps, then left the room. He wasn't worried; it would only take a couple of minutes to run downstairs to grab a beer from the fridge. Impulsive by nature, he'd started to read the mail and forgot he left the water running. When he rushed back upstairs, expecting a flood, he found that the faucet had been turned off—just before the tub would have overflowed.

Another time, he'd known something was wrong the instant he entered the room. His bathroom was white ... all white. But now, the wall next to the tub glowed red from ceiling to floor, a warm light that seem to emanate from no other source than its own.

Just beyond the light, he saw the face of his deceased wife, Courtney. He felt no fear, just wonder at the flood of memories seeing her image brought. The summer they married, right after his graduation from Fort Valley State College. The tough years of medical school at Meharry. Getting him through his residency, paying off the student loans, and settling into a loving and serene routine along the way. They only thing they wanted, but never could seem to have, was a baby. But they were both young, and decided not to worry too much about it.

Everything in their world had been perfect ... until the day Courtney came home from her annual physical. It was ovarian cancer, stage III-C, meaning it had spread throughout her body. The cancer had been detected in a routine tomographic scan. Joe knew that ovarian cancer had earned its name well; the "silent killer" was virtually without symptoms until the advanced stages. But Courtney had never experienced the warnings: bloating, breathlessness, fatigue, nausea. There was little hope of a sustained remission, even after surgery to remove her ovaries and several tumors. Despite his training and experience, Joe was helpless to arrest the disease's progress. He'd never really gotten over losing her, not to this day. And not a day went by that Joe didn't regret their not having children.

Even before he saw her spectral face in the bathroom that night, Joe had revisited their life together in his mind a thousand times, maybe more. In his secret heart, he knew he'd been holding on too tight to her memories. But that was the only way he could make sense of something that stood in contrast with his conservative religious upbringing. His faith and her memory were all he had to hold onto.

∞

Since he lost Courtney, Sunday mornings had always been difficult for him. Until she got too sick, Courtney always brought Joe his coffee and the paper in bed on Sundays, waiting until she heard him stir before heading upstairs with a tray. Today was different, though. Joe woke feeling refreshed and rested ... and thinking of Ashley Heath. Had he dreamed about her, too? He repressed a twinge of guilt. After all, it had been three years. Nothing disloyal in thinking about a pretty woman after all this time. But, it was as though Courtney herself were saying, *"Enough. It's okay to move on."*

After breakfast, Joe went in search of a bulb for the front porch light, humming at the memories of the night before and imagining he heard a bit of ice tinkling as it fell away from his heart.

Seven

Even before he consulted his watch, Klaxton knew it was lunchtime by the rumbling in his stomach. The appointment book told him that he had just under an hour before the next patient was scheduled—time to grab a quick meal at the Chinese buffet in the mall.

He turned on his pager and alerted the receptionist. "Going to grab a bite, Tiffany. I'll be back in time for the two o'clock with Mrs. Hayes."

The practice had gotten off to a much faster beginning than Klaxton or Angie had anticipated. As soon as the lease was signed, they placed ads in all the local newspapers, including the *Journal-Constitution*, plus sent announcements to every major hospital and healthcare office in the area. They were in no hurry, though; the HMO and temp service had burned both of them out, and they were looking forward to a slow, easy buildup of their caseloads.

But within weeks, the appointment books were filling up, and the Staples realized they could have saved their advertising money. A surprising number of their HMO and temp service patients mysteriously found additional insurance and transferred to their practice, and also referred their family members, friends and coworkers.

Despite their fantasies of long, lazy days, from the beginning, they put in hard hours—to the point that they maintained separate schedules during the day, and sometimes didn't even get a chance to have dinner together.

Thanks to a thriving food court at the mall, Lee's Chinese was rarely crowded at lunch. Today, only four or five of the tables were occupied. He found one in a back corner, slapped his *New York Times* down and headed for the steam table.

"Well, Dr. Staples, I'm surprised to see you here!"

He didn't even have to turn around. "Vickie," he said hollowly. "What a coincidence."

"Or maybe birds of a feather really *do* flock together," she replied.

Klaxton had done his best to stay clear of Vickie since the housewarming. He'd known women like her before. They were trouble with a capital T, and he'd been on his best behavior since breaking up with Stephanie. Even in her dull white receptionist's uniform, it was impossible to ignore Vickie's attributes. But he was giving it his best shot. Another woman was the last thing he needed —especially right under Angie's nose, and especially since she seemed to have chosen to ignore what, if anything, Ashley told her about what happened at the party. Get involved with another woman? No way, Jose.

His plate brimming over with char siu and dim sum, he gave Vickie a polite nod and returned to his table.

"Is this seat taken, Dr. Staples?"

What could he do? Fighting a sigh, he said, "Of course not. Please." He rose slightly as she sat, and vowed to keep the conversation neutral. From the receptionist's heaping plate, he could see that she also had a healthy appetite, and there was a comfortable silence as they dug into the food.

"So, tell me, Vickie," Klaxton said after a few minutes, "how long have you been working for Dr. Fry?"

"A little over two years," she answered, reaching up to smooth her shoulder-length hair. "I'm from New York, too. I moved down here to go to Spelman."

Part of the Atlanta University complex of historically black colleges, Spelman enjoyed national prestige. "Spelman. Wow," he said, genuinely impressed. "I would never have taken you for a blueblood. Doesn't tuition there run about the cost of a Beamer 7-Series?"

Vickie chuckled. "Not if you qualify for a scholarship. I'm straight out of Brooklyn. Brownsville, actually."

Klaxton whistled. "Brownsville. I know the area. My hat's off to anyone who's able to get up out of that jungle. What was your major?"

"I was pre-med, but I dropped out in my second year."

"Why?" he asked, genuinely curious. "Graduating with a good GPA from a school like Spelman, you could've had your pick of any medical school in the country."

Vickie sighed and dabbed at her lips with her napkin. "It ... just wasn't me. I found out I'm not the doctor type, really. My real love is show business."

"Show business? What kind of show business?" This girl was a lot more complex than she seemed on the surface.

"The scholarship didn't cover all my expenses, so I earned a little money singing at the local clubs. But my night job took too much time away from school. The next thing I knew, I was falling behind, and that scholarship faded into thin air."

Vickie grew quiet, then picked up her fork and began toying with it. "Maybe I wanted it that way."

"You really love singing enough to give up a scholarship?"

Her nod was accompanied by a confident smile. "Singing is who I am. Only special people get to see the real side of me. Most people think I'm rough and tough. That's the side of me I *let* them see."

"Like a wall?" Klaxton asked. He understood walls.

"Um, more like a defense mechanism." She smiled again and gave him a sideways glance. "That's what I call it, anyway. But it's my self-expression. How I communicate spiritually ... with myself, and other people too."

"That's deep," Klaxton said.

Her voice turned softer than before. "People say that if God blesses you with a talent, and you don't use it, He'll take it away. Singing is my talent. So I keep on singing. Nights, weekends, whenever I can."

Klaxton, for once, could think of nothing to say, so touched was he by her sincerity.

"So," she said after a moment, and carefully picked an egg noodle from the plate in front of her. "Now you know how I ended up in Atlanta. What brought *you* down here?"

Klaxton's answer was always ready. "Angie and I felt like there was just too much going on in New York. That Atlanta would be a better place to raise a family. So we moved here to get a fresh start and—"

"Well, Klaxton, what a *pleasant* surprise. Enjoying your lunch?"

Ashley. "Hi," he croaked. "Just grabbing a quick bite between appointments. Have you eaten? You remember Vickie ... from the housewarming?"

He's screwing her. Ashley made a mental note of that, then allowed "Uh huh" to creep from her lips.

Klaxton whipped his head around to Vickie and gave a nervous chuckle. "Vickie, this is Ashley Heath, my wife's best friend. She was the one hanging off that white hockey player's arm, remember?"

An embarrassed silence ensued until Ashley gestured at the to-go bag in her left hand and said, "Don't let me interrupt. I was just doing a little lunch-hour shopping and decided to grab something to take back to the office. Gotta run, you two have fun." She walked away, pulling out her cell phone as she went.

"What's up with her?" Vickie asked. "You'd think *she* was your wife, with all that attitude."

"Nothing. That's just how she is ... and nosey besides." He glanced at his watch. "Sorry, Vickie, I've got to run. Got a two o'clock. I enjoyed our chat, and best of luck with your singing." *If I hurry, maybe I can catch her and explain*, he thought as he hurried away.

∞

Vickie watched him race after Ashley. Yes, she sure *did* remember Ashley Heath from the party. She was the one who'd made the scene with the drunken intruder. Kicked the hussy out on her ass. And just as Ashley was doing so, Vickie happened to see Klaxton, saw his horrified face.

Was the drunk girl one of Klaxton's other women? Vickie wondered. No other scenario made sense.

She stayed for a while, nibbling at her food, but now, her mind was on other things.

∞

Klaxton was sweating as he raced the Mercedes' engine. He'd done nothing wrong, but it would be hard to convince Angie of that after Ashley got through with her. For the first time since he broke it off with her, he missed Stephanie, wished he could talk to her.

Stephanie had been his confidante, and kept her mouth shut, too. But since the party, she'd been calling him at home and the office, leaving nasty messages on his pager, alternately begging for a reconciliation and threatening physical harm.

What was he supposed to do? He couldn't call the cops. Innocent or not, he was an ex-con to them. They would always be his enemy. And he sure couldn't talk to Angie about this. Especially when she seemed to have forgotten about the incident at the housewarming. Either that, or she didn't want to talk about it. But he had to keep Ashley from stirring that up again. Had to!

He suddenly felt overwhelmed. And, like always, he was all on his own.

Eight

Klaxton spent the rest of the afternoon seeing patients, grateful the appointments kept him busy. But in between checking ears and throats, or every time he paused to write a prescription, his mind kept going back to what happened at lunch. To keep the panic at bay, he practiced his explanation in his head: *I went to grab lunch and ran into her, honey. She sat down at my table. What could I do? Be rude? Shoo her off like some bug?*

It was true. But even to him, it sounded lame.

Once or twice, between appointments, he stuck his head in Angie's office; each time she was on the phone, but waved at him cheerily enough. He came back from his four o'clock to find a note on his desk in her childish scrawl: *"K, honey ... Going for rounds at Crawford Long. Dinner out tonight?"*

Klaxton wasn't sure how to take Angie's apparent ignorance. Maybe she was waiting to sack him at dinner.

Or maybe she's waiting for me to say something first. But if he brought it up and, by some miracle, she and Ashley *hadn't* talked, he'd be telling on himself. Angie seemed to be gifted at denial, even over what happened in New York. On the other hand, what if his lunch with Vickie turned out to be her last straw?

What in the hell *am I going to do?*

"Doctor? Did you say something?"

He jerked his head toward the voice and saw his patient, an elderly woman who'd come for her diabetes checkup.

"Oh? No, Mrs. Moore, I didn't say anything," he said quickly, and reached for his otoscope. "Here, let's check your hearing next."

With an inward sigh, Klaxton decided to keep going with the flow. If Angie didn't bring it up, neither would he. And if she did ... well, he'd cross that bridge when he was about to drive off it.

∞

Later, Klaxton stopped to inspect the IV bag hanging from the post of the metal-framed bed, then flipped through the pages of the chart he held.

"Hey, Roy. How they treating you in here, big man?" he said to his young patient.

"He's been sleeping a lot since he came in," the anxious mother said before the groggy child could answer. She placed her hand on Roy's arm. "Is that normal, Dr. Staples? I've done a lot of reading and I know that some children ..." She caught her breath. "... some children don't—"

"I think he's out of the danger zone, Mrs. Baker," Klaxton said in his most soothing bedside voice. "But I'd like to keep him a bit longer. Roy's going to need plenty of rest, and he'll need to get his medicine by IV for a while." He flipped on the overhead light.

Blinking from the glare, the boy shifted in his bed. "This needle hurts, Dr. Staples. When can I get it out of my arm?"

"Hopefully soon, Roy," he said. "You're still my main man, right?"

"Yes, sir," Roy replied with a weak smile.

"Then you'll be back shooting hoops before you know it."

Klaxton scanned the chart for Roy's most recent blood pressure and temperature readings. A moment later, he closed the chart and nodded reassuringly. "Everything looks better here, Mrs. Baker. His blood pressure's normal, and his temp's under contr— Oh, excuse me."

He pushed his lab coat to one side to expose his vibrating beeper and fought a gasp when he saw the number displayed.

"Thank God for you, Dr. Staples. I don't know what we'd have done if you—"

"It's okay, Mrs. Baker. That's what I'm here for," Klaxton said, distracted. "There are going to be a lot of doctors helping me to take care of Roy, but I'm his primary physician, and you can expect daily visits from me. In between, if you guys need anything, just let the nurses know."

"Is there anything I need to do, Doctor?"

Klaxton smiled and walked into the corridor; she followed him. "Ma'am, you're doing everything you can, and so are we," he said, keeping his voice low. "I'm pretty sure he's past this crisis, and I think that new medication regimen is going to help avoid another one."

She glanced back at the open door before speaking. "I hate to ask, Dr. Staples, but ... Roy doesn't like this hospital food. The nurse said I'd have to get permission from you to get him something from McDonald's downstairs."

He smiled, wishing all questions were that easy. "No harm in that once in a while. Roy will probably like that. Sure, that's fine. No more than once a day, though." He gave her shoulder a reassuring pat, and she went back into the room to tell Roy the good news.

∞

He had walked only a few steps down the hall when he heard heels clicking against the tile floor and a familiar voice call out, "Klaxton, slow down. I need to talk to you!"

Although she was a far-from-welcome sight, Stephanie looked more scrumptious than ever in a beige silk mini dress and lace-strap sandals. She switched her Fendi purse from shoulder to shoulder as she struggled to catch up, attracting the attention of more than one passing resident.

"Klaxton, we have got to talk!" she hissed, finally managing to grab hold of his arm.

He tried to keep walking but she stepped in front of him, blocking his path.

"Stephanie, leave, or I'll call security," he barked at her.

"You mean to tell me that after all the stuff we've been through, you can't give me five minutes? Remember me? I'm the woman who was there for you when your ass was in prison and your name was mud in New York City. I even testified for you. I was *there* for you. Why can't you be here for me?"

The word "prison" stopped him. He glanced around, then turned back to her and whispered, "Stephanie, do you think throwing guilt trips at me is going to change things between us? Or maybe that humiliating me at the hospital is going to get you on my good side?"

She took a deep breath and lowered her voice. "I didn't want to come here, but you won't return my calls and pages." Her face hardened. "You should be glad I came here instead of your house. Your wife probably wouldn't like that much."

Klaxton glanced up and down the deserted hallway, saw that the staff lounge next to him was empty, then looked back at her. "Okay. Five minutes. But you better not make a scene. Let's go into the lounge here."

He led her inside and closed the door. With a snarl, he pressed her against the wall, gripped her shoulders and leaned in close.

"What the hell's wrong with you?" he hissed. "We had an agreement. You broke it, and it's over. Don't think you can intimidate me by blowing the whistle to my wife. Do you really think she's going to leave me after all we been through together?"

Tears welled in her eyes. "I ... I need you. I don't have anyone here but you. You're why I moved to Atlanta."

"Stephanie, I did what I had to do. It's finished! And I don't backtrack. You have to get over it."

She tried to break away, but he held his grip. Her tears spilled down her cheeks, but her voice held firm as she said, "Well, how do you *expect* me to act when you come over to my place, make love to me and toss a check on my dresser like I'm some two-dollar whore? Klaxton, no matter what, I didn't deserve that. You owe me an apology."

"An apology?" He loosened his grip but kept his eyes fixed on her face. "So *that's* what all this is about? Well, let me fix that. I'm so freaking sorry! Now will you get your ass-for-hire out of this hospital before I have you committed? You're even crazier than I thought." He let go of her and moved toward the door.

Stephanie was sobbing now. "You've changed cities, *Dr. Staples*, but you're still playing the same old stupid games. You're the kind of niggah who only loves himself. You never loved me—or Cheryl either." She stopped crying, and her eyes narrowed. "Remember the party? I told your wife on the phone that you didn't love *her*, either."

Her confidence lifted at the shock on Klaxton's face, and she pushed ahead. "You played it off real cool that night, *Doctor*. You should be *real proud* of yourself. That was an Emmy Award performance. So you say it's over? That you did what you had to do? So I guess I'll do what *I* have to do. I wonder what your patients would think if they knew the *upstanding* Dr. Staples is an ex-con? What would that woman down the hall think if she knew her son's doctor did time for murder? If she knew what Cheryl said on my *answering machine* the night she died?"

He reached out to grab the back of a nearby chair, missed, nearly lost his balance. "You told me you destroyed the tape—"

"Maybe I did, and maybe I didn't." She turned away from him and moved toward the lounge door. "Still think I'm crazy? I'll show you what crazy is."

"I-I'm warning you for the last time, Stephanie … Don't mess with my livelihood. That'll be one move you won't live to regret. I'm warning you. Don't go there!"

She whirled around, eyes blazing. "Don't go there? Then where do you want me to go, Klaxton? Want me to go away? How 'bout this? Since you're so quick to throw money at me these days, why don't you throw fifty grand my way? I'll be on the next plane to LaGuardia, crawl back under my rock, and you and old girl can live happy ever after. Call it hooker severance pay and use it as a tax deduction. That'll keep me away *and* keep my mouth shut."

He gasped. "Fifty thousand dollars? Where am I going to get that kind of damn money? You can't be serious!"

Stephanie's eyes pierced him. "You're the one driving the hundred-thousand-dollar car and living in a million-dollar house. You're a smart man, Klaxton. You'll figure it out. And believe me, brother, I'm dead serious."

They stood for a moment, locked in stare-down mode. "What are you going to do, Klaxton?" Stephanie hissed. "Kill me like you killed Cheryl? I'm not afraid of you."

She turned and strode toward the door.

"Why should you be afraid of me?" Klaxton called out. "I'm a doctor, not a killer. You know that!"

She halted, seemed to be listening, and he allowed himself to hope. "Why are you doing this to me?" he said. "I was good to you. Gave you everything you ever wanted. If I was still in your bed, we wouldn't have a problem, would we?"

She never turned around. "Remember to bring cash. I don't want another damn check from you. Oh, and if you can't get the cash? Wait and see how much it's going to cost you later. If you don't give me the money, I'll mess your reputation up so bad, you won't be able to get a job as a dogcatcher."

"I told you, I don't have that kind of money!"

Just before the door closed behind her, he heard her heels clicking rapidly down the corridor. He stared at the door, thinking, *Ah, hell, another Prozac case.*

And a bad dream starting over again.

He never told Stephanie he loved her. Never! They were drawn together by Cheryl's death. The sex just happened. He never lied to Stephanie, never said their alliance was anything more than mutual convenience and pleasure. Just needs.

This isn't my fault, his mind screamed at him. *But ... what if what she's telling the truth? What if she kept a copy of that answering machine tape?* If she did, she could ruin him!

Klaxton breathed deeply and tried to regain his composure. Fortunately, Roy had been his last patient. But he couldn't put off going home forever. Soon, he had to face Angie and find out what she knew. *If I can't think of a cover story, I'll just have to come clean with Angie. There's no way I can pay Stephanie that much mon—*

The realization hit with gut-wrenching suddenness. He'd just told Stephanie he couldn't pay her. What if she believed him, and was heading to find Angie right now to blackmail *her* for the money?

Unaware he was moving, he raced to the elevator and punched the down button. When the door slid open, his wife was standing there.

"Hi, honey," he sputtered, hoping his surprise looked pleased, not terrified. "What are you doing at St. Joe's? I thought you were at Crawford Long."

"Had an emergency delivery here right in the middle." Angie gave him a wide grin and a kiss on his cheek. "When I finished, I thought I might catch you and we could get some dinner somewhere."

Catch me. His stomach lurched and he forced a smile. "Dinner? Perfect timing. Let's do it." Unlike Stephanie, Angie would never make a scene in public. And even if he couldn't feel her out, dinner would give him a few more hours to plan his story—and keep her far out of Stephanie's reach, too. He took her arm as the elevator door opened.

"By the way," she said casually. "Guess who I think I saw in the lobby just now?"

His heart stopped.

"Remember, that friend of Cheryl's from New York? Stephanie Rogers, the one who testified at the trial?" She shrugged. "But I thought, 'What in the world would *she* be doing here?' Whoever she was, she looked a little upset. She gave me a long look as she walked by. Like she recognized me. And she said, 'Hello,' friendly-like. I kept trying to think where I'd seen her before. I don't think she's a patient. I always remember them."

"You gotta be hallucinating," he scoffed. "Even if it *was* her, so what? Atlanta's a big place. The mecca for black Americans, remember? What kind of food are you in the mood for?"

Her eyes and her dimples shifted into a smile. "I ... I guess you're right. And now that you mention it, I'm starving. What about Loca Luna?"

"You got it, beautiful lady," he said, tightening his grip on her arm as they headed for the exit.

∞

Angie knew it was better to keep Klaxton from knowing she was upset. But she was barely able to pay attention to what he was saying. If that *was* Stephanie, why was she at the very hospital where she and her husband worked? Were the ghosts of their old life in New York back? And if that *wasn't* Stephanie Rogers, she still thought she remembered the woman from somewhere ... somewhere recent.

But she hadn't expected a straight answer from Klaxton. Before their marriage, they were inseparable. Before their world in New York had crumbled, they were still close. Now, the tension between them grew each day. He never asked her how she was holding up. Not once. And she didn't know how to ask him what was wrong now, or why he looked like he'd seen a ghost a minute ago.

The pictures flashed in her mind, clear and bitter-cold, and her heart flipped in her chest. *I recognize that voice. That's the same trifling heifer that called me the night of the party! And he knows damn well who she is!*

Fuming silently, Angie walked beside him to their car, a sour lump in her throat.

Nine

Ashley Heath, attorney-at-law, always arrived at work early—at least half an hour before the associates, and sometimes as early as seven. She understood, better than her mostly Caucasian male colleagues, that long hours were part of the dues one paid for making partner. Ashley also discovered that early morning, before the distractions of phones and office drop-ins, was a great time to catch up on paperwork, case research and brief-writing.

Today was a seven a.m. day, and with good reason. The latest rumor in the firm's active rumor mill was that she was in the running for promotion from senior associate to junior partner. And the rumor mill's record for accuracy was nearly perfect.

"Don't blow it," she told herself, shrugging off the massive leather briefcase holding hardcopy files of all her active cases. "Can't afford to let your guard down after you've made it this far." She rubbed her aching shoulder. "If you make partner, girl, maybe you'll even have your own intern to drag this case around for you."

After a huge lucky break on her first case with Johnson & Browne, LLC four years ago, Ashley's goal was to make partner. Sure, she'd known it was a long shot. The prestigious firm was founded in 1903, and even in the twenty-first century, elderly white men dominated it. Ashley joined it right out of law school. That was her first big break. She wasn't a fool; she knew it was her grades and position on the *Law Review* that made her a good diversity hire. But still, she felt lucky to get the offer. The firm needed help with a tobacco case. It was messy and complicated, a viper's nest none of the partners wanted to touch. She took on the challenge with no illusions or false expectations.

"Of course you won't be lead attorney," Robert Browne had warned. "You'll be working under Thomas McMurry, and the case-work alone will take another six months. If your performance is satisfactory, there will be other opportunities for you."

Big break or not, Ashley wanted to tell Robert Browne Esquire to stuff his kind offer. In his day, Thomas McMurry had been one of the firm's top litigation attorneys. But after his wife died he took to drinking, and drinking some more. McMurry was kept on, but given cases nobody else wanted. Associates and interns handled everything except the actual arguments, and everybody was reasonably happy with the arrangement, McMurry most of all. Not having to work hard gave him more time to drink. It was Ashley's turn to be happy covering for a has-been lush.

Yet she knew she could distinguish herself, and set herself to research, discovery preparation and drafting briefs with the zest displayed only by those who are both talented *and* as-yet untried. Her hard work paid off; she earned McMurry's gratitude and respect, and when he was sober, he talked to her about past cases, courtroom techniques and the experiences that had put him, at one time, at the top of his field.

All this proved fortunate for Ashley when he had a fatal heart attack in the men's room on the day of opening arguments. The trial was postponed for two weeks. Ashley used the time to convince the firm that she was fully prepared to argue the case.

Initially, the partners were amused by the green attorney's chutzpah. *Unthinkable*, Robert Browne himself had said. But after reviewing her notes and quizzing her, they agreed to let her proceed; there was certainly no one else in the firm prepared to take it on at that point.

Their amusement turned to amazement when Ashley, working from her enhanced version of McMurry's original preparation, executed the case flawlessly—garnering a $10 million judgment for the client and an aura of awe for Ashley. A few thought it was beginner's luck, but from there on, her place in the Johnson & Browne hierarchy, albeit junior, was unquestioned.

It's amazing what luck, timing and hard work will bring, Ashley thought. *And oh, long legs and a big smile don't hurt, either.* Grinning, she adjusted the skirt of her designer suit and settled in for a day of hard work.

That she also happened to be an African-American female didn't hurt, either. Atlanta had long been America's stronghold of black economic success, and the city relished its motto of "The City Too Busy to Hate." Citizens elected their first black mayor in the early '70s. Mayor Maynard Jackson ushered in a new era of opportunity for black professionals and businesspeople. Many NBA and NFL players made their homes in Atlanta, and singers, actors, entrepreneurs and other well-to-do blacks congregated in the city reconstructed by carpetbaggers a century earlier.

After her victory in the tobacco case, Ashley was given a couple of minor-league entertainers as clients, local rappers and vocalists who earned just enough to keep themselves in minor trouble most of the time.

"As you can guess, these aren't the kind of clients Johnson and Browne usually solicits," she'd been told. "But the entertainment industry is lucrative, and we feel we shouldn't turn them down. If you take on these clients, we'll be willing to extend your contract another six months."

"And after that?" Ashley inquired.

"We'll see," was the answer.

She knew these were second-rate opportunities—the kind of stuff the big boys felt beneath them. If she hadn't already known, she would have figured it out when one of the Harvard-educated junior partners said offhandedly, "It makes sense, you being young and African-American and all. You'll be able to communicate with them."

"With my own kind, you mean?" Ashley retorted.

Of course the partner protested, but the truth had been spoken. Ashley was in no position to enlighten him further on her opinion of his political correctness. But that was okay. That junior partner's time would come.

Besides, there were other advantages. Being the first African-American female in the stodgy, tradition-bound firm was just the kind of challenge Ashley relished. As it happened, though, one of her rap clients hit the big time and blew up again, this time in a major way. That meant big bucks for the firm—and a firmer hold on her position. After the old men saw how she handled that, there was no more talk of "extensions." She was in for good.

If the rumor mill was right as usual, she was about to advance to the next rung.

I hope. Ashley sighed.

It was nearly eight-thirty now. People were beginning to drift into the building. And outside her cubicle, Ashley heard her secretary arrive and put her purse away. As always, Mary's first task was to check the answering machine; its annoying beeps carried through the closed door between them.

She pressed the intercom button. "Mary, good morning. Could you bring me a cup of coffee, please?"

Her voice was courteous, but cool. Although she had no proof, she suspected that her white secretary resented fetching coffee for her. When one of the partners summoned the older woman to bring coffee or perform some clerical task, Mary responded with promptness and charm. Now that she was assigned exclusively to Ashley, her manner was noticeably cooler—and slower. Whether it was because she was a woman, or black, or both, Ashley didn't know. But she made it a point to have Mary bring her coffee every morning anyway.

If Mary was a racist or anti-feminist, though, she was clever enough to mask it. "Good morning, Ms. Heath," she said. "I'll bring your coffee soon. I have a couple of messages for you, too."

Ashley knew she had to play the courtesy game, too, or she'd come out looking like the villain. So, when Mary brought the coffee, she forced a smile. "Thank you, Mary. And, oh, would you get Dr. Bowen-Staples on the line for me?"

Mary smiled a tight smile in return, reached across her and pressed the speed-dial button.

Ashley took a sip of her coffee and almost choked. She reached for the sugar packets and stirrer Mary had placed beside the cup. So much for trying to appear in charge.

"Dr. Bowen-Staples is on line one," Mary said.

"Thanks, that'll be all," Ashley responded, noting that Mary had already started out the door.

The second the door closed, she grabbed the phone as though it were a lifeline. "Hi, girlfriend!"

Something was up. Angie's usually whispery voice was positively booming into the receiver. Probably best to lose the extra pair of ears outside the door.

She asked Angie to hold and pressed the intercom button: "Mary, I almost forgot. Could you please run these papers down to the mailroom for me? They have to go out this morning."

Mary retrieved the stack of papers from Ashley's outstretched hand, her manner bordering on pleasant as she asked, "Will there be anything else?"

"No, that will be all for now. Just put the phone on voicemail while you're gone. And, oh, pull the door shut on your way out. I don't want to be disturbed for a little while. That's great, thanks."

Ashley removed her hand from the receiver as soon as the door closed. "Sorry 'bout that. Every now and then, I have to show her who's the boss around here."

"Ash, things are going so well!" Angie exclaimed.

Ashley's eyebrows rose. *Considering what I told her at the party, she sure seems to be in a perky mood.* Yet as long as Ashley had known her, denial was Angie's way of dealing with problems. She still had to tell Angie about seeing her husband and Vickie, though. Couldn't let Angie be the last one in her office building to know.

"I-I'm glad to see you so happy," she said. "But—"

Before she could finish, Angie blurted, "Guess what? Klaxton and I are going to try for a baby again."

Ashley didn't know what to think; months before, Angie had told her she was unable to have children. *Well, she's an obstetrician. She should know.* "Hey, that's great."

"Did I tell you that after the party, Klaxton and I made love like our lives depended on it?" Angie's voice was higher, almost shrill now.

"Well, I—"

"Girl, it's been like that all *week*." The normally shy doctor's words were falling over each other. "Last night after we made rounds at the hospital, we went to Loca Luna for dinner, and then came home, turned our pagers off, and Klaxton took the phone off the hook."

When she heard the giggle, Ashley shook her head. No, it just wasn't the right time to tell her friend what she'd seen at the mall the day before. "Well, ah ... I suppose that might explain why you sound so giddy," she said instead.

Angie chuckled. "Oh, and by the way, Ash ... I think Dr. Fry downstairs has a thing for you. He asked about you last week. Wanted to know all about you—including whether you were really serious about Richard Perry. What'd you *do* to him at the party?"

"Don't you go trying to fix me up with anybody," Ashley said. "As you know very well, I prefer to find my own men, thank you. Besides, he's too old for me."

"Oh, he's not *that* old."

"Angie ..."

"Okay, okay! I won't push. But if you change your mind and want to come back to black, let me know and I'll arrange for you two to just *happen* to be at the same place at the same time. Okay?"

"Don't hold your breath."

Laughter billowed over the phone, then Angie said, "Girl, you'll wake up and smell the coffee. Wait and see. By the way, what time's your hair appointment today? Five, right?"

"You know when it is," Ashley said. "Remember? You're the one who told me to change it so we could hang." A short silence, then Ashley said, "Angie ... sweetie. Are you *sure* things are all right with you and Klaxton?"

It was a moment before Angie replied, and her answer wasn't what Ashley expected. "Why would you ask something like that?"

"It's just that ... I worry about you sometimes."

Ashley heard a beep on the other end, and Angie's voice turned serious. "It's the hospital, Ash. Got to go."

Ashley put the phone down, leaned back in her chair, laced her red-tipped fingers together and tried to wish away the uneasy feeling in the pit of her stomach. For the next fifteen minutes, her case files went ignored.

Ten

The day at Buckhead Medical Associates finally ground to an end. As Angie grabbed her bags and hurried off to The World of Curls and Books, Klaxton was entering his landlord's office.

He tapped his finger on the opaque glass of the reception-room window. A moment later, the window slid open and an irritated voice said, "Sir, would you please not ..."

Vickie's reprimand trailed off when she saw who it was. "Hello, Dr. Staples, I didn't know it was you. People have been banging on this window all day. Patients, delivery guys, pharmaceutical reps, you name it. You'd think they'd see the sign. It's staring them in the face."

His eyes followed her pointing finger to the lighted button mounted on the window frame. He pretended to peer at it, smiling at her. "Miss Heath, I regret it, but I'll have to disagree. That bell has a placement problem. It's down there, where *short folks* can see it. And I'm *up here*." He straightened his six-foot frame to illustrate, bent down again and glanced around the reception area to make sure they were alone.

Vickie smiled back and leaned away, but not before returning his smile. Her breasts strained against the tight white polyester of her uniform.

He glanced at the area behind her, "Ah, is your boss in, or do you have the place to yourself?"

Without taking her eyes off his, Vickie pressed the intercom button and said, "Dr. Fry ... Dr. Klaxton Staples is here to see you."

"Let him in and show him into my office. Tell him I'll be right with him. I'm finishing up with my last patient."

"Yessir," she said, and turned back to Klaxton: "Both our nurses have left for the day. I'll take you back."

She unlocked the door to the exam rooms and led the way, teetering sensuously on her three-inch heels while thinking, *I wonder if it's true what people say about the size of a man's hands and feet.* That, of course, wasn't the right question to ask. Still, she couldn't resist putting a sway into her walk as she escorted him down the hall.

Klaxton followed, watching her butt swing from side to side with greater enjoyment than he knew he should have. To take his mind off the view from behind, he asked, "Do you folks always keep the reception door locked?"

"Yeah." She looked back at him, stopped and whispered, "Dr. Fry's kind of funny about things like that. He likes for the doors to be locked at all times, even when we're seeing patients."

Klaxton's forehead furrowed. "Is he afraid someone will try to rob the office?"

His question brought a giggle. "Rob? I don't think so. This is Buckhead! It's fairly safe around here. Anyway, if someone ever tried it, they wouldn't find much. Most of our patients have insurance, so there's hardly any cash. No drugs, either—at least, not the kind most addicts would steal. Mainly antibiotics and local anesthetics." She lowered her voice and added, "But I have an idea of what he might be so nervous about protecting."

He entered the door she pointed to, realized that it was the office lab, empty at the moment.

She closed the door and turned toward him. "If you really want to know, I think he feels like someone might want some of those weird paintings he has in his office."

Klaxton remembered and nodded. "I recall thinking the artwork in his office looked rather expensive—"

He couldn't get another word in. Clearly, Vickie had been saving her suspicions for someone who could appreciate secrets.

"Oh, it's waaaay more than that. He's not into stuff just because it costs a lot of money. I mean, you see how he dresses!"

Klaxton fought to keep a straight face as she continued. "No, it's not how expensive they are. He stares at them every time he goes in his office. And he's always dusting them, like he thinks his housekeeper isn't doing a good enough job. I know better— Mrs. Caldwell keeps the place immaculate!"

Warming to her subject, she breathed, "I think he's one of those … uh, obsessive-compulsives, you know? Right after I came to work here, the poor guy almost had a stroke when he ran into a spider web hanging from the back entrance! He practically *ran* to get a broom to take it down! Ever since, he checks all the doors and windows himself every day before work." She shook her head. "He's a nice man, but he can be a little weird sometimes."

"Well, *weird* or not, I'm sure he's wondering where we are," Klaxton said, not quite knowing how to react to the uninvited confidences.

They headed to Joe's office. "I'll let you in, and you can wait for him here," Vickie said, and opened the cherrywood door and stepped aside.

"You sure it's all right?" Klaxton asked. "Him being funny about things and all?"

Vickie waved her hand in the air. "Oh, no, he'll be fine. Remember? He told me to."

When she was gone and he could think again, Klaxton took a closer look at his surroundings. In New York, he often attended private auctions, ones generated by the need to liquidate assets in a hurry. Some of his day-trading buddies had gotten caught like that. He'd never had to host an auction of his own, but he *had* attended enough to know that his initial impression was true—Joe's collection included some fine examples of African and Egyptian art. He recognized some of it as being from East Africa, including tribal masks that looked authentic. Of course, they couldn't be. In his pre-auction research, he'd never seen pieces of this age and quality for sale, only for display.

A few minutes later, his appraisal was interrupted as Joe strode into the room and reached out his hand. "Sorry I haven't been up to see you yet. How are things going upstairs? I've seen the parking lot. It's been full, man. That's good, eh?"

"We owe you, Joe," Klaxton replied. "I knew this was a good location, but we never expected to be so busy so soon. Actually, the reason I came by today is business—landlord-tenant business, that is." To Joe's surprised look, he added, "Angie asked me to stop by to see if you had the exterminators put down some kind of roach bait or something in our offices."

Joe shook his head, concern on his face. "No, I had the building treated when I bought it. Not that it needed it, but I figured it would be easier to do while it was empty. They spray outside once a month, but they don't spray the inside unless we request it. But if you think we need it, I can have them out here tomorrow."

"Oh, no, it's not a problem. Angie just found something that looked like salt spread around in the corner of her office. No one owned up to spilling anything there, so I thought it might be roach or ant powder."

Joe thought a moment. "Well, I'll ask Mrs. Caldwell, but I'm sure it's not insect powder. She'll be quite upset about any mess like that, I assure you. And she'll have it cleaned up first thing tonight when she comes in."

"Sounds great, man." Klaxton grinned. "Anything to keep the wife from worrying. When she worries, I'm not a happy man ... you know."

Joe returned the grin. "I vaguely remember."

Klaxton turned to go, but stopped at the door. "Oh, something I probably ought to mention. I'm sending you a patient."

Joe's eyes widened. "Thanks. What's her diagnosis?"

"That's the problem. I can't figure out what's wrong with her. She's having a lot of generalized muscle pain. When she came to me, she'd been seeing a chiropractor for a couple of months without relief."

"Has she seen anyone else?"

"I sent her to a neurologist and a rheumatologist, and between us we've run every test we can think of. But she's getting worse."

"Worse how?" Joe asked, already wishing he had the letter in his hand and the patient in his office. "You said pain. Where? Any other symptoms?"

"Fatigue, muscle weakness, headache ... what you'd find in about a hundred disorders. Weight loss, too. I suspected lupus or fibromyalgia, but the tests came back negative. Hell, *every* test has come back clean so far!" Frustrated, he threw up his hands. "Man, this one's got me."

"Does she live around here?"

He shook his head. "She's from somewhere in Africa. Doesn't speak English. But the daughter said she claims someone put a spell on her." He chuckled. "You know, our people live on the most advanced continent in the world here, and over in Africa they're still running through the bush believing in some hoodoo-voodoo mess."

"That's interesting," Joe said quietly.

"Anyway, the woman wants to go home—back to Africa—but the daughter says there's a civil war going on back there."

"She's right," Joe said. "It *isn't* safe to travel in some areas of Africa right now."

Klaxton nodded. "Anyway, take a look at her and let me know what you make of it. Vickie was just telling me that you got a new tomogram unit. Maybe it will tell us something."

Joe smiled. "Maybe it will. For the money I paid for it, it ought to. But it's worth it to me. I treat a lot of pain in my practice. And I don't like to prescribe a lot of pills." Dropping the file he held onto the desk, Joe added, "I'll be happy to take a look at her. But if I can't find anything, I'll probably refer her to a specialist in tropical diseases."

Klaxton grimaced. "I thought of that, but you know how long and drawn-out that kind of evaluation is." He looked at Joe with concern. "If you don't find anything, I'll go ahead and make a psych referral. But I don't want to do that until everything else has been ruled out."

"I understand."

Klaxton said goodbye and headed upstairs, his mind wandering. His body, though, was focused on the memory of Vickie's scent, and her swaying walk. Grumbling, he unlocked his office and headed for his private shower.

∞

Joe's patients had left, his staff was gone for the day, and he had literally no reason to go home. He walked over to his golf clubs, set up his practice green and grabbed his putter, intending to hit a few balls.

But then he changed his mind—about the putter, and about his chances with Ashley Heath, the focus of his thoughts. Based on her charming assertiveness at the party, if she'd been interested in seeing him again, she would have. He was easy to find through Klaxton or Angie, her friends. And if she hadn't by now, he'd likely said or done something to make her think he wasn't interested in another meeting. Gwyn and Denise, his office nurses, accused him of that once, when they saw an attractive pharmaceutical rep's interest in him, and he was too blind to notice it. But even when they told him, he didn't feel a spark with the woman, charming as she was.

So what if Ashley *was* one of the few women he'd felt anything for since Courtney died? Neither the world, nor the women in it, revolved around him. What did he, a struggling internist past his youth, have to offer someone as young, beautiful and successful as Ashley anyway?

He smiled, realizing that his tendency to pick the sourest grapes in the bunch was getting the best of him—again.

No, the best thing was to stop thinking about her and get his mind on something else. The box behind his desk called to him, and he considered that. Since the box was delivered by special courier the week before, he'd been too busy. But he knew that wouldn't satisfy his soul tonight.

Maybe he *should* go home. Perhaps work on his pet project—a treatise on African-American social issues in the new millennium.

Perhaps *that* would take the sting of rejection out of his mind for a while, and give it a chance to subside in his heart.

He picked up his briefcase and walked to the door. As he reached for the light switch, he hesitated, then turned around, re-moved the picture of Courtney from the shelf and put it in his desk drawer, fighting the stab of guilt the action brought. Moments later, he entered the exit code on the back door's keypad, tapping the wall next to it three times before he did, as always.

"I'm still here, Doc," Vickie called out. "And hey, what's that noise I just heard?"

He jumped and called back up the hallway, "Oh, I'm sorry, Vickie. I-I was just tapping for good luck. I thought you were gone."

"No, I have some claims I need to transmit before I leave."

"Well, don't stay too late."

As he walked to his SUV, he considered what Klaxton had told him about the powder Angie found in their office. *Roach bait? What next?*

Eleven

The stench of burned hair, lye and perm solution greeted Angie as soon as she opened the glass-paned door of Montrease's World of Curls and Books.

She signed her name at the bottom of the five o'clock appointment list. Using the stubby, string-tied yellow pencil as a pointer, she counted the names already on the list, then looked at the ceiling in annoyance. "I'll never get out of here before dark."

Angie spoke more to herself than to the women sitting in the waiting area, gossiping. Each of them held a copy of Bernice McFadden's *Sugar*, a best-selling novel about a young woman's battle with infidelity. Montrease, who loved books as much as she loved hairstyling, had created a bookstore in her beauty shop. The walls of the renovated bungalow were lined with hardbacks, and many of her regulars attended her monthly reading group. A stack of the next month's selection—*Temptation* by Victoria Christopher Murray—lay on the glass table in the middle of the large room.

The sight caused Angie's annoyance to grow. She'd forgotten it was the first Friday of the month. She enjoyed the book club, but she had other plans for tonight. Tonight was going to be special. It had to be. If her suspicions about Stephanie were true, she had to make every moment count tonight. But by the look of the packed waiting area and the books, dinner would be late.

"Girl, I *know* I didn't see you turn your face up in the air when you looked at my appointment book." Montrease appeared next to Angie with a thundercloud on her face.

Angie started. "No, of course not, Trease. I ... just need to get out of here at a reasonable time tonight, that's all." As she spoke, she shrugged her damp raincoat from her shoulders.

Trease scowled. "Don't tell me you didn't read the book!"

"I read the book," Angie said. "It was a great read. All I'm going to say is Sugar should be ashamed of herself. I can't bel—"

"Save it for the discussion," Trease said. She looked Angie over. "I – I – I *likes* that. Red is your color, Angie." The women in the waiting area turned their attention to Angie as Trease continued. "Just what a woman of your stature ought to wear. Dress to impress, I always say."

Angie blushed, knowing every ear in the shop was listening now. "Trease, I ... can't stay for the discussion tonight."

Trease stopped sashaying long enough to place her hands on her generous hips. "What's your hurry, girlfriend? That fine hunk of husband waiting at home with his motor running?"

Angie smiled a schoolgirl smile and blushed even harder as she hung her coat on the rack by the front door. "Well ... we do have a special evening planned."

Trease opened her mouth, but another voice broke in.

"Angie, what's up, girl? Trease, don't tell me you're running behind again!" Ashley's voice cut cleanly over the noise from the hairdryers.

"Oh, my!" Trease said to Angie. "Here comes your friend, the black Janet Reno."

"I heard that," Ashley snapped. "Don't start hating on a sister just because I'm about to come up!"

The grinning Trease took Ashley's raincoat and placed it on the hook next to Angie's. "Oh, girl, I was just playing with you. Don't take everything so serious. I'm glad to see black folks doing well for themselves. Did you bring your book?"

Ashley waved her copy in the air.

With that, Angie gave up trying to hurry Trease and headed to an empty chair. Chuckling, Ashley followed, calling out, "Hey, heifer!" and hugging her friend before taking the chair next to her.

Angie looked at her watch. "You're late, Ashley. You're never late."

I'm not late," Ashley protested. "You know Trease operates on colored people's time. So I just add thirty minutes to my appointment. Besides, when the book club meets, she always drags behind."

"Speaking of dragging behind," Angie said with a smile, "have you given any more thought to Joe Fry? He sure is easy on the eyes, as my grandma would say. And I keep telling you he's interested in you."

Ashley sighed. "Is this going to lead back to the matchmaking conversation we had earlier? I've already told you he's too old for me." *Or did I?* Ashley couldn't remember, but it wasn't that important. It was Angie she worried about. She never got a chance on the phone, but somehow, she had to tell Angie that her man was cheating on her—shoot the messenger or not.

"Well, I don't think he's too old for you," Angie said. "According to Klaxton, Joe's receptionist thinks he's a little weird. But he impressed *me*."

This was the opening Ashley had been hoping for. "Hmm, Klaxton said that, did he? I guess she told him that during their cozy little lunch at the mall last week."

Angie swiveled her head to look directly at Ashley. "What did you say?"

Ashley straightened in the chair. "He didn't tell you? I guess I shouldn't be surprised. It's just that when I saw them having lunch last week, they looked a little too ... cozy for my taste."

Angie shrugged. "I'm sure it was harmless. You know how friendly Klaxton is. He'll sit down and talk to anybody."

"And he does it even more often if the *anybody* is a female."

Though inwardly furious, Angie fought to stay calm. "Ashley, don't start with me. You're making a mountain out of a molehill. What day was it that you saw them?"

"I think it was Monday," Ashley answered, watching her friend's face.

Angie's face relaxed a bit. "That was the day I had to skip lunch. Okay. So why are you just now telling me this?"

"I called you as soon as I walked out of the restaurant," Ashley told her. "But your receptionist said you were busy with patients. And I tried to call you that night, but I guess Klaxton *conveniently* took the phone off the hook." She paused a moment, "Look, you're my girl and I love you like a sister. But you can be a little naive sometimes."

"What do you mean—?"

Ashley interrupted with a sigh. "I'll tell you. For as long as I've known you, you've tried to make it seem as if you and Klaxton live this perfect little life. And maybe the average person might believe that. But not me."

She dropped her eyes for a moment, wondering if she should tell Angie that Klaxton had once made a pass at her, right after she and Angie met. But no. *Not now, and probably not ever.* She raised her eyes back to Angie's. "Look, I know you're a grown-ass woman, so I'm not telling you to run out and get a divorce. I just think you need to take a step back and look at what's really going on."

Angie fought to keep her breathing even. Why was she playing this silly game with Ashley? No, it wasn't silly, and it wasn't a game. On the drive to the restaurant last night, she had willed herself to believe nothing was wrong. But there was, of course. There was plenty wrong—with her! Later, after they'd made love, she'd spent most of the night thinking about ... her past. About how people would blame her for it.

Not even Ashley knew. No one could know. If Klaxton found out— *No, he can never find out!* And she couldn't risk Ashley going to Klaxton out of concern. Angie would rather die than live without Klaxton, and Ashley could never understand that.

She took a deep breath and blew it out. "You keep asking me what's *really* going on, just like I'm keeping something back from you. I swear, Ashley, you remind me of my father. He's always preaching, 'Angie, you're too weak, you need to be stronger, you need to do this, you need to do that.' That's one of the reasons Klaxton and I moved here—to get away from that. So, as my friend, please lay off, okay?

"Anyway," she added, smoothing the hem of her dress, "for your information, things between me and my husband are better than ever. Like I *said*. We have a beautiful home and our practice is booming. And who knows? We might even have a baby someday soon. My life is rolling along just fine, thank you very much."

Angie's last statement was wishful thinking. Just that morning, she'd seen the results of yet another negative pregnancy test. And there was truth in Ashley's words. Painful truth. But there was no way she'd share that with Ashley. No, she just wouldn't understand.

Ashley shrugged. "Lay off? No problem. I'll let your marriage be exactly that—*your* marriage."

Laughter erupted from the back of the salon as Trease walked into the waiting area. "Okay, ladies of Curls and Books, are you ready to start the discussion?" Her question was greeted with enthusiastic chattering.

Trease gestured to the two vacant salon chairs. "Angie, honey, I know you're in a hurry. I can do you and Ashley while we talk."

"Trease," Ashley began as she and Angie were seated and draped, trying to shift her thoughts away from the conversation with Angie, "do you think Sugar is related to the man who lives next door to her?"

"Girl, yes!" one of the women from the waiting room jumped in. "That got to be her daddy. He look just like her."

"*Old girl* was wrong for sitting up in that window like that," Ashley agreed.

"Some women will do anything to get your man," Angie said, her voice harsh.

Ashley bit her lip.

∞

Trease was magic. Within minutes, she had shampooed Angie's long tresses and was at work on Ashley's short hair. As she wrapped Ashley's head in a towel she said, "Ladies, I think we all agree that *Sugar* is an excellent book that deals with some very real issues."

"Men!" Ashley chimed in. "No-good men." She risked a glance at Angie, but her friend's face showed no emotion. So Angie's next words almost knocked her out of the chair:

"Trease, I agree that some of Sugar's wounds can be related to men. But as a doctor, I think that certain external factors, like stress, are the root of most marital problems."

Trease, spraying oil sheen on Ashley's hair, gave Angie a pointed look. "What? You saying this is like some kind of disease we all can take a pill for and be better tomorrow?"

When Angie didn't reply, Trease said to the room, "All you ladies have made some great points. That's why, for our next book, I've chosen an inspirational. And this time I have a real treat for you. I haven't confirmed it yet, but I'm trying to get the author to come in."

The room filled with applause.

"And ladies, don't forget your copy of our next read there on the table in the waiting area. I stuck your receipt in the book."

After the last of the women said goodbye, Trease turned back to Angie and Ashley. "So Ashley, tell me about that brother Angie introduced you to. Was he *light* enough for you?"

Ashley gave Angie a gentle glare, to which Angie responded with a grin.

"The *brother's* name is Joe," Ashley said to Trease, her tone purposely mild. "And actually, there's not much to tell. He's not *young* enough for me. But I can say that he's a very nice man. A perfect gentleman. And on top of that, he's well-spoken and handsome."

Ashley noted, with surprise, that she'd just spelled out all the qualities she'd always looked for in a man.

The only stylist left in the shop besides the owner, putting the finishing touches on an elderly woman's tortured bouffant, poked out her lip. "Girl, if you're fool enough to shoo this man off, shoo him my way."

Beaming, Trease and the stylist high-fived and chanted, "Sweet chocolate sugar!"

Angie's face lost its buoyant expression, and the plastic apron covering her clothes rustled and shifted. Her hand emerged from under it, holding a buzzing pager. She glanced at it. "Trease, can I use your phone? Mine's in the car. It's Klaxton. I told him I wouldn't be here long. After the discussion started, I forgot to call him to tell him I'd be late."

Ashley tried to hide her distaste as Angie punched numbers into the cordless Trease handed her.

"Hi, honey, sorry I'm running late," Angie cooed. "I'm almost done, and I'll be there as soon as I can."

The change in her voice stunned the other two women. Seconds before, she'd been a self-confident physician having a great time. Now she sounded like a little girl hoping to quell her daddy's anger.

She listened a moment, then said, "So the exterminator hadn't been in my office, like you thought? ... Salt? Is that what Joe thought it was?"

Angie glanced nervously over at Trease and Ashley. They seemed engrossed in conversation.

When she heard Joe's offered solution, she said, "Mrs. Caldwell? Baby, I don't like that woman. She makes me nervous."

Klaxton sighed so loud, Angie was afraid the other two women could hear it through the telephone line. She lowered her voice again. "Look, honey, it was nice of Joe to offer, but I'd feel better if we got our own cleaning people."

Trease had finished with Ashley, who wandered off to the far end of the room and was checking out the new-releases bookrack.

"All right, baby, we'll talk again at home," Angie replied, and impulsively planted a kiss on the phone's mouthpiece before she clicked off.

Trease took the phone from Angie's hand and whipped off her client's apron, scattering hair trimmings everywhere. Placing a hand on her shoulder, she nudged her up from the chair. "Angie, you're done."

Angie reached into her purse for her checkbook, but Trease placed her hand out to stop her. "I know you're in a hurry, but step to the back for a minute."

"But, Trease," Angie protested, "I'm late. Klaxton is waiting on me to come home so we can eat."

"It will only take a minute. Girl, come on."

Trease led Angie to the area in back where she mixed the chemicals she used on her customers and said, "Who put salt in your office?" Her voice made it clear that Angie's reply wasn't optional.

"Trease, that was a personal conversation," she sputtered.

"Salt," the portly hairdresser repeated, ignoring Angie's remark. "People use salt when they want to put a spell on someone pretty. It dries them up and makes them look old. Girl, you better watch that. You'll look a hundred years old in no time." Montrease snapped her fingers to illustrate. "I've seen it done before."

Angie sighed and waved her hand under her nose. "You've been inhaling too much perm solution back here, Trease."

"Folks use salt to take someone's man or woman away, too, you know," Trease insisted. "And you mentioned that Mrs. Caldwell. Is someone trying to take your man from you or something?"

Ashley had just come around the divider separating the mixing-room from the rest of the shop, and heard only the last question. "Trease, you just hit the nail on the head," she said. "I was trying to tell her that earlier, but she wouldn't listen to me."

Without warning, Angie began to weep frustrated tears. "Look, I really appreciate you two looking out for me, but ... I don't know why everybody always seems to think that I'm nothing but a weak little, naive girl, or that my marriage needs fixing. Klaxton ... he told me just the other night not to listen to what people say in the street, because they're just jealous of what I've got. I think he's right!"

"I know, honey," Ashley began, but Angie cut her off. "Well, in case you two are wondering, Klaxton's not going anywhere! He loves me. He always has, and he always will. Maybe other women really *are* jealous, and that's why they want him. I know that," she added, glancing at Ashley through brimming eyes. "I'm not a fool." Her look turned hard. "I can take care of myself."

"We know, baby, we know," Montrease said, patting her shoulder. "We just don't want you to have to do it all by yourself. That's one of the reasons I formed the book club. It's a way of getting women together and exploring some of the issues that we *all* deal with."

Contrite, Ashley said, "I'm sorry, Angie. I really *was* only trying to help."

Trease frowned. "But honey, if what you told me is true, you really do need to watch your back. I'm telling you, putting salt in somebody's workplace," she shook her head, "whoever did it is *not* your friend."

Ashley gave Trease a hard look. "Salt? Did I miss something?"

Trease nodded, then explained what Angie had said.

While she and Trease continued trying to console Angie, Ashley's mind spun. She didn't buy Trease's notion of Angie being under a spell. That was ridiculous. But she *did* think something odd was going on, and the attorney in her kept insisting that Klaxton was the root of the problem. "Look, ladies, it's been a long night," she said. "I've worked like a dog all week, and I'm tired. Let's all go home."

Angie looked at her with surprise. "Ashley, you're never tired. You coming down with something?"

"Maybe I am," Ashley said with a secretive smile. Taking Angie's arm, she added, "Nothing that a good doctor can't fix, though."

Trease picked up on her meaning, but the guileless Angie didn't. "Well, you'd better come see *me* if you're sick! You know where I am."

"Yes ... I do." Ashley smiled another furtive smile, took Angie's arm and led her to the checkout desk, Trease following and muttering what sounded like an incantation under her breath.

Twelve

Ashley made the call just as soon as she left the World of Curls and Books. *Better now than to wait until Monday morning,* she decided. Besides, she didn't want Mary to know she was making a doctor's appointment—something like that could get out to the rumor mill and into the wrong person's ears.

Instead of the easy call she expected, all Ashley got was frustration. And frustration's first name was Vickie.

"Oh, Ms. Heath," the receptionist chirped, "you're lucky you caught me. I usually have the answering service on, but I'm working late. But to answer your question, I'm sorry, Dr. Fry isn't accepting any new patients without a referral."

No need to wonder if Vickie remembers who I am, Ashley thought. "I understand," she said, working to keep a light tone. "But I think he'll make an exception for me."

"I don't know about that, Ms. Heath. Even his regular patients are experiencing a long wait for an appointment. The earliest—"

Ashley didn't make a habit of taking no for an answer, especially from a secretary who thought wearing clothes three sizes too small was an acceptable way to entice married men. "Look," she said, "I know you might have a little trouble following, so let me know if I go too fast. I'm going to see Dr. Fry. I'm going to see him on Monday afternoon. Tell him that I'll be there at three o'clock. If he should inquire, just tell him that it's personal, would you, darling? Be sure to get that message to him."

"Well, I'll need some insurance information from you just in case he *is* able to see you. Which you probably shouldn't count on. He's—"

"Tell you what. Let me explain what 'personal' means: that I don't need to give you any insurance information. If I need to see him on a professional basis while I'm there, I'll pay cash. But Dr. Fry and I will work that out. Okay, *sweetie*? Thanks again for your time. Good-bye."

She hung up the phone, remembering how Vickie's head had tilted toward Klaxton's in the dim restaurant. "That little slut knows I'm Angie's friend," she muttered. "I guess she thought taking me through that little drill would intimidate me or something." She smiled. "They always let the good hair and light skin fool 'em."

Realizing she had more important things on her agenda than taming Vickie, she headed home. Fortunately it was late, and the light traffic allowed her another chance to revisit that conversation. "I'm *not* going to let some lowdown home-wrecker stress me out," she whispered.

But no matter how confidently she said the words, they ripped open an old wound. She took her hand from the steering wheel long enough to stroke the fabric of her bottle-green designer skirt. *Ashley, you did well,* she thought.

She pulled down the sun visor of her red BMW, opened the mirror and teased her layer-cut hair, and pressed her lips together to spread her bronze lipstick evenly. That done, she retrieved her cell phone from the passenger seat and dialed with her right hand as she steered with her left.

After a short series of beeps, the recorded voice told her she had a new voice message. She pressed the button to retrieve it while passing a truck, and returned the phone to her ear.

The message was brief and indecipherable, but the voice belonged to a man ... a man she thought she recognized. A man who was very drunk.

She swerved to miss a hubcap and pressed the number four to bring back the message. What she really wanted was to throw the phone out the window. But it wasn't the electronic device she was mad at; it was Richard.

"Watch where you're going, idiot!" The shout was followed by the sound of a blaring horn.

In her annoyance, Ashley had crossed the centerline, nearly sideswiping the car next to her. As the car shot past, a man's hand extended from the passenger-side window in a middle-finger salute.

Instead of yelling at the speeding car, she yelled an obscenity into the phone. She caught herself, ashamed of her immaturity yet still pissed. The last time Richard got drunk and started calling people, she had to get up in the middle of the night to bail him out of jail.

"I'm not in the mood for *that*," she said to the windshield. "Matter of fact, I'm fed up with his tired ass. And to think I might have been in ..."

She didn't finish because she realized that, even though she'd hoped for more, the chances of that happening had just evaporated out the window.

She threw the phone into the passenger seat and checked her watch. *Good. They're not on the road this week. He should be home. Think I'll make a little pit stop.*

With the needle hitting eighty and nearing the Peachtree Street exit, she could see the entrance to the gated community where Richard lived. She nodded at the gatekeeper as he clicked the lock to let her drive in, knowing it would do no good to ask the elderly white man if Richard had driven out lately. The old fart barely knew he was on the planet. So she just smiled and waved at him, and parked on the street in front of Richard's building.

She removed her keys before getting out of the car. No matter how good the neighborhood, everyone wanted a BMW, and she didn't feel charitable about donating hers. Smoothing her hair into place, she walked up the shrubbery-lined walkway, bounded up the short flight of steps and knocked on the front door.

Sixty seconds later, she was still knocking. Taking a step back, she took a small notebook from her purse and began writing:

> *It's been fun, but I think it was a bad idea mixing*
> *business with pleasure. You're a great dancer, and*
> *one hell of a hockey player, but this will never work.*
> *Get some help with the drinking before it costs you*
> *your career. I'll have the firm assign you another*
> *lawyer. I think this is best for both of us. See you in*
> *the office someday. Your friend, Ashley.*

Slipping the note under the front door, she turned and walked briskly to her car, relief and regret creating a bitter mixture inside her.

When faced with a dilemma like this, most women would go home, pour a glass of wine, run a hot tub with Warm Vanilla Sugar bubble bath, light a scented candle and escape reality for a while. But that wasn't in Ashley Heath's nature. She did rev up her BMW and head home—but this time, with her mind on the man she planned to see on Monday: Dr. Joe Fry.

Thirteen

On Monday at three p.m., Ashley rapped lightly on the reception area's opaque window. After a few seconds, she said aloud, "I *know* that heifer sees me standing out here."

The window banged open to reveal Vickie's scowling face. "Look," she snapped, "if you don't mind, please ring the bell! Don't you see that note?"

"What note?" Ashley asked, enjoying herself.

Vickie reared up, leaned forward, stuck her arm out the window and pointed to the magic-markered sign next to it. As she sat down she said, "The note that tells you not to knock on the glass. *That* note. Why don't you read it next time?"

Ashley glanced at the note. "Ohhhh, *that* note. The one that says 'Please do not knock on the window'?"

"Yes," Vickie hissed.

She'd seen the sign, of course; it was hard to miss it. But knocking on the window had brought the desired result. "This hand-lettered thing? I thought it was just some scribbling from one of Dr. Fry's patients." She traced the letters slowly with one Tikki Punch-tipped fingernail. "So unprofessional looking. Surely he hasn't seen this yet! And, by the way, hon, could you let him know I'm here? It's Ms. Heath."

"Ms. *Heath*," Vickie said, "Dr. Fry is well aware of the problem of *inattentive* patients tapping on the glass instead of ringing the buzzer. And, I assure you, he is also well aware of the corrective measure I've taken."

Smacking her forehead in mock astonishment, Ashley exclaimed, "Oh, right, now I remember *you*! You were the one having the cozy lunch with my best friend's husband the other day!"

Vickie shot back, "What can I do for you, Ms. *Heath*? Do you have an appointment? As I think I *told* you already, Dr. Fry is booked solid."

"As I just *said*," Ashley returned, "let Dr. Fry know that Ms. Heath is here, *please*."

"We work on appointments in this office, *Heifer*," Vickie yelled, not caring who heard her anymore. "If you want to see Dr. Fry, you schedule an appointment!" She slammed the appointment book closed to punctuate her meaning and glared at the woman, her breath coming in shallow gasps.

Joe heard the exchange and dashed toward the sound, thinking it might be a medical emergency. "What's going on?" he shouted when he neared Vickie's desk.

The sight of the woman who'd occupied his thoughts since the Staples' party locked in a staring contest with his receptionist stopped him. Vickie looked ready to go right through the window and punch Ashley out.

"Hold on a minute," he said, giving Vickie a slow wave of his hand he hoped would soothe her temper. "Hey, Ashley. This is a nice surprise. What brings you by?"

Ashley relaxed and turned to face him with a charming smile. "Hi, Joe. If you can spare me a few moments ...?"

Calmer, Vickie addressed her boss. "I told her that you were booked up. It ain't my fault she doesn't listen."

Joe took a deep breath and said quietly, "Ashley, Vickie's right. I *am* booked solid. Every one of my exam rooms is occupied, and I really must see these patients before I'm through for the day. But I don't have to make rounds at the hospital until six o'clock. If you don't mind waiting, why don't I take you to my office? We can talk in between patients."

"But, Doc, you've—"

"That'll be fine with me," Ashley said, glaring at Vickie. "But I really don't want to mess up your schedule. Would it be better if I come back another day?"

"It's no problem," Joe replied. *There's no way I'll let you go now that you're here.* "No problem at all." He reached past Vickie to click the lock to the waiting-room door. "Come on back."

As they walked down the hallway, Joe was certain he'd taken at least three of the daggers Vickie was directing Ashley's way.

"Please forgive my receptionist," he whispered to Ashley. "She's very protective of me, I'm afraid."

"Oh, I wasn't *maaaad.*"

He turned to her with a questioning look on his face, and she smiled. "Joe, you know and I know that anyone who works for a doctor thinks the doc is royalty. But, really, it's *attorneys* who can do no wrong."

He laughed, realizing all over again what a very attractive woman she was.

They reached his office, and Joe pushed the door open for her. "I won't be too long. Make yourself at home." Heart pounding at her nod and smile, he nodded back and closed the door.

∞

There were several comfortable-looking chairs in the room, but Ashley was too restless to sit; the triumph of one-upping Vickie had her batteries too highly charged right now. She began to examine her surroundings.

The room was dominated by a U-shaped mahogany desk surrounding a high-backed chair of burgundy leather. The desk had a smoked-glass top and a computer monitor inset directly into the desktop. The person in the chair had only to look down to see the entire screen and keyboard simultaneously.

"Nice," she muttered, and made a mental note to get a desk just like that when she made partner.

The cherrywood and leather chairs on the other side were impressive in their own right, and fine antiques. "Unless I miss my guess," she said aloud, knowing she was correct. When she wasn't in the courtroom or at the mall, shopping, she was browsing in antiques galleries.

A putter in one corner showed that Fry was a golfer, and there were indications of many more interests on the cherrywood bookshelves lining three walls of the office. The Sumerian sculpture, African artifacts and volumes of ideological, theological and archeological books—all displayed a deeper side of this more and more intriguing man.

Ignoring the side chairs, Ashley settled into Joe's chair to think about what she'd seen. Her eyes wandered and came to rest on a large painting of a little boy and a woman across the office. She smiled when she realized the little boy was Joe, at maybe ten or twelve years old. The woman standing next to him, who had the same distinct lower jawline, forehead and eyes he did, must be his mother. Her expression was one Ashley had seen many times in African-American matriarchs—one of unflinching integrity, dignity, pride and honor.

Both the boy and the woman were dressed in their Sunday best, and the youngster, emulating his mother's stern expression, already resembled the man of character and accomplishment she had recently met.

Ashley sighed and resumed her search for other clues of Joe's past. Meanwhile, she asked herself again why she'd come here today. Her caseload was jammed full; it wasn't as if she had nothing better to do than sit here and wait on the convenience of a busy man.

Well, part of it was to put that bitch on notice about Klaxton, Ashley admitted. But the other reason she was on guard was that, for once, the rumor mill had failed her. There had been no word from on high about a promotion, and it was difficult for her to concentrate on her work in the vacuum created by such resounding silence. Since she couldn't keep her mind on work, following up on her interest in Joe Fry was the next best option.

And then, there was the salt. To protect Angie, she had to know if Trease's superstitions about the use of salt to put a hex on a beautiful woman had any basis in fact. More specifically, if the landlord of the building where the substance was found took such things seriously. Or if his cleaning lady did. Sure, she was attracted to Joe. But her legal mind wouldn't rest until she had answers to those questions.

When she first sat in Joe's chair, she didn't notice the open box next to it. She spun the chair around to investigate, bumping the computer mouse with her elbow as she did so.

"Wow, what do we have here?" Ashley reached down and picked up one small figurine, then another. She reached for a third, but withdrew her hand as though she'd been burned. "Man, I'd hate to pay his insurance premiums. This stuff is *expennnsiiiive!*" Well, at least she figured so. Even though ancient in appearance, the items were in excellent condition. And unless she missed her guess, those were real emeralds in the eyes of the statuettes.

With her hands thus occupied, her thoughts continued to race, thinking about seeing Joe without the noise, the buzz, the booze of a party scene—to see how he reacted to her without all those distractions around. He was even more handsome than she remembered. She smiled. *And not so old-looking, either.* And, so far, the vibes had been strong and positive. *For whatever that's worth.*

While she thought, she kept looking through the box. Along one side of it was a leather notebook, similar to one she'd once seen on a trip to New York. The auctioneer's book used at Sotheby's to record sales was of fine-grained leather, just as this one was.

Ashley carefully slid the book out of the box, and was soon enraptured. "Samples from the Tigris and Euphrates areas? 1300 BC? Wow!" Ashley glanced back at the box. She'd seen *pictures*, but never thought she would ever see the real thing.

Still looking at the book, Ashley unconsciously spun the chair around, bringing her gaze in line with the computer screen. When she bumped the mouse earlier, she had unknowingly deactivated the screen saver and revealed the document it hid. Most screen savers were on a timer; if she'd waited just a few more minutes to turn around, she might not have noticed what was underneath. Now, her curiosity in full control, she began reading.

According to the header, the e-mail was sent today, from someone named Aratha Munami, the chief curator for the state museums of Egypt. What she read caused her mouth to fall open:

> *My dear friend,*
>
> *To answer your question, salt has been used in rituals throughout recorded history. In ancient times, many societies considered it more precious than gold, and wealthy people used it not only to preserve and season their food—much as we do today—but also to*

prevent and treat disease, and to thwart evil spirits. It is commonly assumed that the latter use has been discarded, but this is not the case in many countries, including several in Africa. There, many tribes believe salt is capable of precipitating the downfall of shamans, warlocks and witches, and it is still used frequently in many of their rituals for that purpose.

As to your specific question, only the intent of the person engaging in the ritual determines whether the use of salt is for good, or for evil. Might I recommend that you refer to some excellent references on the subject, such as ...

Half of the long string of impressive-sounding titles weren't even in English.

"Wow," Ashley whispered, eyes narrowed. "Well, I guess that answers one question—if the good doctor didn't take it seriously, he wouldn't have e-mailed an expert in Egypt about it."

But still, did Joe do that because he believed in it, or because he was worried that someone else did?

She didn't want to be caught snooping, particularly in light of what she'd just read. While waiting for the screen saver to come back on, she carefully replaced the book and other objects in the box, then moved to one of visitor's chairs, picked up a medical journal and opened it. Her eyes gazed blankly at the text—it might as well have been in Sanskrit—while she struggled to understand what she'd just seen.

Fourteen

Joe's last patient, a woman who listed her age as seventy-seven on the intake form although she looked closer to ninety, was the one Klaxton had referred to him. She was accompanied by her daughter, who unfortunately didn't seem to have much more information than Klaxton had.

"Doctor, I know it sounds crazy," the daughter told him. "She keeps saying someone put roots or some kind of voodoo on her back home."

"Roots?" Joe repeated. "Does she have any idea who might have done that to her?"

The daughter, Jarvia, looked shocked at his question. "Don't tell me you take that seriously!"

"I'm not saying I do or don't," Joe replied. "But since your mother does, I have to take that into account if I'm going to get the fullest picture of what's troubling her."

Jarvia nodded and turned to the wizened woman, addressing her in what sounded like a tribal dialect.

Joe saw the old woman's face brighten as Jarvia relayed his question. Her answer took a while. Joe leaned back in his chair and waited for Jarvia to translate.

After a few minutes, Jarvia placed her hand on her mother's arm, turned to him and said, "I know this will sound silly, but Mother keeps saying ... well, she keeps saying that the name of the person is a word that, in our language, means 'no forgiveness.' Said the spirit-man in her village told her that. But ..." Jarvia's face turned sad. "I haven't been back to Sierra Leone in a long time. So I'm not sure what she means by that. I'm sorry." She cast a sidelong glance at her frail mother.

"No need to apologize," Joe assured her. "The main thing is that she's identified an actual person in her own mind. If we have to refer her to a ... another type of specialist, that information might be helpful."

Jarvia noticed Joe's hesitation. "It's all right, Dr. Fry. Dr. Staples told me she might have to see a psychiatrist. I understand. There's no shame in it. I'll do anything to help her get better."

Joe understood Jarvia's reasoning. Judging from Klaxton's referral letter, Jarvia's mother was in a great deal of pain. Klaxton's orders for Lortab, a potent narcotic, were for the maximum dosage. Joe made a note to get with him later and discuss lowering the dosage long enough for him to try other remedies.

Joe told Jarvia that he wanted to try tomography, explained how it might help with a diagnosis, and added that he wanted to run some other tests. "I might refer her to a tropical disease specialist next," he said, choosing his next words with care. "I hope you understand that we might have to take a slightly unconventional tack if the conventional methods don't identify the problem."

"I don't care," Jarvia said. "If I have to, I'll even bring the spirit-man to America—if I have to go get him myself!"

"I'm sure it won't come to that," he told her, hoping he was right.

After helping Jarvia wheel her mother to the front and arranging for the tomography, Joe headed to his office, where he found Ashley sitting in one of the side chairs, her back to him, reading the Bible. He stood with a quizzical smile on his face, unsure what to do next.

When Ashley had finally given up trying to read one of Joe's medical journals, she'd noticed the Bible, sitting on the same ornately carved side table as the old painting of Joe and his mother. She could tell that this Bible wasn't just for show. Its large, illuminated pages were dog-eared from use and had several bookmarks. Unaware of the door's noiseless opening, she flipped to one of the bookmarks, happening on the Book of Zephaniah. Intrigued by the mention of salt in the description of Sodom and Gomorrah there, she grabbed up the heavy book and headed toward Joe's desk, intending to read the e-mail again and try to make some sense of it through the scriptures. That was when she saw Joe standing in the doorway.

"Oh, hi, Joe!" she said, jumping in spite of herself. "I was just reading your Bible, and ... your chair looked a lot more comfortable than the ones on this side of the desk."

Joe nodded and sat in his chair as she rushed to replace the Bible on the carved table.

"Please don't feel you have to stop reading, Ashley. It's a good book," he said, smiling.

"Now that you've finally got a minute, I'm more interested in talking to you," she said, reclaiming the visitor's chair. "I'm not much of a Bible reader anyway. It just looked interesting."

"Well, if you don't read the Bible, I highly recommend it," Joe said. "Not only God's inspired word, but also a fascinating historical document." He took the stethoscope from around his neck and placed it on the desk. "I'm sorry you had to wait so long. Now, tell me what brings you here."

She took a deep breath. "I hope you won't think I'm meddling, but ... Angie is my friend. A *good* friend. And I guess sometimes I feel a little protective of her." She grinned. "Kind of like a receptionist might feel toward the doc she works for. It's about the salt Angie found in her office."

To his confused look, she rushed to explain. "While we were at the beauty shop Friday, Angie called Klaxton to tell him she was running late, and he mentioned that he'd talked to you about it. I ... maybe this sounds silly, but Trease—that's our hairdresser—overheard Klaxton and Angie talking, and made a big deal about it."

"How so?" Joe asked.

"She said ... someone might be trying to work a spell on Angie. That tore my girl up a little bit, if you know what I mean."

The look on Joe's face told her he did.

Remembering the e-mail from Egypt, Ashley was careful with her next question: "And ... I don't believe in this voodoo-and-roots stuff myself. Do you?"

Joe rocked back in his chair, looking thoughtful, remembering the things he'd seen in his house since Courtney's death. Finally, he said, "You might say I've been ... involved in spiritual matters since I was a child. And these days, I'm not surprised by what I hear or see people do. Or what they believe in. But ... to believe in something gives it power over you. For myself, I believe there's a God, yet I acknowledge the existence of evil too."

He leaned forward, and his dark eyes bore into hers. "What one person considers a bunch of hooey, others might find fatally real. Do you get what I'm trying to say, Ms. Heath?"

Ashley nodded, "Joe, 'Ms. Heath' is so formal—for judges and clients, not for my friends. Call me Ashley." She smiled. "At the party, you said you never met a stranger. Were you serious about that ... or was that just a line you use on all the women?"

This time, Joe's smile was bashful. "No, I haven't forgotten a word of what I said. I just didn't want to presume too much."

Their eyes met, and Joe shifted his eyes away. To occupy himself, he began shutting down his computer.

"Don't tell me you're shy," Ashley said.

He glanced up at her. "Where did that come from?"

"Well, if I'd looked at the typical brother the way I just looked at you, he'd have been trying to push up on me by now."

Joe grinned. "I'll take that as a compliment. In you, I see a beautiful woman to whom I'm very much attracted. But I also see a woman who demands respect. I'd never disrespect you or myself by acting like a street-thug. Pushing up on pretty ladies, as you put it, isn't my style."

"Just what *is* your style, Joe?"

He thought a moment, then decided it was worth the risk. "Would I be a typical brother if I said that I've had an image of you etched into my mind since the night of the party?"

"Ah ... that's interesting." Without realizing it, Ashley's voice lowered. "I guess that's what I picked up on the first time I met you. So why *didn't* I hear from you before now?"

Joe shrugged. "I presumed you were either taken, or you only dated a ... certain type of man."

She chuckled. "Well, I'm certainly not taken. And that hockey puck you saw on my arm the other night was a client, nothing more. But you're partly right," she added, holding his gaze. "I was impressed with you, too. You're not like most men I meet. If you were," she flashed him a smile, "I feel sure I would have heard from you. But since I didn't ..."

"Hmmm ...?" His reply was bland, his demeanor anything but.

She had an ephiphany, and leaned back in the chair. "Well, I ... I don't guess I really came here to talk about the salt. I don't believe in that kind of stuff. It's just that it was bothering Angie. What I really wanted ... I guess ... was to ask you out."

"Would you like a cup of coffee?" Joe asked. As he spoke, he got out of his chair and headed toward the door. "I forgot to offer you one, and I could use one myself."

She laughed and nodded, and yelled at his receding back, "Cream and sugar in mine, please!"

"Got it," he called out.

When he returned, a uniformed woman was following him, holding a tray with two steaming mugs, sugar and creamer dispensers, napkins and spoons. She had a nametag announcing her as Denise Whitby, RN.

Ashley gave Joe a wary look. "If I'd known you needed help, I would've come with you."

"That's all right," Denise piped up. "I was just on my way out, and hated to see this coffee go to waste." She turned to Joe. "Okay, I'm out the door. Just put the cream up before you go, and I'll take care of the rest tomorrow."

Joe nodded. "Thank you. Should I walk you out?"

"No, Gwyn is leaving, too. We'll be fine. You two have a good evening, and I'll see you tomorrow."

Ashley looked at Joe as the nurse left the room. "You sure did get *helpless* all of a sudden."

He took the visitor's chair next to her. "On the contrary. I *really wanted* a cup of coffee, and I *was* embarrassed that I hadn't offered you any. Denise was in the kitchen when I got there, fussing about wasting half a pot of coffee. When she saw me pouring two cups, she insisted on helping me." While he spoke, he added sugar and cream to his cup, stirring the brew as though his life depended on it.

"Uh-huh," Ashley replied, leaning over to add cream and sugar to her own cup.

As she did, she saw him tap the side of his cup with the spoon. The actions were deliberate—*tap … tap … tap.* Joe glanced up, noticed her watching, but only smiled sheepishly.

"Joe, you're a hard man to figure," Ashley said.

"That's the same thing my mother says," he replied, leaning back in his chair. "Now, back to what we were talking about. I just want to know one thing."

"What's that?" She stopped stirring her coffee and waited.

"You surprised me. I never thought a woman as … that a woman like you would be interested in someone like me. I'm sure you have your choice of men, brother or no. Why me?"

When Ashley didn't answer immediately, Joe said, "Don't go quiet on me. After all, this is the new millennium. Remember? It's okay for a woman to ask a guy out."

The look on his face was so abject and hopeful at the same time, Ashley had to laugh, doing a spit-take with her coffee. "Okay, you pass the test," she finally said, grabbing one of the napkins to wipe coffee off the desk.

"Good!" he said. "And I would be delighted to go out with you, anytime, anywhere. But I must warn you, I'm not much of a socialite. Going to the Staples' party was rare for me. Besides work, I really don't do much else."

She cast her eyes down, then back up at him. "I had a lot of fun with you at the party. And it's pretty obvious to anyone who spends any time in this room that you're a man of many and varied interests." Nodding toward the putter in the corner, she added, "I like to shop. You have a mindless hobby, too, I see. So maybe we can just go get a bite to eat and have a few laughs some night."

He smiled, trying to slow his racing pulse. "I'd like that. Shall I give you a call?"

"Sure. By the way, I meant to ask you ... is that your mother with you in that picture?" She pointed to the painting.

"Yes," Joe replied, glancing fondly at the image. "She's very special to me. I haven't visited her in a while. I'm looking forward to seeing her over Thanksgiving."

"That's nice. You're from Middle Georgia originally, right?"

He nodded. "And you?"

"Atlanta. Born and raised. When I was little, I dreamed about what it would be like to live in a small town. It's probably a happier place to grow up than the city."

She hadn't meant to reveal so much, Joe suspected; she cast her eyes down and examined her nails.

"Small towns have their appeal, but they have their problems too," he said. "More than you might think."

"Maybe so," she murmured. Then she said with forced cheer, "Now, about that date?"

He checked the ornate clock on his desk and thought for a moment. "Let's see ... How about dinner tonight at eight? That will give me time to go home and change after rounds."

"That sounds great."

Joe smiled. "Okay. Give me directions, and I'll be there at eight sharp."

Her eyes turned playful. "How about if I pick *you* up? I saw that tank you drive parked out at the side of the building. I want to take you for a *real* ride."

Instead of being insulted, he laughed. "I see you're a new age woman after all."

He wrote the directions to his house on a yellow notepad, handed it to her and walked her out the back entrance, and watched as she scratched off in the red Beamer, smiling at how good he felt about tonight, but hoping that Ashley was right: that the salt in Angie's office didn't portend tragedy.

Fifteen

"Dr. Staples, that was your last patient," Tiffany said as she placed a stack of charts on Klaxton's desk.

He looked up from the file he'd been reading. "Really? Is Angie almost finished, too?"

Tiffany put her hands on her hips. "Have you been too busy to notice? Dr. Angie canceled her patients and sent her staff home right after two o'clock."

"Probably an emergency at the hospital," he conjectured.

Tiffany shrugged and placed a file in his inbox. "I'm putting the charts you asked for *right here*." She was all too familiar with his tendency to misplace things.

He looked at the stack. "Where did all those come from?"

"Well ... *you* said not to turn anybody away, right?"

"Yeah, we need to keep the momentum up while it's flowing. No patient flow, no cash flow."

She smiled. "I got your back, Doc. All the claims from today have already been transmitted. You know, we saw over fifty people today. Fifty-three, to be exact. I think that's our highest yet."

"Tiff, that's what I like about you," he said, returning her smile. "You're on it. And thanks for remembering those charts." He reached for the first one on the stack. "Keep up the good work. You're going to be on the list for a raise real soon." Noting her pleased surprise, he added, "You're always the first to get here and the last to leave. Don't think I haven't noticed."

Her smile widened. "Thanks, Dr. Staples. Oh, and don't forget ... Vickie's waiting to speak with you."

"Did she say what she needed?" He stood quickly and removed his starched white lab jacket, then hung it on the coat rack near the door.

"Nope. Just that she needed to talk to you. She's been in the waiting room for about twenty minutes. I told her you were still seeing patients, but she wanted to wait."

He returned to his desk and lowered himself back into his seat. "That's fine, Tiff. Tell her to come on back on your way out. And, oh, what did you do with the lab report on ... on the kid with meningitis."

She removed the top document from a tray labeled "Lab Reports" and handed it to him. "Doc, I'm out. Do you want me to lock the front door on my way? There's no one else out there besides Vickie."

"No, that won't be necessary," he said, peering at the report. "I'll be right behind you." He looked up. "On second thought, go ahead and lock it. Vickie can take the back stairs when she leaves."

Klaxton continued to read the lab report until he heard the *clickety-clack* of spike heels in the corridor. Vickie, wearing a very short, red silk miniskirt and matching handkerchief top, appeared in the doorway.

Klaxton looked up slowly. "Come on in, Vickie. What's up?"

"You tell me," she replied with a devilish look. "I'm on my way to my night job, and I just wanted to invite you to stop by the club later if you're free and catch my act. I'm doing some Billie Holliday tonight." Without being invited, she entered and took a seat in front of him, crossing her legs slowly. "'You're My Thrill,'" she sang softly, her eyes holding Klaxton's gaze. "Like that?"

"Nice voice," he replied, stunned by Vickie's boldness. But she must have known that Angie was gone for the day ... along with the last patients and the rest of the staff.

"Too bad you can't come," she said in a seductive whisper. "I'd love for you to see my act."

This was a come-on. No doubt about that. The question was, was it also a setup? She had certainly set it up for privacy. He felt himself growing irresistibly interested. Still, Angie was waiting for him, probably planning a special evening. She'd been doing that almost every night lately.

His look was guarded, but Vickie saw the interest in his eyes. She gave him a reassuring smile. "Remember? I owe you for lunch anyway. Happy hour, drinks on me?"

"Uh ... No. Not today. I'm kind of burned out. Maybe next time."

Her smile was coy, but she must have decided she'd tortured him enough; looking around, she said, "Nice place. One of the most elegant offices I've seen in a long time. Beats our office by a mile."

Klaxton followed her gaze. The contractor the Staples chose had carved out a spacious office area, which they'd decorated in off-white and sea green. The softly upholstered leather sofas and chairs in the waiting room were as refreshing to look at as they were comfortable. Over the massive sofa was an exquisitely framed print of *By the Bayou*, one of Angie's favorites.

Remembering Angie helped Klaxton hold it together when his eyes turned back to Vickie. "Thanks. We were going for the tranquil look when we picked everything out."

"Well, it's lovely," Vickie said. "I heard that your wife left early. So why are you working so late?"

"I could ask you the same thing, couldn't I? Joe running a slave-work camp down there or something? I saw the cars out there during lunch. You guys working through lunch?"

Vickie shook her head. "No, on the contrary. We weren't very busy today. I had some claims I needed to get caught up on, so I ate at my desk. Besides, Dr. Fry was tied up back in his office talking to that uppity Ashley Heath most of the afternoon."

When he didn't answer right away, Vickie smiled and continued. "Some people'll just do anything, you know? She called Friday evening, claiming she needed to see him like it was medical-related. But I know she just wants to give him some. Girls know these kinds of things." She rolled her eyes for emphasis. "We may all play different games, but the objective's always the same."

He was out on the limb. He knew it. But suddenly, he no longer dreaded the fall. "And what objective is that, little sister?"

By way of answering, Vickie walked over to his desk, placed her hand on it, leaned forward and said, "I see a very attractive man in front of me who I wish would stop running and give a sister some time."

All thoughts of Angie disappeared, replaced by the sight of Vickie's long ebony tresses hanging so low, they almost touched his hand across the desk. "Ahh ... I wouldn't call it running. Just say that I'm sparing you some trouble."

"What if I like a little trouble?" Vickie said, her eyes glinting with fun, and something else.

Joe might still be in the building, might come by any moment to discuss the patient with the mysterious illnesses. He had to see patients, then get home. He had promised. But work would have to wait. Everything would have to wait. He closed the chart, laid it on the desk, and rocked back in the oversized chair.

That was all the invitation Vickie needed. She moved around the desk, took a spot behind the chair, placed her hands on his shoulders and began massaging them. Unsure at first but more confident when he didn't move away, she slid her hands past his shoulders and down to his chest. Her action brought a soft moan from him.

"Why are you so tense? This spot right here is really tight." As she spoke, she worked her hand to an area just below his scrub-suited neckline.

Eyes still closed, he whispered, "You're something else."

He hadn't spoken the words, but moaned them. Vickie felt giddy with her victory. "Are you sure you don't want to take up me on that drink I offered earlier?" she breathed into his ear.

"I've got to go by the hospital when I leave here."

"All work and no play makes for a dull life," she said in her good-little-girl voice.

"What was it you wanted to talk to me about?" As he spoke, he took a discrete whiff of her sweetness.

"Oh, nothing. Just an excuse to be near you. From where I'm standing, looks like I picked a good day. You look like you need some company."

He slowly spun the chair around to face her. "So, what? ... You came to take care of me? Do you really think you can handle all that comes along with the territory?"

Before she could answer, he snaked his hands under her short red skirt and pulled her astride his outstretched legs. Looking her dead in the eyes, he gently stroked her soft, round bottom, pushing all other thoughts from his mind.

She lowered herself just enough to grind against him. Slowly rocking in a circular motion, she opened her eyes and said, "Looks like you stopped running, Dr. Staples."

In response, he pulled her close enough to kiss lips that were already open for him. "If you want to know the truth, I think I've been running toward you, not away."

Holding her securely, he gently spun the chair around until she was sitting on the edge of his desk, easing up her skirt as the chair turned. He opened her legs wide, and his sharp intake of breath revealed his acknowledgement of how beautiful her body was. Reaching out with his fingers, Klaxton rubbed her inner thighs lightly, occasionally running his fingers underneath her lace thong, teasing her.

When he began to stroke her, she gasped and pulled away slightly, leaning over to kiss him on the earlobe. "Don't start something you can't finish," she whispered.

When he hesitated, she gave an encouraging smile. "Remember, I'm not a kiss-and-tell kind of girl."

He rose to a standing position and reached over to remove a condom from the back of the lower desk drawer, wincing when he recalled that he'd put them there, thinking he'd never need them again after his breakup with Stephanie. Pushing the memory away, he handed it to Vickie to open as he untied his scrub suit bottoms. She removed the condom from its moist package and slowly rolled the latex up the shaft of his erection, bringing another moan from him. When she finished, she leaned back and spread her legs wider, and he lowered his body to the edge of the desk.

The telephone rang, its tone shrill and punitive in the turgid silence. They jumped apart and Klaxton grabbed for the receiver, struggling to get his breath under control.

It was his private line; it was Angie. "Hello, baby!" he whispered. As he huddled over the receiver, his scrub bottoms still around his knees, he barely noticed a resigned Vickie tiptoeing out the door, high heels in hand.

∞

While Stephanie sat parked in the freezing-cold outside Klaxton's office, she forced herself to dig back into her memory. Had Klaxton really killed her best friend and gotten away with murder? Had he used Cheryl and abandoned her, then did the same thing to her ... and was now doing the same thing to another unsuspecting woman?

She had pulled in over an hour ago, just as dark was coming on, determined to know who owned the red Volkswagen—except for Klaxton's Mercedes, the only other car in the lot at this hour. In her heart, she knew it was another woman. The moving shadows she'd seen in the dim-lit, second-floor window confirmed that. And she remembered....

The night of Cheryl's death, she'd just gotten out of the shower when she heard her machine go off. Thinking that maybe her nine-thirty had cancelled, she snatched a towel from the towel warmer, wrapped it around herself, opened the bathroom door wide to let the steam out and went to check her messages.

But when she punched in the number for the dating service, she got a shock, listening in disbelief as the operator told her the news: her fellow call girl, Cheryl Jaworski, had been found unconscious by firefighters after neighbors reported smoke coming from her apartment door. She was at Lenox Hill Hospital, in critical condition.

"I knew you'd want to get over there right away," the switchboard operator, Melanie, told her. "She ... She hasn't got any family here. Actually, no family that I know of. She never talked about her family."

Choking out a tearful thank you, Stephanie disconnected and ran to her message machine. The first message was from a sobbing Cheryl. "Call me, please! The test came back positive, and Klaxton, he ... he's not happy about it. Oh, God, what am I gonna do?"

Her stomach lurching, Stephanie glanced at the display. The time of the message was six thirty p.m. The display now read eight-eleven.

Stopping only to throw on jeans, boots and a sweater, Stephanie grabbed her jacket from the hall closet and headed out in search of a taxi.

The twenty-minute ride to the hospital seemed like an eternity. Finally, she was ushered into a small room, and a doctor came in. From the look on his face, Stephanie knew it was too late.

On the way to the hospital, she had called Klaxton to meet her there. Now, the two walked silently to the room where Cheryl's body lay. She was face up, her hands crossed on her chest. Her white-blond hair was disheveled and her face was pale, but there was nothing else to indicate that she was dead, stone dead.

Stephanie leaned over and kissed one pale cheek, putting her hand over Cheryl's; the flesh was still soft but no longer warm. She stood silent for a moment, then brushed by Klaxton. Considering Cheryl's last message, Stephanie was sure he had some heavy emotions, and Stephanie was too numb with both grief and shock to help him.

Afterward, Stephanie found out that Cheryl's death wasn't an accident. Her friend had been killed by a lethal injection of narcotics. The fire had apparently been set to cover the killer's trail. Hearing that, Cheryl's message took on ominous overtones.

"Klaxton, did you kill her?" she'd asked bluntly. "You had a key to her apartment. You're a doctor. You have access to drugs. And Cheryl had just told you she was pregnant."

"Steph, that's not true—"

"Don't lie to me, Klaxton. I got it from her own lips!" Stephanie had yelled. "She called me right before ... before whoever killed her got to her. How do I know *you* didn't go over there and take care of her so you wouldn't have to tell your wife you'd gotten another woman *pregnant?*"

"Stephanie, I *swear* to you I didn't kill her!" he said, pleading. "I was going to see her that night and talk about the— But I couldn't get away from the house. You've got to believe me. I didn't kill her!"

In her work, Stephanie had met many deceitful men. And sure, Klaxton Staples was no better and no worse. After all, he lied to his wife about his affair with Cheryl. But ... his voice and his posture convinced her. Not to mention that he had an alibi. She'd taken him at his word, and never asked again. Even more, she stood by him through the trial, and destroyed the damning answering machine tape. "If I ever find out that you lied to me," she'd told him, "I swear before God, I'll kill you my damn self."

Tonight, sitting in her car parked in a dark corner of the lot, knowing that his lying ways never ended, she accepted a bitter truth. Klaxton was a dangerous man and someone had to stop him. She owed that to Cheryl, and to Klaxton's newest woman. Maybe she didn't have the tape anymore, but there was still plenty she could do. Plenty.

Her eyes narrowed as she watched a woman enter the parking lot from the rear of the building, smoothing down her skirt as she walked. Klaxton exited only minutes later. Neither of them noticed her as they got into their cars and drove off, one after the other.

She blinked tears back. What she'd just seen made her stomach roll into a knot, but it gave her the courage she needed.

He dropped me for a whore nearly young enough to be his daughter, she thought, and her eyes turned into slits. *He can keep the fifty grand. I have something better in store for him.*

A glance in her rearview mirror showed her what she didn't want to see—the eyes of a woman who was disintegrating from self-pity and alcohol. But the revenge for what Klaxton had done to her would be bitter, and sweet. First, she'd find out who that little chippy was and have a private chat with her. Tell her the kind of man she was messing with. And then ... Well, she didn't know what to do after that. "But," she muttered, "I will surely figure it out!"

She reached beside her for the familiar bottle and twisted off the cap with one hand. After two good swigs she blew out a breath, cranked her car, turned on the headlights and sped off into the darkness.

Sixteen

All I ever wanted was to love someone and have them love me back. The words weighed heavily on Angie's heart as she collapsed onto the king-sized bed. If she could give him a child, Klaxton would love her unconditionally. She was sure of that! From the first time she met him, he spoke of his desire to have a family. *A big one*, he'd said. She could still remember how his eyes glowed that day, full of dreams and promise. Yet all the wishing in the world wouldn't make her infertility go away.

As quickly as she hit the bottom of that familiar pit, sudden anger pulled her out. Why was *she* always the victim? Was it really her inability to conceive that kept pulling Klaxton away from her? Or was it … the other thing? The thing she couldn't let herself think about.

She might as well have asked the wind to stop blowing. The memories came back, slicing at her like jagged pieces of glass, and she turned facedown on the bed and moaned. Somehow, he must have found out—something she'd accidentally said, or maybe her father had said. "It's not fair," she whimpered, reliving the way she'd felt after each time it happened.

Life had never been fair to her, she thought bitterly. She had studied this. Hell, she'd counseled patients in the same situation to get help. But not her. No. That could never be. She was and always would be a victim. Even when her subconscious screamed for her to speak of her childhood, shame kept her penned up. To speak the words would acknowledge what Angie had buried away in a cave, out of existence, just to survive. For the thousandth time, she told herself that she was a member of an educated family with money. And things like that weren't supposed to happen to girls like her. But they did anyway.

"Sins of the father," she whispered, and was gripped by a sudden insight. Could *that* be her punishment for not being able to have a baby? Could Stephanie Rogers' sudden reappearance be part of that punishment?

Seeing Stephanie getting off the elevator at St. Joseph's was like seeing a ghost rise up out of the tomb. *And,* Angie told herself with a sinking heart, *Stephanie wouldn't follow Klaxton all the way to Atlanta unless something was going on between them.* That much she knew. Victim or not, she wasn't stupid.

Angie had always suspected Stephanie. Even after the trial, during the three years he was at Elmira, Angie had passed Stephanie more than once in the parking lot, or in the hall outside the prison's visiting room. If they hadn't been having an affair before the murder, surely something must have started up afterward. Why else would she visit a married man in prison? But when Angie got up the nerve to ask him about it, he'd told her, *It's a free country, Angie. People can go anywhere they want.*

Long-concealed anger and hurt overwhelmed her. If Stephanie's showing-up was punishment, she had to do something to circumvent it, had to move forward to protect the man God had sent to deliver her back to sanity. With clearer certainty than she'd ever had before, she knew that protecting Klaxton from her past was the only thing that could save their marriage ... and their dreams to have a family of their own. So she could never tell him what had happened to her as a child.

Using a tissue to dry her eyes, Angie forced herself to think about the past weeks. The housewarming party, when the strange woman called, invaded her home and bragged about having an affair with Klaxton. When Ashley told her about Klaxton's lunch meeting with the hussy from Joe Fry's office. And the biggest blow of all—seeing Stephanie, best friend of a murdered prostitute, roaming the halls of one of the very hospitals Angie and Klaxton saw patients!

Her stomach clenched. *I have to do something. I have to!* But what? Confronting Klaxton would do no good. He'd deny everything, as always. Her head felt like a rain cloud, full of tears wanting to fall. She blinked them back. *No more crying. No matter what.*

She had finished early at the office and, on the way home, picked up two takeout orders of his favorite dinner from Bone's, the Buckhead steakhouse he adored, for a candlelight supper in bed. Stopped by her favorite lingerie boutique on Pharr Road and dropped a couple hundred on a gorgeous lilac silk-and-charmeuse number that she knew would make him drool. Had even run into the SunTrust branch near the house and changed two twenty-dollar bills into singles. Tonight, she would give him a show he wouldn't soon forget!

All that was before she called his office. When he hadn't phoned her by five thirty, she jumped into the shower, made up her face, curled her hair and put on her sexy lingerie. With leaden feet, as though already conceding a battle she hadn't known she was fighting, she set up the feast from Bone's on the gateleg table in their master suite. Riesling was chilling on the floor beside the table in a silver bucket of ice, and jasmine-scented candles burned in the silver candelabra, filling the air with their subtle and exotic aroma.

By six thirty, he still wasn't home. She called him on his cell phone first, then his pager, and only tried his private office line as a last resort. He answered, but something wasn't right. He sounded breathless. *Guilty.* And everything she'd forced to the back of her mind came rushing out.

To her question, he answered, "Got hung up going over some lab reports."

There'd been a silence before he continued, as if he needed time to gather his thoughts. "I'll be home soon, baby. Honest."

Honest. She gave a sour chuckle, remembering that.

She wanted to question him further, beg for reassurances. But that would only make him later coming home. The past had taught her that.

They'd seemed so close after Cheryl's death. Like allies in society's war against black men. His time at Elmira, while Angie helped the lawyers work on his appeal, brought them closer. But the palpable tension between them since the move to Atlanta was growing, not diminishing. She wanted to blame it on the overtime they both worked to build up the new practice. But she couldn't. Not anymore. Not after the way he'd sounded on the phone.

A sharp pain in her right side made her take to the bed again. She clutched a Porthault pillow and gasped. She was an ob-gyn, and perhaps knew too much, knew it could be anything from appendicitis to endometriosis to cancer. But that, she had to keep to herself. She never mentioned it at her own gyn checkups, for fear of the questions she could never answer. So the pain, too, was part of her punishment.

She forced her mind away from the physical pain and back to Stephanie. She had to think, had to have a plan to deal with that. What was she doing here anyway? Even if her profession, or her family, or a man had brought her to Atlanta, why would she be running around one of the hospitals where Klaxton and she practiced medicine?

The more Angie thought, the more it hurt. The more she considered the mess she was in, the more tears she shed. She loved and hated his ways all at once. But most of all, she hated the women that chased after him.

Fuming, she rolled off the bed, wincing, popped the cork on the Riesling and poured herself a glass of the sweet wine and drank it down. Then, trying to ignore the tiny, ice pick-like needles in her belly, she curled her knees into her chest and hugged herself. With the jasmine-scented candles perfuming the air, Riesling on her breath, she lay alone in the oversized master suite, waiting for her man to come home.

Seventeen

From the confidence she displayed in her stride to the full-length mirror in her bedroom, no one would guess that Ashley had less than two hours to get herself together.

Driving home, she conducted a mental inventory of her wardrobe, rejecting most outfits in her closet. By the time she pulled into the driveway of her apartment building, she'd narrowed her choices to what she was looking at: a peach chiffon shirt and brown leather mini, accented by a pair of pumps that made her calves as deadly as a 38-special in a Clint Eastwood movie.

"Maybe more like a semiautomatic assault rifle," she mused, turning to view herself from the side. If her perky breasts weren't enough to knock him out, certainly her bodacious curves and solid, well-toned thighs would. Ashley took one more look in the mirror, assured herself that every hair was in place, then grabbed her keys from the dresser. Barely twenty minutes later, she rang the doorbell on Joe's front porch.

Joe let her in, walked over to his CD player and removed the disc he'd been listening to. "Do you mind? You're providing the wheels, so I'll provide the music."

On the way to the restaurant, Ashley glanced down at the CD player. "So you're really into this Terrence Blanchard, huh? I had you figured as more the classical music type."

He gave her a sideways glance. "Why would you think that?"

"Just from watching you, that's all."

"Well, I guess the old cliché is true," Joe said. "You can't judge a book by its cover. Take you, for example. You're beautiful, articulate and intelligent. Not many people ... or at least an old dog like me ... would think of a hip-hopper like Kid Dog being your client."

Ashley gave him one raised eyebrow and a glimpse of a grin. "I can tell Angie's been talking about me."

Joe smiled and nodded. "Perhaps a little."

"Well, just to underline the truth of that old cliché ... under that hardcore look, Kid Dog's a talented artist who gives a lot back to the community. Goes to show you never can tell."

"That's true, so true," Joe replied, and settled back to enjoy the ride.

∞

Café Intermezzo was far less crowded than Joe expected. They had only a ten-minute wait for a table, and soon they were sitting in front of steaming plates of pasta with shrimp and garlic bread.

"So, tell me," he said, picking up a piece of the bread, "what is it that makes a woman like you take an interest in a man like me? A just plain Joe?"

Ashley twisted a rope of noodles around her fork and smiled into the bowl, making Joe wonder if he'd already asked that question. "No offense intended," he added quickly. "At this moment, I'm happier than a kid who just found his favorite toy under the Christmas tree."

"No offense taken," she said, and looked up at him. "You know, you asked me a similar question earlier, but I think I've got a better answer now." She took a deep breath. "Okay. Why I'm interested in you? The answer is … I don't know. Well, really, I *do* know. You're different from so many of the men I meet around Atlanta. Not the run-of-the-mill Mac Daddy players chasing every pair of legs that looks good under a skirt."

Joe's surprise was genuine. "Are there a lot of men like that around here? Players?"

Ashley's face reflected her annoyance, but not at Joe. "Remember, I grew up here. I don't feed into all the hype about Atlanta being 'the city of black prosperity' like some politician or other's always claiming. There's a whole bunch of fake brothers running around here that don't have a pot to piss in, let alone a back door to throw it out of. And a lot of them are dressed up in Armani suits they can't even afford to pay for."

She reached for a piece of garlic bread; instead of taking a bite, she started twisting small pieces from it. "You remember what you said in the car? About people not always being who we make them out to be?"

Joe nodded. "Right. But being who you are is a lot less stressful, I've found."

She put the roll aside and leaned forward. Her voice barely above a whisper, she said, "To get back to your original question, you are not a 'plain Joe,' and you never will be."

Taken aback at the compliment, he gave a nervous chuckle.

She fished a melting piece of ice from her glass and aimed it his way. "Hey, are you laughing at me? What's so funny?"

He ducked. "Be careful. You wouldn't want to hit some innocent bystander, would you?"

She pulled back at his warning and placed the ice between her lips instead.

"That's what I like about *you*," Joe said, settling back into his chair. "You respect the people around you, at least the ones who've earned it. I hope I always earn your respect."

Embarrassed, she averted her eyes.

But Joe wasn't fooled. Neither was he finished. "I noticed that the first night I met you at Angie and Klaxton's party. How willing you were to go around helping me pick up other people's garbage. All dressed up and dignified, and doing something you didn't have to do."

"Well, I was just helping Angie out," she murmured.

"I notice that about people because I'm like that, too," Joe said. "I guess I owe that to my mother. She'd say, 'Son, if you want respect, you got to give it first'."

Ashley thought how distant she and her family had become, and it made her sad."You and your mom are close?"

He paused. "Used to be. But it's different now. We love each other. Of course. But going home's kind of a heartbreak. Especially since ... my wife died."

"I'm so sorry, I didn't know—"

"It's all right, really," he said. "It's been several years. But it's ... I guess there are so many memories back home. Courtney and I grew up together. I owe my mom a visit, but it's ... still not easy."

He used the thick cloth napkin to brush nonexistent crumbs from his lips. "Enough about me. How about you? Do you have family here in Atlanta?"

"My mom lives here. But I don't see her much. What you said about how hard it is to go home to see your mother? It's funny, but it's almost as hard when you're in the same city." She picked up her fork, but made no move to begin eating again. "As you can probably tell, I'm biracial."

"Well, if you think about it," Joe said with a soft smile, "most brothers and sisters can say that, at least a little."

She felt her face grow warm. "Well, not exactly like that. Mine comes from a little closer on the family tree than slave days. My mother's white, my father's black. Dad left me and Mom because he had another family."

She looked at her plate. Joe wanted to speak, but forced himself not to. He wanted to hear it all.

Not looking up, Ashley continued. "Mom turned against her own family for him, and when he left, it hurt so bad that she started drinking. His leaving pretty much shattered her. And it ... damaged my trust in men. Especially black men."

"I see."

She returned her eyes to meet his and forced a half-grin. "Do you really? For a long time, I swore I'd never date a black man. I mean ... if I couldn't trust my very own father, what black man *could* I trust? But after ... meeting you ... I don't think it was black men. I think ... it was just me wanting some kind of revenge."

She put down her fork and picked up her glass. "Dating *white* men didn't bring me a whole lot of happiness, either. I *did* care for a few white guys. But it seemed like there was always a fence there ... a fence *I* put up. Like I didn't want to get hurt like my mother had." She took a sip from her water glass, buying a moment to collect her thoughts.

"So, did the fence keep the hurt out?" As he said the words, Joe realized that his question was aimed at himself as much as Ashley.

She nodded. "On the outside, yes. It did keep the hurt away. But on the inside ..." She returned the glass to the table, but kept her hand on it. "It was worse when I was younger. Been called everything from a zebra to half-breed. Started to dress down so I wouldn't draw attention. A t-shirt and loose jeans, hair pulled under a baseball cap ... my trademark."

Pressing his elbows on the glass table and resting his chin on his fists, Joe smiled. "I can't imagine you dressed like a tomboy. You really liked dressing that way?"

"*Like* had nothing to do with it, Joe. Or maybe it did. I didn't like who I was." She shrugged. "But when I got out of high school, things got better."

Joe's smile faded a bit. "But you still didn't trust black men?"

She dropped her eyes again, feeling her cheeks grow warn. "Well, I didn't, no. But I'm not sure I feel that way today. I ... I guess if I still did, I wouldn't be running my mouth like this to you, would I?" The warmth that had begun in her face was now flowing all over her body. Uncomfortable, she forced a smile and said quickly, "Joe Fry, I can't believe I've been going on about myself this long, and I completely forgot what I really wanted to talk about tonight."

"And what's that?" Joe asked, eyebrows raised.

"Remember what I came to your office about?"

He nodded.

"Trease—Montrease, that's my hairdresser—she's convinced someone's trying to put a spell on Angie. I tried not to worry about it, and Angie hasn't said anything else about it. But ... I have this feeling that she's buying into it."

"Okay," Joe replied. "But how do I fit in?"

"Well, you own the building, and Mrs. Caldwell works for you. Your housekeeper, right? And Angie acted a little shaky about her. So that made me think—"

"Mrs. Caldwell is harmless," Joe said. "She's a bit eccentric, that's all."

Ashley noted Joe's evasion. "What do you mean, *eccentric*? Eccentric, like she believes in that roots-and-voodoo business?"

"*We-l-l-l,* she does have her beliefs," Joe said. "But she'd never hurt anyone with it." He put his fork down, reached across the table and placed his hand over Ashley's, sending tingles up her arm. "Ashley, I know Angie's your friend. But ... just like you know *her,* I know Mrs. Caldwell. There's nothing to it. It'll all work out."

"Well, Joe," Ashley returned, "truth-time: what do *you* believe about roots and voodoo ... and spells?"

He smiled. "As I mentioned before, I believe in things like that only to the extent of the power they hold over other people. Remember me saying that things aren't always what they seem?"

She nodded.

"I like to find out what makes people do what they do. What motivates them, what affects them physically and spiritually. Other than that, I don't really take the ... roots-and-voodoo stuff too seriously."

Ashley smiled and changed her mind. There was a great deal to explore about this man, and she didn't want his growing attraction to her, and vice versa, derailed by further talk of spirits and spells—not the bad kinds, anyway. Time enough to pursue that later. Tonight, she had other decisions to make.

Eighteen

Klaxton lay restless on the bed, his mind kaleidoscoping. Angie still hadn't come home. It was relatively early yet, but he'd been so tired, he threw off his work clothes as soon as he got home, shrugged on a pair of worn Levis and an Atlanta Falcons sweatshirt and collapsed on the bed. He expected to crash and burn, but sleep was proving elusive. The headache wasn't helping, or the list of worries he kept going through.

At the top of the list was Stephanie. Or rather, the lack of her. In the weeks since their confrontation at the hospital, he hadn't heard from her, and that very night, he and Angie had reconnected. *Man*, he thought, *supper from Bone's, and sexy lingerie, too!* It was almost like old times. Even the sad news that Angie wasn't pregnant after all had brought them closer. And she would never know that her phone call had saved him from making a terrible mistake with Vickie, of promising Vickie far more than he could give her. He would always be grateful for that.

Still, he wondered why Stephanie had dropped out of sight. No phone calls, no pages, no more unwelcome visits. Maybe she found someone else. The idea was comforting. After all, he wished her no ill. Maybe their troubles were behind them.

Well, most of them, Klaxton thought, rolling onto his side in search of a more comfortable position.

Angie had adapted to their new life in Atlanta. *He* was the one who hadn't been able to move on. Even now, lying in this massive bed, he could close his eyes and be back on the narrow cot at Elmira, right down to smelling the Clorox used to mop the cement floors and hearing the grunts and snorts of other inmates as they slept. Even here, at times it seemed as if the new life he and Angie worked so hard to create was made of sand, not rock. He should have known better than to continue the affair with Stephanie after she followed him south. Now, he found her silence ominous.

And ... *Vickie.* No sooner had he dealt with the Stephanie, he almost walked right back into the same kind of trap. What happened that night wasn't all his fault. Vickie had come after him with a vengeance, and he'd been tired and preoccupied, not on his guard. But he knew she was trouble from Day One. And after their brief encounter, she'd become even more aggressive, as though determined to finish what they had started that day.

He looked over at the digital clock and was amazed to find that it was only ten twenty-four p.m. His head throbbed harder now. Klaxton strictly avoided medicating himself: an occupational hazard that caused many good physicians to fall. But he wished for an antidote to the pains, past and present, spiritual and physical, that plagued him. Some of that pain, he admitted, came from the long past.

Klaxton rarely talked about his upbringing, because he didn't want people to look down on him or pity him. But times like this, it was hard not to. He was only eighteen months old when his mother died of what the grownups called consumption. When he was a little older, maybe five, his grandmother, Ma Mae, explained it was a lung disease, tuberculosis. That was the first time he wanted to become a doctor—so he could cure that scary-sounding disease and save the lives of other kids' mothers.

He didn't have a picture of his mother, but he knew what she looked like. "Evelyn was the most beautiful woman you can imagine, Klax," his father would say as they lay together on the rollaway bed in Ma Mae's parlor. "Skin the color of molasses and hair like spun chocolate. And she was tall, just like you're going to be someday."

Klaxton loved hearing how he'd been named after Adam Clayton Powell Jr., a New York congressman and the son of a prominent African-American minister. But according to his father, his mom insisted on making *her* son's name unique.

"She said, 'This boy is not just going to be a junior,'" his father would recount. "She said, 'Let's spell Clayton with a K, for 'King,' because that's what he's going to be—a *royal* child.' When the nurse wrote the name down for the birth certificate, your mama made sure she knew to spell Klayton with a K. But I guess the nurse didn't have very good handwriting. When your birth certificate came back, it was spelled K-L-A-X-T-O-N. I guess that nurse's Y looked like an X to the typist. But when your mama saw that, she got a big grin on her face. She said, 'That's it! Klaxton, with a K *and* an X! He's one of a kind!'"

It made Klaxton happy when his dad talked about this, but it also made him sad. Ma Mae was good to him and he loved her, but he still wished he could have known his tall, beautiful mother with the molasses-colored skin. His father was a traveling salesman, on the road most of the time. But sometimes he'd show up at Ma Mae's and sleep on the rollaway in the parlor.

When Klaxton was six, Ma Mae died, and his dad took him to New York City. They lived in a small high-rise apartment in Harlem. There was a little girl there, too. His dad told him she was his sister, but Klaxton wondered how that could be. Her name was Charlotte—an ordinary name. And she didn't look like his father, or like the picture he carried in his head of his beautiful mother.

Their father worked sporadically. Sometimes they had no electricity and, once, no water for about a week. But helpless to leave, they became wary allies. When their father was home and drank too much and passed out, they took care of him.

Then came the day—the horrible day. Their father was passed out in the bedroom when the knock came—a sharp rap on the door, followed by "Open up! Family and Children's Services!"

Terrified, they clung to one another; neither had the nerve to go to the front door.

More knocking, followed by a loud boom, and the door crumpled inward. Two policemen, pistols drawn, charged in first, followed by two women. White people, all of them. Klaxton could see his father standing in the bedroom doorway, groggy and drawn-looking, wearing only boxers.

"Mr. Staples, we have come to place your children in foster care," the woman said, and reached out to pick Charlotte up.

Before Klaxton could ask, "What's foster care, Daddy?" he saw his dad spring forward. Shouts, scuffling, three short bursts like firecrackers—and their father fell to the floor, blood pumping from his chest.

Klaxton could smell the gunpowder in that cramped room, and the memory still made him want to cry. Over time, he'd come to understand that his father had been vulnerable because he was black and uneducated, ripe for a beating by a world designed for men like him to fail. Yet he learned from his father's hard lesson.

What happened to his father would never happen to him. No way, no how.

Klaxton never saw Charlotte again. He moved from one set of foster parents to another. Sometimes, a group home. For good or ill, he always had to leave them all sooner or later.

Growing up in New York's public school system, even in college and medical school, he would catch sight of a tall, molasses-colored woman with hair like spun chocolate walking down a city street and wonder, just for a second, if she could have been his mother, so proud and beautiful.

∞

He was awakened from a restless slumber by the phone. He found it in the dark, pressed the cold receiver to his ear.

"Did I wake you, baby?" Angie sounded exhausted.

"Uh ... No, baby. I was just dozing a little. Another late delivery?"

"Umm-hmmm," Angie said. "Twin boys. And the second one took his time coming into this world." Her words trailed off into a yawn. "You know men. Some of y'all are just born stubborn."

"Sorry, baby," he said. "How much longer do you think you'll be?"

"Another hour or so. Just until the pediatrician can take over. I should be finished before midnight. But don't wait up ... You need your sleep. I promise I'll make it up to you."

"All right, baby. Tomorrow's Saturday. We'll sleep late. I'll see you when you get home."

He hung up the phone and scratched his head. He couldn't remember if he'd eaten anything since lunch. Oh, well. He was hungry now.

The phone rang right after he got to the kitchen. "Now what?" he grumbled, grabbing the wall phone. "Yeah?"

"Hello to you, too," a familiar voice purred, and he felt a sudden ice cube of fear trail down his back.

"Vickie? Why are you calling me at home? You know better."

"Hey, Doc, you might want to be a little more courteous to a visitor. I was passing by on my way to the club for my last set, and I noticed you left your garage door open. Or your wife did, I guess—since it's her car that isn't in there. I thought you'd want to know."

"Where are you?" His tone was sharp.

"I'm right outside in your driveway. Aren't you going to ask me in? I have a surprise for you."

He pushed the refrigerator door closed with his foot. "And what might that be?"

She giggled. "Look out your front window and I'll show you."

He strode to the front of the house and pulled back the thick drapes covering the living room windows.

The minute Vickie saw him, she grinned and opened the black leather coat she was wearing. It was clear she'd been drinking—the simple motion made her stagger. It was just as clear that she wore nothing under the coat.

Angie could be home within the hour. Thinking fast, he ran to the alarm panel, punched in the code, then opened the door. His frustration turned to fascination when he saw her, saw the flashing at her navel. He reached out, childlike—the diamond navel ring twinkled like a moonbeam.

Vickie shrugged the coat off her shoulders and flipped the off switch on her cell phone, carefully placing it in her coat pocket. "I *said,* are you going to let a girl in out of the night air?"

"No! Ah, Angie'll be home any minute. Go home. We'll talk later."

"I can't stay long anyway. I'm on my way to the club for a set. Come on. Just for a second."

He had to get her away from the front door. Even without the light on, she was clearly visible in the moonlight to any passerby. "Drive around back and I'll let you in."

"I'm not good enough to come in through the front door?" Her voice lost its playful tone, taking an edge that would have been sinister had it not been for a slight slurring of the words.

"Come on, stop playing before someone sees you out there! If one of my neighbors saw that ugly little car, I *know* they'd know it ain't mine. Pull around back."

He shut the door before she could answer and headed back upstairs, holding the phone, trying to think of what to do next, an eerie combination of sorrow and uneasiness wrapping itself around him. Vickie had been drinking and might not be in her right frame of mind. He couldn't leave her alone outside, but he sure couldn't invite her in.

Halfway up the stairs, he knew what to do. The only thing to do was get her away from the house, and he knew just the place. If Angie came home in the meantime, he'd tell her he'd been in the basement. Angie never went into the basement, said she hated it down there.

Instinct made him remove his gun from the bottom nightstand drawer and tuck it into his pocket. Over Angie's protests, he'd bought the gun right after they moved to Atlanta. The 9 mm automatic's cold weight pressed against his hip as he moved down the steps. He wasn't afraid of a woman who'd had too much to drink and was only half his size, but there was no way he'd go parking in a vacant lot this late without some reassurance against other possibilities.

Irresistible Impulse

Hoping she'd done what he said and pulled to the back of the house, he decided to meet Vickie at the basement door.

At the bottom of the basement stairs, he saw headlights round the driveway and stop just short of the basement door. His relief didn't last long; the phone rang and he answered instantly, fearing Angie was on her way home.

But it was Vickie. "Where are you? It's cold out here, Klaxton. Open the door."

"Hold on a minute," he said. "Gotta turn off the alarm system." He was outside and getting into the passenger side of her car before she could get out.

"Turn up the heater," he told her, rubbing his hands together. "Let's go for a ride."

"That's more like it." Vickie put the car in gear and soon they were on the road. From time to time, she allowed the car to weave. Fearing they'd be stopped, Klaxton kept one eye on her, and one on looking for police cars.

Finally, they approached an unlighted parking lot in a deserted strip mall. "Turn right here," he said. "Take a left at the light. Pull in up there."

As soon as the car came to a stop, she shifted her shoulders just enough to make her coat fall and reached her arms toward him. He jerked away. Fog had rolled in behind the moonlight, and he could see nothing except, in the center of her navel, the glittering diamond stud. He was grateful. If he couldn't see her nakedness, he'd be able to do what he had to do.

"Vickie. I think we need to talk."

She allowed her arms to fall back into her lap. "About what?"

"I don't have much time. I gotta get back before Angie, so I'll make this quick. I shouldn't be here. You shouldn't be here. We both know I'm a married man. And, in case you don't know it already, you need to understand that I'm not going to leave my wife. Not now, not ever. What happened between us at the office was a mistake. *My* mistake."

"Way to make a woman feel like crap, don't you think?" Her voice dripped acid.

He swallowed, drew in a breath and let it out slowly. "Don't get me wrong. In a different life, we might've made a hell of a pair. But I've made a lot of mistakes in my life, and it's time for me to think before I act.... Vickie, I don't want you to get the wrong idea about me. About us. If nothing else, I owe you honesty. I don't want to see you get hurt."

Even in the deep darkness, he saw tears in her eyes as she pulled the coat closed and hugged her shoulders.

And suddenly, he found himself talking to her just as he might have talked to his lost sister. As if Charlotte was Vickie's age, and was on the verge of making a serious mistake. "Don't settle for some guy that just wants to get it on every now and then. Find yourself someone who appreciates you for who you are. Someone who loves not just your physical beauty, but the girl who got that college scholarship and gave it up for her dream. Who holds down a day job so she can spend her nights pursuing that dream. That's what you're really about, Vickie. Not just some quick lay with a dude that already has a wife. You're way better than that."

She never replied, just started the car, and then pulled back into traffic. This time, he noted with relief, the car never strayed over the centerline.

They were entering his subdivision when he put out his hand. "Let me out here."

She stopped the car, her face damp from tears, and watched as he walked into the darkness.

∞

He used the few blocks' walk to his house to regain his composure, but it only lasted until he reached the house. He'd hadn't taken his keys when he left, and couldn't remember if he'd locked the basement door behind him. But, he remembered now, he'd left the lower-level alarm system off and the garage door in front wide open. If Angie *had* come home, he'd have a hard time explaining all that. But her car wasn't in the garage, and for that, he was grateful.

The basement door yielded instantly to his touch, and he heaved another thankful sigh. He replaced the gun in the nightstand before crawling under the covers, feeling certain sleep would no longer elude him. He was right. Finally, he had done the right thing, and his reward was a peaceful and almost instantaneous slumber. He never noticed Stephanie emerge from the heavy drapes at his bedroom window and stand watching him as he slept.

Nineteen

Angie tossed restlessly, kicking off the satin duvet as she dreamed of her eighth birthday. After the movie, there'd been a big outdoor picnic with a birthday cake, watermelon and fried chicken with all the fixings. It was July, and the bugs had tried to make a meal of her. Her mother was cleaning up the kitchen, so Daddy took her upstairs to help her get ready for bed. She was itching all over from the bug bites, and sleepy, too.

"Do I have to brush my teeth tonight, Daddy? I'm so sleepy," she murmured as he placed her on her canopy bed.

"Well ... since it's your birthday. But don't tell your mama."

"Can I sleep in my birthday dress, too? *Please*, Daddy? I'm too tired to put my jammies on."

"No, honey. We have to put some medicine on those mosquito bites."

"Ohh-h-h ... Daddy, they don't itch that bad anymore," she whimpered, curling herself into a fetal position, not knowing why she felt so scared. But he pulled at her limbs and finally succeeded in getting the layers off—pinafore, dress, slip, panties, shoes and socks. As he undressed her, his hands became soft and caressing.

Still drowsy but somehow energized, she heard him twist the cap off the big pink bottle of calamine lotion.

"This is going to feel a little cold at first," he said in a whisper, and began applying the chalky liquid in short, gentle strokes to her tummy, her arms, her legs, her midsection. When she felt his fingers go to her private place, she squirmed. He stopped, shook a little more lotion onto his hands and started rubbing again. An unbidden but pleasurable sensation washed over her as she drifted in that state between wakefulness and slumber. This was wrong, wasn't it? Touching her private place? And where was that ringing noise coming from?

"Daddy no!"

One hand came up to cover her mouth, and the soft murmuring continued.

∞

"Wake up, girl, it's a beautiful Saturday morning," Ashley said into the phone. "I'm going to Phipps Plaza for a little shopping. Wanna go?"

For a moment, all she heard on the other end was the moaning of someone suddenly roused from a deep sleep. But that was okay. She had plenty to occupy her mind while Angie woke up. In a few short hours, she and Joe had reached a comfort and closeness Ashley hadn't felt in many years. She didn't want to think about where it would lead, or what it meant; she just wanted to enjoy it while it lasted. So she turned her thoughts to her favorite pastime when she was happy—and when she was sad, for that matter: shopping. The two friends hadn't seen much of each other lately, and even their telephone chats had been hurried. But, today, Ashley was determined to pin Angie down. She was up for some girl talk about this man, for real!

Joe Lester

"So I really need—okay, want!—to find something special to wear," she told Angie.

Her answer was a muffled, "What time is it, girl? I had a late night last night!"

"A quarter to nine," Ashley chirped. "Don't waste this wonderful day lying around like a potato! If you get up and get a shower, we'll have enough time to stop at Starbucks and be at the mall when they unlock the doors at ten. Beat the Saturday crowds."

"Uh ... Klaxton and I were planning to sleep in today." Angie reached behind her as she spoke, but felt only bed linens. She turned over with difficulty; his keys weren't on the nightstand. Sighing, she turned back over. "Sure, why not? But I've only had about five hours' sleep, so you do the driving."

"Fine, see you in thirty."

Angie struggled to sit up. "Birds need longer than that to bathe, girl. Give me an hour."

"Okay, but let's skip Starbucks so we can be at the mall when the doors open. Have coffee ready when I get there."

A scant forty minutes later, Ashley—dressed for a day of heavy-duty buying in jeans, sweatshirt and Nikes—rang the Staples' doorbell in short, staccato bursts, hoping Angie hadn't rolled back over and dozed off again. As she waited, she gazed at the front entrance and wondered for the hundredth time why anyone would buy a house with no corners. *Looks like a Holiday Inn Deluxe*, she thought, shaking her head.

Klaxton, dressed in running gear, opened the door. "Hi, Ash. What's up?"

"Morning, Klaxton." Ashley stepped around him and entered. "Would you tell Angie I'm here?"

With a resigned *huff*, Klaxton turned toward the stairs. "Honey, Ashley's here."

"Honey, is that you?" Angie appeared at the foot of the stairs. "I thought you'd already gone."

Klaxton gave her a peck on the cheek. "My pager went off early, and I couldn't get back to sleep. You were resting so well, I didn't want to wake you. So I decided to come down here and read the paper."

"I guess I did sleep pretty hard," Angie said, nodding hello to Ashley. "Took a couple of sleeping pills and was out like a light. I bet my man's made coffee already, Ash. Want a cup?"

Coffee, yes. Spend a minute more than I have to with Klaxton, no. Ashley looked at her watch. "I'll get some coffee at the mall, if that's okay with you."

Angie turned to Klaxton. "Baby, I'll call you when we're almost done. I know we planned to spend the day together, but I'll be back soon. You don't mind, do you?"

Ashley's stomach knotted at Angie's almost-pleading tone, but she managed to stay quiet. *No need to get in the middle of something I can't fix.*

Klaxton glanced at Ashley. "Don't keep my wife out all day. All right?"

Ashley waved her hand. "Klaxton, I'm just going to let that blow on by."

∞

As soon as they were in the car, Ashley placed a hand on Angie's knee. "Girl, I know you've been busy, and me, too. We've got a lot to catch up on! I had a wonderful time with Joe the other night, and we're going out again. Can't wait to tell you all about it!"

"Not that I *mind* hearing this again," Angie replied, "but you told me something *very* similar last week." She gave her a distant smile.

Ashley suddenly worried that it might have been inconsiderate of her to drop so much sunshine on her friend without asking how she was doing. Even discounting the early hour and lack of caffeine, Angie wasn't acting right. "Sweetie, are you okay?"

Angie glanced out the passenger side window. "I'm fine, just working a lot of hours." A pause, then, "No, I'm not fine. Not really. I ... sometimes I feel like the walls are caving in on me. One day last week, I cancelled my appointments and just drove around. Hardly remembered where I'd been when I got home."

Ashley bit her lip. "Why don't you take some time off?"

A long pause. "Klaxton insists we can't until we get the practice really built up."

What she didn't know, and Angie longed to tell her, was that she feared the past was coming back. Cheryl Jaworski's death. Klaxton's incarceration. And now, her fears about Stephanie Rogers. She couldn't tell Ashley, of course. Ashley had scant respect for Klaxton as it was; telling her would destroy the little civility they had between them. And her man came first.

The sun was blinding. Angie turned away from the window and glanced over at Ashley. *Even if I did tell her, she probably wouldn't believe it—or believe that any sane woman would put up with it.*

Ashley held back as long as she could. When she heard Angie sigh, she took her chance. "Do you mean to tell me that you look so tired because of work? Is that why you have to take medication to help you sleep? Because Klaxton thinks you need to kill yourself to get the business going? Angie, listen to yourself. When you were talking to Klaxton before we left, it sounded like you were talking to your daddy, and he was about to punish you."

"Ashley, I—"

"If you need a break from work, take one. Do what you need to do *for Angie* for a change."

Ashley was so intent on making her point, she almost missed the exit to Phipps Plaza.

She found a parking spot and turned off the engine, and Angie turned to face her, near tears. "Ashley, you're right in a lot of ways. I'm ... tired."

Ashley bit her lip and waited. She didn't have to wait long.

"I know part of the fault is mine. If you didn't badger me to get my hair done, I'd probably just pull it back in a ponytail and go around without makeup in scrubs all the time. And I'm not very good company when I'm feeling that way. That's why I didn't stay for the book discussion at Trease's yesterday."

Ashley sighed. "I thought you left early because you had an emergency at the hospital."

When Angie didn't answer, Ashley pushed forward. "That doesn't matter. Angie, I'm sorry. I just wish you'd told me sooner. It's not good to hold this kind of stuff in. I remember a few weeks ago, you said things were going so great between you two. What happened?"

Angie lowered her head. "I ... don't know." *I can't tell you about Stephanie, I just can't!*

Ashley weighed her next words carefully. "Once you guys get settled in, hire an associate. That'll give you two more time to spend together."

This brought more tears. "It's not just that, Ash. I ... I'm not a mother yet. And I don't see it ever happening. And there are days when Klaxton and I can't get enough of each other, and then the next night, he's sleeping in the basement."

Ashley handed Angie a tissue she'd pulled out of her purse. "Life doesn't always abide by the timelines we create. I know how much you want a child, but ... do it for the *right* reason."

After the words came out of her mouth she paused, amazed at her nurturing tone. *Damn*, she thought, *Joe must really be rubbing off on me.* She wanted to see a smile on Angie's face. "You know that old saying, right? You have to endure a little rain if you want to see the rainbow? But hey, in the meantime, there's shopping—and chocolate!"

Angie grinned through her tears, then pulled down the visor to check her makeup. "I've heard that first part ... But I think you made up that last, girl."

"Nope," Ashley replied, grabbing her bag and opening their doors. "I got that from a very reliable source. Now let's get to the shopping. We'll do the chocolate later. And maybe," she added, thinking of her date that weekend, "the rainbow part right after that."

∞

Four hours later, they emerged from Lord & Taylor laughing and laden with shopping bags. Ashley had Nicole Miller and Parisian bags in one hand, Guess and Louis Vuitton in the other. Angie, draped even more heavily than her friend, had two Lord & Taylor bags hanging from one arm, a small bag from Tiffany's and three large bags from Prada dangling from the other. It was the first time in weeks that Ashley had seen Angie genuinely smile.

"Child, I thought you were going to clean out the candle department," Ashley joked as they loaded the backseat of her car. "You trying to light a fire under Klaxton or something?"

Angie smiled but didn't look up. "Something like that, I guess. You know how much I love candles. Besides, they don't ever go bad." She lifted her eyes to meet Ashley's. "And who knows? I really enjoyed the last party we had. If Klaxton and I ever get the time again, we might have another one." She waved a hand at the backset. "And we'll have plenty of romantic lighting."

"Ain't that the truth," Ashley agreed, letting her eyes rove over the small mountain of bags.

Laughing, they got back in the car to head home.

∞

The shopping spree *had* been just what she needed—a stress-free break from reality. Both her pager and her cell phone had been blissfully silent the whole time.

Angie frowned as she suddenly remembered promising Klaxton that she'd call him before they left the mall. *Maybe he won't be too angry* she thought. *I'll just tell him I forgot.*

Inside the house, Angie called Klaxton's name, but there was no reply. She dropped her bags at the bottom of the staircase and headed to the kitchen. She and Ashley had grabbed a bite of lunch and several lattés at Phipps, but now she was hungry again.

The big house seemed so empty. Every sound echoed. The emptiness reminded her of how her hopes of being pregnant had been dashed so recently. It wasn't even three o'clock yet, and she hated drinking alone, but she needed to relax.

Wine glass in hand, she sat at the kitchen table. Only then did she notice the note in her husband's familiar scrawl: *Hey, baby, had to make a quick run to the hospital. See you soon. I love you, Klaxton.*

Angie smiled. It was rarely a "quick run" to the hospital for either of them, so she probably had time for a bubble bath before he returned. *No matter what Ashley thinks, Klaxton grew up in foster care, and he promised he'd never leave a child of his own. If we had a child … yes, that's what we need to keep us together.*

She put the cork back in the wine bottle, replaced the bottle in the refrigerator and took her full glass with her, humming as she headed up the stairs.

Twenty

Face it, Joe, you're in trouble now.

And he was. Mrs. Caldwell had overheard him making reservations at Dante's Down the Hatch, and she wasn't happy about it. "Dr. Joe," she said, shaking her head as she pulled a sheet of chocolate chip cookies from the oven. "You should have told me sooner. I could have cooked up a fine dinner for you and your new lady. Win her heart for you like that!"

She placed the chocolate chip cookies on a wire rack on the counter to cool, yanked off one oversized oven mitt and snapped the wrinkled fingers of her right hand. "Just like that! She is special, no? I never knew you to take a lady out since Miss Courtney passed. You let me cook for her, she will be yours forever. Just give me a little warning, that's all. After your fine dinner, you bring her back here for some of my special gris-gris cookies, okay? I will leave 'em on the counter and I will be sleeping away. You two won't disturb me, no way."

Chuckling, she removed the other oven mitt.

"Thank you," he answered absently. "That's very thoughtful, Mrs. Caldwell. They smell delicious. But you didn't need to do that, not at all. You put a special love potion in them, is that right?" He winked at the elderly woman and slipped a cookie into his mouth.

"All that I cook is made with love," she said, wiping her hands on her apron. "That is the best ingredient."

"Sounds great, and next time I promise to let you know in plenty of time to cook up a full meal for us. How do I look?" He pointed to the black v-necked cashmere Polo sweater he was wearing over a starched white shirt and charcoal gray trousers.

She gave him a rare smile. "You look like a prince. In my country, you would be wooed by all the women in those fancy clothes."

Joe couldn't resist. "Is it true that in your country, a man can have as many wives as he wants?"

Her face turned serious. "Different countries have different customs. It is true that in Sierra Leone, a man is allowed to have as many wives as he can provide for. 'Provide for' is the key phrase, though—not like here." She took off her bifocals, folded them and slid them carefully in her apron pocket.

Joe nodded, knowing she was alluding to the many men in America unable and unwilling to provide for one wife, let alone two.

"But," she added, "When I married Ernest, who was not from my country at all, I was never jealous of what he did for other women. I was only concerned about what he did for *me*. Ernest never disrespected me by bringing any diseases home to me, and he never paraded any women around town in my face. But I realize I was lucky to find a man like him. Since he passed on, I have been alone. And I will never find a replacement for my Ernest. There are no two people alike. Sometimes better to leave well enough alone."

She scowled darkly and turned to go.

"I-I don't understand," Joe said, and she turned back around.

"Dr. Joe, the same evil that destroys families in Sierra Leone destroys families all over the world. Jealousy. *Jealousy* is the prince of all evil."

He sighed and nodded. "I have to agree with that."

She walked back to him. "As you make your way in this world, you must listen to the voices inside your head."

He was shocked. How could she know about the voices? The ones he'd heard, off and on, since Courtney's passing. *Surely she's speaking figuratively.*

She continued, and her next words put the lie to his assumption: "Believe me. I would never kid you. It is too serious. If you feel evil lurking about you, acknowledge its presence. But remember that evil has no power unless we give in to it. The Devil never does his own dirty deeds.... He leaves that task to human beings."

Klaxton popped into Joe's mind, and that perplexed him. His tenant might have a few habits he didn't approve of, but Joe didn't consider him evil by any stretch. If there were evil forces surrounding him, they had to be due to the weird events happening lately—not to Klaxton himself.

Still, Mrs. Caldwell's words bothered him enough to evaporate the light mood he'd been in. "Well, Mrs. Caldwell, whatever magic potions are keeping the demons at bay, I'm grateful. And I hope they prevail tonight."

She shook her head. "You been dealing with demons you do not know about. You think I do not know, but I do." She ignored his surprised look and added, "There is a ghost that lives right here in the house with us."

"Oh, surely—"

"She is not an evil ghost. She is a good spirit. I think she probably lives here *because* of you. To protect you."

"Mrs. Caldwell, no—"

The woman crossed her arms and bore on. "She even helps me fold clothes. I leave a basket in the laundry room, and when I come back a few minutes later, they are all folded." She shrugged. "You may have another explanation. Yet strange things happen around here. Lights on when no one has turned them on, shadows walking on the wall at night."

The old woman's eyes turned guarded. "I have seen her. She's very pretty. Not every night, but some nights lately, I can see her in my room, pushing a baby carriage like a shadow."

Desperate to change the subject, Joe said, "So, my sweater is okay?" He smoothed the sleeves with nervous hands. "I tried several on, but settled on this one."

Mrs. Caldwell finally gave up. "I am sorry, Dr. Joe. I did not mean to go on a tear, as they say around here. Like I said, this is a good spirit. And good spirits protect us from evil ones." Shaking her head, she added, "Yes, as I said before, you look like a prince. Remember next time, I will cook for you and your lady friend. They put too much salt in the food at those restaurants. Bad for you."

Joe's grin faded. Mrs. Caldwell had mentioned her aversion to too much salt before. Frequently, in fact. She was the only non-tenant who had access to his office building, too. Was it possible, even remotely, that Ashley was right—that Mrs. Caldwell put the salt in Angie's office? He decided to try to find out.

"There's nothing wrong with salt in moderation," he said. "Salt is a necessary mineral in the body."

"Humph. Salt is just like medicine. Go back to your Bible. They used to rub newborn babies with salt to keep them from getting diseases. I bet you tell people to soak in salt water for an infection. Salt is powerful stuff!"

Her voice rose with something that sounded very much like fear. "In my country, if you want to do something bad to somebody, you give them salt. In their food, or just throw it on the ground in front of their house. Does not even have to touch them to do its work. If you want to protect them, you do the same, but … you do it different."

"That's preposterous," Joe said carefully. "How can something that doesn't even touch someone harm them?"

Her face closed. "Well, there are those that believe, and those that do not. But, Dr. Joe, if I ever saw salt near someone I loved, I would watch out for them. Or, I would be glad to see it, because that would mean that—"

The phone rang, startling both of them. "I'll get it," Joe said, walking to the kitchen phone. "It might be Ashley. She might be running late."

But it wasn't Ashley. It wasn't anyone. Or at least, anyone willing to announce themselves. All he could hear was breathing on the other end. Finally, he hung up in disgust and returned to Mrs. Caldwell. "You know, I keep intending to get Caller ID. That would come in real handy with all the prank calls I've been getting lately."

She nodded. "Perhaps that is a good idea. Ms. Ashley is lucky to be spending the evening with a man of your integrity and consideration. You have a positive glow about you this night."

"Thank you," he said, and walked over and gave her a rare hug, noting that she had a surprising amount of strength in her short body when she wouldn't release his hug.

"True love does not come around every day," she whispered in his ear. "Do not let it pass you by if it comes again. Listen to an old lady who only had one chance. Do not miss *your* opportunity." Only then did she release him from the embrace.

After a moment, he said, "Since I lost Courtney, I've done a great deal of soul-searching. I … I guess you noticed that I took her picture down. It wasn't easy. I'm still not really sure I'm doing the right thing."

The old woman shook her head. "Your wife had a good spirit. I never knew her, but I felt her spirit in this house from the beginning. That was three years ago. It is time to let her rest in peace." She paused a moment, "All those things I see? I think she is trying to tell you so through them."

Joe's head reeled. Here was another person who was saying she'd seen these manifestations too, and also sensed their source as Courtney's spirit.

It was too much to deal with, Joe decided, and gave her a smile. "You always seem to know the right thing to say."

She nodded and smiled back. "We all need to walk in someone else's shoes once in a while. Well, Prince Charming, the cookies are in the cookie jar, and I am going to go upstairs and get out of your way. You show her a good time!"

"Yes, yes. I will. Thanks for everything."

With a last look that seemed part-smile, part-grimace, she walked into the deep shadows of the stairwell just as headlights bounced off the dining room window.

Joe opened the door just as Ashley was extending her finger to ring the doorbell.

"Right on time!" he said, and glanced appreciatively at her outfit—an off-the-shoulder, tomato-red sweater dress.

"Were you that anxious to see me?" she replied, a cat's grin on her face.

"Anxious to see you? Always." He took her coat and hung it on the rack behind the door.

Ashley looked past Joe into the spacious dining room on one side of the house, then turned around to take in the living room on the other side of the foyer. "I didn't tell you the last time I was here, but you have a really nice place!"

"Thank you," Joe said, taking her arm and drawing her toward the kitchen. "To be honest, it's really bigger than I need. But ... I thought I'd need more room when I bought it."

Ashley noted the sadness in his eyes. "Well, it's bigger than my little condo space, for sure. A lot for just one person, though, I guess."

Joe forced a smile. "I'm not completely alone. Mrs. Caldwell lives in. And, as of this week, we have a new addition to the household. Come on, I'll introduce you." He flipped the light switch at the stairwell and guided her down the basement stairs.

Ashley squealed like a first-grader when she saw Joe's new roommate—the beagle puppy his mother had given him during his visit home the previous weekend. Even in the dim light of the basement, it was easy to see the puppy's tail wagging enthusiastically in his mini-kennel.

She knelt down and reached in to pet him, cooing unabashedly, then stood up and demanded, "Why in the world are you keeping this precious little baby cooped up down here?"

"I told Mother that if I took the dog, it would have to be an outdoors dog," he answered. "Mrs. Caldwell's so fastidious, I didn't think she'd take kindly to dog hair and ... well, you know ... all over the house."

The puppy began to whine, and Ashley insisted, "Joe, you open that cage and let him out this instant!"

The second the kennel door opened, she reached in and gathered the puppy into her arms. "There, there, sweetie," she cooed. "I won't let him keep you all locked up like that anymore." She turned to Joe. "What's his name?"

"Solly. Short for Solomon." Joe grinned shyly. "Mother's big on Bible names."

Ashley nuzzled the puppy and cooed, "You're named after the wisest king in the Bible, did you know that? That's perfect. With those eyes, I can tell you're a smart dog." She was rewarded with several well-placed licks.

"I hope he *is* smart," Joe said. "I'm thinking about training him so I can take him hunting when I go back home to visit. Beagles make good hunting dogs."

Ashley gasped. "You can't, Joe! This is no hunter. He's a pet. He needs attention and love." She stroked his fur as if to demonstrate. "After five minutes with him, I'll just bet Mrs. Caldwell won't be able to say no to him either. What were you *thinking?*"

Smiling, Joe reached down to pick up the mini-kennel. "All right. We'll leave him in the kitchen until we get back from dinner, okay?" He looked at his watch. "Hey! We need to get going. Our reservation's for eight."

∞

Over dinner at Dante's, Ashley regaled Joe with stories about the pets of her childhood years. When she turned the conversation to her work, Joe said, "Being an entertainment attorney must be interesting."

She speared a cube of French bread and dipped it in the fondue pot. "Well, that seems like what my law firm wants me to specialize in. All my clients lately are rappers. You heard about J.P. and Kid Dog from Angie. Their music's big-league, but they're definitely not what I'd call fun to work with. Not my kind of men."

"Well, what *is* your kind of man?" he asked, working to keep his voice nonchalant.

She smiled. "Guess I asked for that one. Okay, if you'd like to know, *my* kind of man knows who he is, and knows what matters to him." She gave him a level gaze. "And he always, always tells me the truth."

"The truth?" Joe stared into his plate. "And what kind of truth are you expecting from *me*?"

"For starters, what you're thinking right now."

He looked at his plate. "I don't know.... Thinking about what?"

"I think you know, Joe. Ever since the party, I've been attracted to you. You know I like you a lot. And I think that's mutual. Correct me if I'm wrong."

He glanced away, then back to her. "You're not wrong. But there are a lot of things I have to tell you. Things you need to know."

"So tell me." She wasn't smiling anymore.

"It's nothing bad. It's just that, for a long time … since I was a kid, really … I knew I was different."

"Different how?"

He gave a nervous smile. "It's hard to explain. My family … I guess you could say my family was very religious. When I was a little kid, maybe about six or seven, I was called to preach."

She cocked her head. "Preach?"

"Yes."

"Well, I never imagined anything like that about you," Ashley said. "You sure you weren't just a mouthy little brat?"

"No," he said, laughing. "In fact, I was pretty shy. Church was about the only place I spoke up. But when I preached, everyone listened. It wasn't something I could have stopped, even if I wanted to. The words came out of me, just like God was telling them to me. Pretty soon, my family was getting invited to other churches so I could preach. By the time I was ten, I was preaching at tent revivals all over Georgia. In fact, that's what I planned to do with my

life—be a full-time preacher. But ... that ended when I turned sixteen."

"Wait, let me guess. Girls?"

He sighed. "In a manner of speaking. All the boys my age cared
about was money and girls. None of that mattered to me. But when
I was sixteen, I met a girl who changed my life forever."

"Joe, most boys start liking girls at some point. That's
normal."

"No, it wasn't *all* girls, just one girl. Courtney."

Ashley nodded, recalling that his wife's name was Courtney. "I
see. And she *did* change your life, didn't she?"

"Yes. By the time we started college, I ... I guess I was
disillusioned with preaching by then. No, it was more than that. It
seemed like there was a bigger drive in me—to become as successful
as I could to make Courtney proud of me. I majored in chemistry,
she got her degree in education. Both of us could have been teachers.
But I wanted more."

He smiled at her, and her return smile encouraged him to go
on. "After I did my internship in Nashville, we moved back to Georgia and bought the house. Planned to live happily ever after."

He paused, but Ashley couldn't reply. She was pretty sure she
knew where this was going, and her heart sank. *He can't get into a
serious relationship because he's not over his dead wife. Oh, Lord,
what have I gotten myself into?*

Joe cleared his throat. "I, uh ... Courtney died three years ago.
Cancer. No woman has— I've thought about pursuing a relationship
from time to time, but each time, it didn't work out. It was always
me. Whenever I thought about trying to find someone like Courtney, I ... I knew it just wouldn't happen."

He stopped, wondering if he was saying too much. But no ... if he was ever going to make it work with another woman, he had to be straight with her. "Ever since her death, it's been ... empty. Like part of me died with her. I always wonder why she had to die, and why I lived. Why I, as a doctor, couldn't save her. That ... maybe I wasn't worthy of loving anyone else."

And finally, Ashley found her voice. "Joe, if this isn't what you want ... being with me ... or if it's moving too fast, I'll understand."

His eyes widened. "No. What I mean is that ... this time, it's different. When I'm with you, I hate telling you goodbye. And when I'm not with you, I'm already looking forward to being with you again. There's ... peace surrounding me. I mean ... I know it's too soon ..." He sighed. "I guess what I'm trying to say is, I don't know where this road is going but ... I *do* know that I'm willing to travel down it this time. If you are."

She covered her mouth with her hand, fighting sudden tears.

"You said you wanted honesty, so I wanted to let you know how I feel," he said, his words rushing. "And I hope you know I'd never deceive anyone I care about."

Ashley pulled her hand away from her mouth. "So where do we go from here?"

Joe laughed in his relief. "How about back to my house? I've got homemade chocolate chip cookies and milk, *and* a baby beagle pup straight off the farm. Besides, you drove."

She nodded, eyes shining. "Joe Fry, I can't think of anywhere else I'd rather be tonight."

Twenty-one

Vickie Renfroe had been with a lot of men, but never told any of them about her hopes and ambitions. Sure, many of the guys she went out with were musicians themselves, but long, thoughtful discussions weren't a part of how they spent their time together. Most of all, no man had ever respected her. Not really. Not until Klaxton. The fact that he passed up the opportunity to sleep with her because of his commitment to his wife only made him more desirable in her eyes.

Of course it wasn't the ideal situation, given that he was a married man. And his rejection the week before had hurt. Vickie's mother had been cynical about men, telling her, "There are two kinds of men in this world—men with balls and money, and men with balls and no money. Go for the balls *and* the money, honey." For a long time, Vickie had operated on the assumption that her mother was right. But here was a man with all that and more: Dr. Klaxton Staples possessed a conscience, too.

She knew it was a bad idea to fantasize about being with him, but she couldn't help thinking how great her life would be if they could be together. With his money and her talent, she could realize her dream of a singing career, and have a loving and caring man at her side, too.

She sighed and returned to the real world. To get through this next set, she had to keep her head out of the clouds. It was Friday night, and Hairston's Supper Club was packed. Vickie's weekend workplace was popular with the over-thirty crowd. Thursday was ladies' night; Sunday night was amateur night for standup comedy. Vickie and the band, the Soul Groovers, performed three nights a week, with a late set close to midnight on Fridays and Saturdays, which drew the biggest crowd of all.

She stirred her watered-down margarita and tried to clear her mind of extraneous thoughts. The first set had been one of her better ones, hot and soulful at the same time, and her pulse was still racing. To perform well again, she had to compose herself and start the next set from a serene place. *Not always easy to do in this smoke-filled joint.* "Mark, you sure do make a good margarita," she said to the bartender.

"That one's special, just for you," he replied, smiling as he wiped the counter. "Not everybody gets the good tequila. I save that for my favorites."

Mark was an excellent bartender. Not only did he have a deft hand at the shaker, but he was a good listener as well. "By the way," he asked her, "how's it going with that doctor of yours?"

She sighed. "I don't know, Mark. Tell you the truth, sometimes I think it's going, sometimes I don't."

"Why's that?" he said. "He's not married—?"

"No, no, he's not married. He's just real busy. I only get to see him at lunch, usually." *And ride around with him at night.*

Mark smiled. "I guess it was inevitable that if you kept hanging with them doctors, you'd finally catch you one."

Suddenly bothered by the lie she'd just told, she said, "Look, I guess I can tell you, but will you promise to keep your mouth shut?"

He nodded.

"Okay, he *is* married. But I don't think that's going to be much of a problem, 'cause it isn't much of a marriage, if you know what I mean."

Mark had been a bartender too long to pass judgments. Still, he liked Vickie, and what she just said concerned him. "If that doctor-friend of yours don't work out," he said with a wink, "just remember, I'm still here. I ain't hooked up with nobody. Just patiently waiting on you."

She blushed. "Oh, you! You're old enough to be my dad. But I adore you. You know that, right? Just help me find the right guy!"

His expression turned solemn. "Vickie, you don't need a man to take you away from here. One of these days, you're going to make it to the big-time all by yourself. You got it goin' on, girl, and don't you ever doubt it. You're bringing it from your soul, little sister."

"Nice show, Vickie."

The unfamiliar female voice broke over the jukebox music. Vickie swiveled around on her stool to find a nervous-looking woman standing in front of her. The woman clutched her small purse so tight, Vickie could see her whitened knuckles in the dim lights around the bar.

"What can I get you, pretty lady?" Mark asked as he sized up the newcomer.

"Nothing, thank you," the woman said, keeping her eyes on Vickie.

Mark saw the look, and decided it was time for him to bow out. "If you need anything, just holler," he said smoothly, then eased away.

"Thanks for the compliment," Vickie said, wondering about the woman's intense gaze. "Do I know you from somewhere?"

"No, we've never met. I'm Stephanie Rogers." The woman's voice was friendly, if cool. "Pretty dress. Did Klaxton buy that for you?"

Vickie's chin jerked. "Not that it's any of your business, but no. I'd ask what it is to you, but frankly I don't give a damn." She swiveled the barstool back around to the bar.

"It's nothing to me, honey," Stephanie said, moving onto the empty barstool next to her. "Let me get straight to the point."

"If there is one, please do."

"Look, I don't mean you any harm. I only came here to warn you about our mutual friend. You know him. I've seen you with him."

Vickie sucked in a breath and whirled to face her. "Okay. *Now* I remember you. The party. *You're* the one who got into the fight with Ashley Heath."

Stephanie's silence was all the encouragement Vickie needed to keep talking. "So? ... You couldn't handle Ashley, and now you want to vent to someone else?"

Stephanie sighed. "Vickie, you don't need to cop a 'tude with me. First of all, I'm trying to give you some valuable information. You're not the only one he's been screwing. And second of all—"

Holding her hand in the stop position, Vickie said, "Let's go back to 'first of all.' I don't recall asking you for a background check on Klaxton."

Stephanie's eyes were dark and heavy, as though she'd gone a long time without sleep. She breathed deeply, her eyes frozen on Vickie, expectant.

"So let me guess," Vickie continued. "You came here to tell me that you and Klaxton are having an affair?" She slapped herself on the forehead in mock surprise. "That's a dumb question. My bad! No, you're here to try and reclaim something you've obviously lost."

Stephanie's dam finally broke. "I tried being nice to you, but since you want to go there … the relationship between Klaxton and me was much more than an affair. An *affair* is what *you* are having with him, dear."

Vickie pursed her lips, rolled her neck and let loose. "Let me make this clear, because you're obviously confusing me with someone else. I'm not Ashley Heath. I'm not going to argue back and forth with you like she did. I'll kick your ass and ask questions later. I advise you to leave while you still have the option of doing so without assistance."

Mark heard Vickie's voice rise over the music, and stepped back over to where they sat. "Everything okay, ladies?"

"I'm straight, Mark," Vickie said, her eyes looking through Stephanie. "She was just leaving."

Mark nodded and walked off, but glanced at them from time to time as he filled a drink order.

Vickie took a quick sip of her drink and pressed a hard look onto her face. "Can I say something before you leave? I don't particularly care for people following me around. People have gotten hurt for less than that."

Stephanie forced a smiled and pushed the barstool back as she stood. "I was trying to do you a favor. I wanted to let you know the kind of man you're dealing with." She toyed with her purse. "I was … there the other night. Saw you drop him off down the street from his house. I … I misjudged you, Vickie. But … I've been where you're trying to get—sex while the wife is away, expensive clothes, the whole nine. Has he offered to pay your rent yet?"

To Vickie's quick intake of breath, Stephanie shook her head. "Don't take it, girl.... It's a bad check that might just cost you your life." Her eyes grew sad again. "Since you know so much, the next time you see Dr. Staples, why don't you ask him where he got the scar over his eye? Ask him what his last address was in New York, too, while you're at it."

"Thanks for the words of wisdom," Vickie spat. "But I don't need them, especially from a jealous-assed *ex*-lover. There's a right way and a wrong way to handle every situation. Had you come to me the *right* way, I wouldn't have had a problem with you. But—"

Now, she saw the earnestness in Stephanie's face, and the hurt, and her tone softened. "Don't get it confused. I'm not mad at you for wanting Klaxton back. We both know what he has to offer.... But you came to me, not even knowing me, and I asked you to leave it alone—"

The bass player was signaling to her from the stage. She turned to Stephanie and said, "I have another set. It's the perfect song for you. So why don't you stick around?"

Stephanie took a defiant sip of her drink. "I may. But please, think about what I'm trying to tell you. I've tried to talk to his wife, and she wouldn't listen, either. But I'm not through with her yet."

"What do you mean by—?"

The bass player called out again, and Vickie had no choice but to head for the stage. Onstage, she pulled up a stool, positioned the microphone and told the audience, "I'm going to slow it down for y'all a little. Make sure you listen to the lyrics. This goes out to all the haters in the room."

As the beat of Jill Scott's "Getting in the Way" filled the air, Vickie looked right at Stephanie and began singing. Before she finished the song's second hook, Stephanie had stormed out.

∞

By no means is this over, Stephanie fumed, walking to her car. She'd taken all she was going to. Klaxton didn't deserve a second chance, and neither did his little hoochie girlfriend. It was clear that Vickie was as blind as she'd once been. The thought that she could have put a bullet between his eyes while he slept scared her, but not as much as it could have. She had only gone to his house that night to talk, had only gone inside when he didn't answer and she found the door unlocked. On the streets, that alone was enough to kill for. But he had also killed her friend Cheryl and her unborn child. Of that, she no longer had any doubt.

The damage done to her, she could live with; this wasn't the first time she'd been dumped by a man. But this time, she'd willingly given up her other well-heeled lovers. Now, she was two months behind on her rent, facing eviction, with no income to speak of.

Yet she wasn't going to worry about that right now. No, that wasn't as important to her as justice for Cheryl and the baby. There was no way she could let him get away with murder. It was time to pay another visit to the *other* Dr. Staples and tell her what kind of man she had really married.

Twenty-two

Earlier that evening, while he decided what to pack, Klaxton thought about what a great weekend this would be. And he wanted to make sure that what he took with him reflected his new attitude.

He was always a believer in projecting a positive image. "The best-dressed man always has a smile on his face and a shine on his shoes," his dad used to tell him. Yet it was much more than that, he knew. Since the night in the car with Vickie, he'd been walking around with a new, deeper sense of joy. He'd resisted an overpowering temptation, had tried to redeem himself by being loyal, caring and respectful since then. That's what led him to make reservations at Chateau Élan, a winery, spa and golf resort northwest of the city. Angie had wanted to go ever since they came to Atlanta, but they never had the time. He forced himself to make the time now, to show her his commitment to their marriage.

He smiled when he looked up at the closet's highest shelves—his old medical bag, the one he bought secondhand as a struggling med school student, rested there. Even though he'd long since graduated to a spiffier Mark Cross bag, he couldn't stand to part with this one. It was like an old friend. But the handle had long ago broken, and he'd been meaning to take it for repairs. He decided to stash it in the trunk of his car before they left. That way, he'd be more likely to remember to drop it off next week.

Seeing it reminded him of his hope that Joe Fry would forgive him for the lie he'd told. One of Angie's ob-gyn friends was covering her patients, but Klaxton didn't have anyone so easy to call on. He'd been pretty sure Joe would be willing to cover for one night—through Saturday morning—but less sure about an entire week-end, maybe more. Sure, he and Angie wouldn't be back in Atlanta until at least Monday. But the odds were in favor of a quiet week-end. And if there were any emergencies, Joe would come through like a champion, and they'd make it up to him later.

Again, Klaxton congratulated himself for the way he handled the situation with Vickie. Stephanie, too, even though he wasn't as sure about that one—yet. *I don't owe Stephanie a damn thing*, he reminded himself. *I always dealt fair and square with her. Once she accepts that I'm not coming back, she'll give up and go away.*

Angie was different. She was his wife, and he loved her. The other women, Cheryl included, came into his life because of his irresistible impulses—urges he didn't intend to give into, ever again. He had far too much to lose if he did.

∞

Angie and Klaxton made amiable small talk all the way to the Chateau, and the farther they got away from the Atlanta skyline, the more Angie seemed to relax. Klaxton exulted inwardly. As soon as they got to their suite, they unpacked with record speed and made love without even turning down the bedspread. Afterward, wrapped in terrycloth spa kimonos, they stood together on the balcony and watched the sun set down beyond the vineyards below them. When the knock came on their door, they were still out there.

To her question, he said, "I forgot. I thought you might like to have dinner in our rooms tonight."

She reached out and stroked his face. "Honey, how sweet!"

"Hey, after all those dinners you've made for me, it was the least I could do."

The waiter laid their meal out on the spacious balcony, dipped in gratitude at Klaxton's generous tip, and departed. While the waiter did that, Angie retrieved the candles she'd brought from her suitcase and lit them, and he gave her an indulgent smile. They sat, still in their robes, and enjoyed the sumptuous array of food and wine. The only sounds were their clinking glasses and the occasional gurgling of their wine over the chirping crickets in the distance … until he looked up and saw her eyes heavy with tears.

"Angie?"

When she didn't respond, he repeated her name and added, "Is anything wrong, baby?" Glass in hand, he leaned forward.

Angie whispered, "Klaxton … please tell me. Is there another woman?" Her beautiful face held an agony that tore at his guts.

His mind raced. *Could Vickie have said something? Or could Stephanie have?*

The only way to head her off was to ask her a question. "Baby, how can you ask me that?"

Angie shook her head and sighed. "We used to talk so much when we first moved here. I don't know what happened." Tears began to spill onto her cheeks. "There's not going to be a baby. Not from my womb, anyway. So what are we doing together? What kind of life are we creating?"

Klaxton pulled his chair beside hers and took her hands in his. "What are we doing? Loving each other. This moment we have now ... isn't it enough?" He released her hands and gestured out toward the softly lit vineyards below them. "We can have more of these. And we *can* have a family. There are ways, you know that. But first, last and always, it's about you and me, honey." His voice was pleading, but, he didn't mind begging.

"I'm ashamed of myself, Klaxton," she said. "I'm so jealous when I see other women around you. Hawking you, wanting you. Wanting what they *think* you and I have. Am I wrong for that? *Am I a fool?*"

"A fool? Baby no, I love you so much. There's no one else, I swear!" He placed his right hand on his heart, meaning every word. He had fought off temptation and burned his bridges; there *wasn't* anyone else. And never would be again!

After a long pause, Angie said, "That Vickie in Joe's office. Stephanie from New York ... Cheryl." She spoke quietly, but her jaw was rigid.

"Cheryl?" he stammered. The gentle reproach in her voice was more hurtful than the most violent of Cheryl's rages. "Baby, that was a long time ago."

Angie shook her head again. "My dad used to always say, 'Those who ignore the lessons of history are doomed to repeat them.' I know Cheryl's dead, but she haunts me. These others ... why are *they* after you?"

He opened his mouth, but she raised her hand. "Don't bother. I see the way women look at you. And the way you look at them. Sometimes I wonder if anything's changed since New York."

She placed her wineglass on the balcony railing and traced her fingertip around the rim of the glass, causing the crystal to emit a small squeaking noise. To him, it sounded like a scream.

"What's changed?" he said. "Honey, *everything* has changed."

She stared straight ahead. When the winter's chill made her shiver, she pulled her robe tighter around her. He went to his knees beside her in silent supplication, but was too terrified to speak.

Finally, Angie said, "Klaxton, I'm going to ask you again: Is there anyone else? For the third and last time." She met his eyes without blinking.

"No, baby. Goddamnit, no! You have *got* to believe me!"

"All right," she said, turning away from him. "If you say so. I'm going to bed now."

∞

Under the lavender-scented sheets, Angie lay stiffly. Before long, she heard her husband's familiar snoring. *How can he be so cavalier?* And how could she be so vulnerable, after all this time? She had waited so long to finally express just how much his past infidelity had hurt her, and her worry that it was happening again. Even now, years later, it was hard to hold her head up in the face of what her husband's unfaithfulness had done to their marriage, and to her. *Another* woman wouldn't have just left a man like Klaxton after what happened with Cheryl. No, any other woman would have scorned him publicly, too. *That's what he deserved,* her logical mind told her.

But that anger, easy to sustain when they were apart, was impossible to hold onto in his presence. Whenever he was near, she melted like butter too close to a stove; his energy consumed her, burrowing into her body and claiming ownership. In her heart, she knew she couldn't walk away from him. Even if he was cheating on her now, she couldn't leave him.

She hated herself for her weakness, but was powerless to change it. Her mother had a reason to stay in an unhappy marriage; she was financially dependent on the man she married. Angie had no such excuse. Even though her father had left her with deep scars, she'd fought for and won independence from him. Meeting Klaxton had given her the will to pull her life back together. Financially, she held the reins; aside from his bad investments, the two trials had taken every dime they had. Yet now, *he* was the authority figure she hated herself for needing.

Deep down, she knew he needed her too—even if he thought he needed other women more. But if Klaxton *was* having another affair, she could never forgive him, or herself.

∞

Just as Angie was beginning to let go of her troubled thoughts and sleep, Klaxton awoke from a turbulent dream. He was already forgetting a lot of the details, but he remembered that he'd done something horrible. He had killed ...

Who? Angie? A woman, that much he knew. She had made him angry, and he feared she would hurt his son. There had been a son, yes. Or was he dreaming of his own boyhood through his father's eyes? Was the woman his mother?

Klaxton felt the sharp pain that presaged one of his throbbing headaches. His mind raced through his past like a pitiless videographer, showing him scenes he wanted to forget, women he wished he'd never met.

Unbidden, the night he met Cheryl raced through his mind. Restless after work, he decided to go to a late-night jazz place for one last, calming drink. If only he'd gone home instead! She was a white woman, his first—the ultimate forbidden fruit for black men in the world he grew up in. He found out the hard way that conniving women are the same, regardless of race.

"But that's all history," he said softly to the sleeping woman beside him. "I'll prove it to you somehow. And I swear, no matter what it takes, no woman will ever come between us again."

The pounding in his head faded, and he dozed off. This time, he dreamed only of her.

Twenty-three

The kitchen had been the last thing on Joe's mind when he bought the house, but now he was glad the room's main window faced east. Morning sunlight streamed through it, lighting up the U-shaped breakfast nook where he sat with the coffee and blueberry muffin Mrs. Caldwell had brought him. The room's brightness lifted his spirits.

The Saturday paper lay beside him. Usually, he couldn't wait to tear into it; the Saturday paper was his reward for a hard work-week, and a way to transition to the weekend. But his thoughts today were of Ashley and their evening together. He imagined her sitting there beside him in the breakfast nook, her hair backlit by the sun's rays, sipping coffee and browsing through the newspaper with him as Mrs. Caldwell fussed over them.

He sighed. Even though he was covering for Klaxton, last night could have gone another way. If he had pressed her, he sensed, she would have stayed the night. But something held him back. *Not lack of desire, God knows.* But ... what?

Fear? Not exactly. Yet he'd found himself hesitant to ratchet up the momentum. There was a tension inside him, but not just sexual. Something rarer—a spiritual connection that he couldn't put a name to. He'd almost forgotten that roller-coaster feeling of being physically infatuated, and, with Ashley, it was already overlaid with a sense of ease, caring and comfort that was virtually overwhelming after three years of self-imposed celibacy and solitude. Despite the urgings of his body, he'd forced himself to wait.

Deep in these thoughts, his coffee growing cold, Joe didn't hear the phone ring.

"Dr. Joe?" Mrs. Caldwell's voice called from the next room. Joe turned to see her approaching with the cordless in her hand. "Your answering service! They say it is very urgent." She thrust the phone at him as if it were a live rattlesnake.

Joe blinked, fully in the present now. "Dr. Fry speaking."

Mrs. Caldwell, watching, saw his face fall as he listened.

"Are you sure?" Joe said. "I just spoke with him yesterday afternoon. He said he'd be back on call before midnight tonight. Well, okay. Please keep me posted, and I'll call you the minute I hear anything at all. Thanks." Joe clicked off the phone and placed it on the table.

"Is anything wrong?" Mrs. Caldwell asked.

"Yeah, there is," Joe said, thinking. "There's been a fire at the Staples' house. And nobody's been able to reach them."

∞

At about the same time, Ashley's cell phone rang on the night table beside her bed. Its shrill cry intruded like a bomb. She lurched into consciousness and grabbed it.

"Hello?" Her eyes widened. "Yes, this is Ashley Heath ... What? ... No, I don't know. Have you checked the hospital or called her cell phone? Is everything all right? ... When you get in touch with her, please call me back immediately! Thank you."

She closed the flap on the phone and rolled back over onto the pillow, breathing hard. After a moment, she punched in Joe's number. "I just got a call from the hospital," she told him when he answered. "They can't find Angie. Have you heard from her or Klaxton?" She listened, then jumped up from the bed. "A what? Oh, my God! ... No. I haven't heard from her since we went shopping. This isn't like Angie. She would have paged me or called my cell. What if they were in the house?"

As she spoke, she raced for her answering machine to see if she'd missed any calls.

"Ashley, don't panic. I'm sure they're all right," Joe said. "You try Angie's numbers and I'll try Klaxton's. If we still can't reach them, we'll ride over to the house. I'll pick you up, all I have to do is get dressed."

He found a pen and wrote directions to her condo on the masthead of the newspaper, carefully tearing them off and shoving them into the pocket of his robe. "I'll call your cell as soon as I'm outside your place."

They disconnected, and he turned to Mrs. Caldwell. "I'll call you as soon as we know something." Then he stood and headed for the stairs. Over his shoulder he called, "I forgot to feed Solly. Can you—?"

"Do not worry!" she called after him.

∞

As always in a crisis, Joe headed for the Bible he kept on his nightstand. He stopped in his tracks; it wasn't there. Glancing around the room, he saw it, lying open, on what he still thought of as Courtney's side of the bed. For a split second, a familiar, sweet aroma filled the room, and he reached out to touch the Bible, as though to reassure himself that it was really there. Then he grabbed a pair of jeans and sweatshirt and dressed hurriedly, remembering at the last minute to get the directions to Ashley's and cram them in his jeans pocket.

Less than half an hour later, Joe and Ashley were turning into the gated community where the Staples lived. Even with the car windows up, they smelled the acrid scent of fire before they saw the thin haze of gray smoke rising into the unpleasantly cold late-winter air.

As they neared the house, Joe noted only a single fire truck, a police car and the charred remains of the structure. It was clear that the fire had raged out of control. All that was left was a series of beams that had formed the curved walls of the front of the house and a huge pile of rubble. Toward the rear of the house's footprint, the twisted remnants of a refrigerator and dishwasher stood in silent testimony that there had once been a kitchen there.

"God! Oh, God!" Ashley cried out.

Joe put his arm around her shoulders and glanced toward where the garage had been. "I don't see either of their cars, so that's a good sign. Pray with me, honey."

They stopped for a moment in a silent embrace while Joe bowed his head and whispered. Then they slipped under the yellow crime-scene tape surrounding the remains of the house. Joe remembered the last time he'd taken a trip up this walkway. It had been lined with holly, barberry and boxwood shrubs; now, that greenery was burnt and trampled.

A heavyset black man wearing a suit walked toward them. His measured stride and serious face told Joe why he was there.

"We're friends of the owners," Joe called out as the man approached. "Have you been able to locate them yet?"

"I'm Lieutenant Brown, DeKalb Police," he said, extending a massive hand. "You are ...?"

"I rent medical offices to the homeowners," Joe said, shaking the lieutenant's hand. "I'm Dr. Joe Fry, and this is Ashley Heath, an attorney who's a friend of the Staples. We were called by their answering service to see if we could help locate them. What happened?"

"Sir, I'm sorry, but this is a crime scene. I'm going to have to ask you to stay back." Brown pointed to the bright yellow tape. "Have you spoken with either one of them?"

"No," Ashley said before Joe could reply. "Why is this a crime scene? Was it arson? Was anyone hurt? What caused the fire?"

Brown shook his head. "I'm sorry. It's still under investigation, and I'm going to have to ask you to leave. There's nothing to see here. If you talk to your friends, please have them call the DeKalb Police or go to the nearest police station."

He handed Joe a business card, then motioned for them to turn around.

Joe shivered as he and Ashley read the card: "Lieutenant Carlton Brown, Homicide Division, DeKalb County Public Safety Department."

"Walk!" Brown ordered, and they complied.

"Fat bastard," Ashley said under her breath. "Give a black man a badge and he thinks he owns the world."

Back in the car, Ashley began punching numbers into her cell phone.

"Who are you calling?"

"A friend at the police department. Someone who might know what the hell's going on."

After a few whispered words, she hung up the phone, shaking and silent.

Joe extended his hand, but didn't speak. He knew what she'd found out, but better to let her tell him when she was ready.

After a few moments, she took a deep, strangled breath. "We need to go to the morgue."

Twenty-four

On the drive back to Atlanta the next morning, both of them were quiet. A hurried cup of coffee and bagel after a mostly sleepless night wasn't enough to make for easy conversation. Angie insisted they head back home, and seeing the hurt still in her eyes, Klaxton didn't have the heart to argue. They silently packed and checked out before eight a.m. His headache was still with him, and the car's purring engine sounded like thunder. He didn't even want to turn on his beloved sound system; the thought made him wince.

So it was even more excruciating to hear the building squeal of a police siren behind them as they approached the exit to the Highway 985 cutoff. A glance in the rearview mirror told him that history was about to come back and bite him on the ass; the Georgia State Patrol car behind them drew close enough for him to see the lone trooper inside, and the vehicle's lights began to flash.

He glanced at Angie and saw her jaw clench as he swerved into the emergency lane and braked.

He brought the car to a stop and pressed the button to roll down his window, willing his breathing and pulse to slow. Beside him, Angie sat taut and coiled like a cobra.

"'Morning, sir. May I see your driver's license, please?" An oversized pair of sunglasses whose surfaces reflected twin images of the Interstate 85 overhead sign hid the trooper's eyes.

Klaxton glanced at the man's nametag and slowly retrieved his wallet, saying casually as he squinted into the sun and proffered the license, "What's the problem, Officer Hightower?"

"Dr. Staples?" the trooper replied. "Is the address on your license your current residence?"

"Ah, no. We just moved into a new home this past summer."

"Let me have that address, sir."

"4517 Willow Spur Lane, in Atlanta. Is anything wrong?"

Hightower glanced past Klaxton to Angie. "Are you Mrs. Staples?"

"Dr. Angie Staples, yes," she replied.

"I'll need to see some identification for you as well, Doctor." He checked the license Angie handed him, and Klaxton could swear he saw relief cross the man's face when he handed it back.

"What in hell's going on here?" Klaxton demanded. This was no routine stop for a speeding violation.

"We received an all-points bulletin from DeKalb County. They're trying to contact you," Hightower nodded toward Angie, "or your wife. There was a fire at your house early this morning."

"A fire?" Angie cried out. "No!"

Klaxton gasped. "Are-Are you sure?"

Hightower nodded. "I regret to inform you that the residence was nearly destroyed." With a glance at Angie, he lowered his voice and added, "A body was found inside, sir. A female." His voice louder, he referred to a piece of paper in his hand. "The firefighters and police attempted to contact you. When they couldn't reach you, there was some concern that you and your wife might have been in the house at the time of the fire."

Klaxton glanced at Angie, raising his eyebrows, and she sputtered, "I ... I turned off our pagers and cell phones in the hotel room last night. I forgot to turn them back on when I packed this morning. And what's that about a bod—?"

"I've been instructed to escort you back to DeKalb County," Hightower said, and handed Klaxton's license back to him. "I'm sure they'll answer your questions. If you'll pull back onto the highway when the way is clear, please. When you see me pull around you, follow me to the North DeKalb Police Station."

Too stunned to reply, Klaxton nodded, and Hightower returned to his car. Angie was sobbing quietly as he pulled back onto the expressway, his heart pounding so loud he barely heard the patrol car's siren behind him. When the patrol car whipped around their Mercedes, his thoughts flashed to his arrest in New York, to the routine ride to police headquarters for "questioning" that ended in a three-year vacation at Elmira Prison. The flood of memories made his hands tremble.

This can't be happening, he thought. *Stephanie!* He hadn't taken her seriously. *It had to be her. Who else would have torched our house?* He'd thought the New York trouble was behind them. He should have known better.

Glancing to his right as he maneuvered lanes, he quietly said what he feared was a lie: "It's going to be all right, baby."

Angie stared blankly into space for a few moments before turning to meet his gaze. "I love you, Klaxton," she said, her voice devoid of life, and turned back to the window.

∞

Ashley was slowly losing her composure, like peeling the layers of an onion, and seeing the burned house had been only the first layer. She stood next to Joe as he signed their names on the visitor's log at the DeKalb County Medical Examiner's Office. A clerk directed them to a waiting room just to the left of the sign-in desk, and they sat, holding hands, without a word.

Finally, they were summoned to a bright-lit, vaulted, stainless steel-clad sanctum that smelled strongly of disinfectant. Inside, they saw two empty gurneys and an array of cadaver drawers just like those on the television crime shows.

The attendant, a redheaded youth with a pimply neck, showed them to a distant corner of the room, where a sheet covered a body on a table. He peered at each of them briefly, then slowly pulled the sheet back. The woman's hair was singed, but otherwise, she looked as though she was asleep.

"Oh, God, it's—it's that woman," Ashley cried. "From the party at Angie's. I-I don't know her name."

"It's not Dr. Angie Staples?" the attendant asked.

"No. No," Ashley said, the words coming in hitching sobs. "Oh, God, thank God, no."

Joe pulled her into his arms, and it was a moment before they were able to follow the attendant out.

∞

Angie was huddled into a small ball on one of the plastic chairs in the waiting room of the DeKalb County Public Safety Department's North Precinct. Her head was facing a window, and she was rocking back and forth and humming softly, giving no sign she heard Joe and Ashley come in.

Ashley had never seen Angie like this. As they moved closer, she recognized the tune her friend was humming: *"Hush, little baby, don't you cry ..."*

"Angie?" Ashley called out, her voice breaking. "Sweetie, are you okay?"

Angie didn't reply, just continued rocking back and forth. But the humming stopped. Ashley took it as a sign of recognition.

"Angie, honey, listen," she said, bending down. "Where is Klaxton?"

No reply.

Ashley looked at Joe, and his answering look told her he was just as lost as she was. But with just as much reason to worry. After they left the morgue, Joe's cell phone rang. It was a Detective Jack Dubose, requesting that they meet him at the North Precinct.

While on the phone, Dubose informed them that the medical examiner's office was searching for dental or fingerprint records to confirm that the body was that of Stephanie Rogers. When they told him the name had no meaning to them, Dubose said, "Well, since you know the Staples, I thought you might know of her. An off-duty cop working security at Crawford Long Hospital found an abandoned car at the hospital's emergency entrance. The car's registered to someone by that name. The car was unlocked, probably left there all night. When he noted a gun and an empty can of kerosene in the backseat, he ran the tag. Nothing definite yet, but it's looking pretty good that she's the woman in the morgue. The dental records will tell us. Or we'll use the fingerprints found in the car."

Joe told Dubose of his brief meeting with the woman the night of the party, then said, "Ah, Detective, I'm glad to know you might have identified her, but ... I'm really concerned about the Staples."

"Don't be," Dubose said. "They've been found, and they're at the police station for questioning."

When Joe turned to tell Ashley, sitting beside him, she let out a sigh, relieved. But just as quickly, her face fell. "Joe, I'm glad Angie's okay, but there is another woman lying in there dead. I—"

Joe shook his head and turned his attention back to Dubose. "We're on our way." Then, he switched off his cell phone. Good or bad, he didn't think he could handle any more news for the next little while.

Watching the uniformed policewoman heading toward Angie now, he realized that good news wouldn't be forthcoming. After exchanging a few words with Ashley, the policewoman escorted Angie away, whispering gently and grasping her by both sagging shoulders.

Before they could take a seat in the small waiting room, a large black man dressed in a golf shirt and khakis came toward them. "Detective Dubose," he said, extending his hand to Joe.

"Joe Fry," Joe responded, and added quickly, "This is Ashley Heath. She's ... the Staples' attorney."

Ashley gave Joe a sideways glance, but didn't say anything as she shook the detective's hand.

Dubose led them to a small room with scant furnishings—a table, three chairs, and a wastebasket. The moment he said, "Have a seat," Ashley said, "No thank you. I need to confer with my clients. I asked, but I still don't know where the policewoman was taking Dr. Angie Staples. And I definitely want to find out where Dr. Klaxton Staples is right now."

"Shortly," Dubose replied. "In the meantime, if you want to remain in here with Dr. Fry, please hold any questions until after I finish asking mine." He picked up a legal pad as Ashley bit her lip, and Joe squeezed her hand.

In the minutes that followed, Joe and Ashley learned of the prostitute's murder in New York, and Klaxton's homicide conviction, incarceration, and subsequent exoneration.

"Is my client being charged in connection with this case?" Ashley asked, unable to stay silent.

Dubose gave her a measured stare. "Which one?"

"When can I see Dr. Staples?" she demanded, ignoring the detective's question.

"Which one?" he repeated. "They're being interviewed separately."

"Interviewed?" She turned a fiery glare on him. "I'm going to talk to both of them. *Now*, please."

"Go back to the waiting room, both of you," Dubose instructed. "I'll come and get you in a moment, Ms. Heath, and I'll send someone to take your statement, Dr. Fry."

As soon as he lumbered out of earshot, Ashley turned to Joe, her eyes narrowed. "I'll be Klaxton's attorney of record. But, I'm telling you, Joe, if I get even a *hint* that asshole had anything to do with that dead woman in his basement, I'll go to work for the DA to get him convicted!"

"And I'll be right beside you," Joe said, pressing her shoulder lightly, yet certain, after what he'd just found out, that his new business partnership was about to dissolve and leave him in a worse financial mess than before.

While they waited, Joe wondered why he hadn't done a more thorough background search on Klaxton and Angie. But he knew why. He'd been so anxious to rent the property, he didn't think about it. *After all, doctors are some of the most trusted people in our society. Right? Yeah. Just like I trusted Courtney's doctors to make sure she stayed healthy.*

But there was something else. Ashley. She acted shocked when the detective told them about New York, but ... how much of all this did she know before today? Ashley Heath made him feel alive and vibrant, and her willingness to provide legal counsel to someone she obviously loathed was commendable. But Joe wondered if he'd gotten too close, too quickly, to someone he didn't know nearly well enough.

He didn't want to think these thoughts, but they came, unbidden, and lingered long after Ashley was finally called to see her newest clients.

∞

Ashley was ushered into the room where Angie was being held, her mind galloping to find the best strategy for the next few minutes. Should she let her friend know that the body in the house might belong to her husband's lover? The one that Ashley had tried to tell Angie about, but she didn't want to hear it? One look at Angie's puffy eyes, and she decided to wait. Better to find out what Angie herself knew first.

"Angie ... honey," she said, taking a seat beside the shivering woman, "everything's going to be okay. Just tell me what you might know about this. About the fire. About ... About anything at all."

Angie was silent. Ashley cleared her throat and tried again. "Angie, sweetie ... they told us about Klaxton's ... problems in New York. That's why he ... both of you ... were brought in. They're probably just, ah, concerned because of that."

When Angie still didn't answer, Ashley squeezed her hand. "Look, sweetie, I need to see Klaxton. And I have to ask you some questions before I go back there. Can you keep it together?"

Angie nodded. "I think so."

"Do you have any idea—any idea at all—what someone would've been doing in your house last night while you were away?"

Angie shook her head and began to weep. "No! We left the hospital together and drove straight to the Chateau."

Ashley handed her a tissue from her purse. "You didn't see ... or hear anything unusual before you left your place?"

Angie shook her head and sobbed into the tissue before speaking again. "No, Ashley, I swear! Klaxton got paged to the hospital before we were finished loading the car. But there wasn't a living soul in the house when I left it to go meet Klaxton at the hospital. I locked all the doors, and I even double-checked the garage door."

"Does anyone have access to your house other than you and Klaxton?"

Angie shook her head.

Ashley gave her a comforting pat on the thigh, then got up and headed for the front desk. Like it or not, it was time to speak to Klaxton.

Twenty-five

Klaxton was pacing the floor when Ashley entered the interrogation room, but stopped when he saw her. "Thank God you're here," he said, happy, for once, to see her.

Before he could say anything else, the other person in the room stood. "Detective Crowley, DeKalb Police," he said, addressing Ashley as he rested his milk-colored hand on the wobbly table for support. "You're Ashley Heath?" He took her in appreciatively, stopping just short of a leer.

Ashley returned his gaze without flinching. He was probably in his mid-thirties, long and lanky, with a reddish-blond crew cut and freckles. If she wasn't mistaken, he harbored a plug of chewing tobacco in his left cheek—a sure sign of a redneck in her book. Her conversation with Angie had shaken her, but she knew how to handle this kind of redneck, and probably a racist, too.

"Hello, Detective Crowley," she replied coolly, extending a hand flashing with diamonds. "My gracious, we sure do have plenty of detectives working today. You're the third, maybe the fourth I've met today. But yes, I'm Ms. Heath. I'm representing Dr. Staples." Standing a little straighter, she smoothed her navy Prada shift and dug a business card from her bag, then passed the card to him. As he read it, she asked, "Detective, what is my client charged with?"

Crowley shot Klaxton a glance, and received a glare in return. "Based on our initial investigation, he's been held in connection with the death of the person whose body was found in his basement."

Ashley's eyes narrowed. "On a charge of ...?"

Another leering grin. "Well, let's just say it's under discussion at the moment as to the specific charge."

"I trust you'll inform me ASAP," she snapped. "If you please, I need to speak with my client ... *alone.*"

"Sure," Crowley said, recognizing that she knew the drill as well as he did. He opened the door to leave.

"Oh, and—?" Ashley called after him. "Do you think you could get us some coffee, *hon*? One black, one with cream and two sugars?"

She pursed her lips into a seductive pout, and chuckled inwardly as Crowley stalked off.

Turning to Klaxton, she saw that his white shirt was soaked with perspiration—a sure sign of panic and fear, and too often, guilt.

"Ashley, get me out of here," he pleaded before she could speak. "I didn't do it, I swear!"

She placed her hand on the wobbly table and gave him a look that had shaken many a client. "Just what is it that you didn't do, Klaxton?"

"Anything! I didn't do anything! All I did was take Angie for a weekend at Chateau Élan. What are they saying I did? You've got to help me!"

His last words came out as sobs, and he rose from the folding chair and began pacing. He made no more sounds, but his chest was heaving.

Ashley considered her options. This was far different from the cases she usually handled. She'd have to come up to speed on the possible charges, from arson to homicide, and sell the case to her firm. It wasn't the niche her partners had carved out for her. But, she had explored new territory for them before—successfully—and they knew it.

Was Klaxton a murderer? Looking at him here, raging and stomping around, she wasn't sure if she wanted to help him. After all, Klaxton Staples was no friend of hers. He was merely someone she tolerated to maintain her relationship with Angie. But Angie was almost like family, and if Klaxton went down for lack of a good lawyer, it was sure to create yet more pain for her friend.

Maybe the fact that he wasn't a friend was a good thing. She could distance herself enough to be professional in her approach. *Yes*, she decided. *I'll do it, and he'll take my lead on it—or he can find himself another attorney.*

She walked over to him, her heels clicking hollowly on the tile floor. "Look at me, Klaxton."

She paused until he complied. "Listen, and listen good. I'm not taking any bullshit off you. If you want my help, you're going to have to be straight with me—"

"I am INNOCENT!" he shouted. "You wouldn't believe what they put us through. We did *nothing* wrong. Whatever happened to that old cliché, 'Innocent until proven guilty'? They got nothing to keep me here on. They took my car, and God knows what—"

"Do you want to get out of this jail?"

She spoke softly, but her calm authority cut through. "Of *course* I want to get out of here," he said, quieter. "Get me out, Ash."

She let her voice drop almost to a whisper as she drew within inches of his face. "If you keep yelling like you were a minute ago, they're going to take you right back to your cell. If they do, your big, dumb ass can just sit there until the bond hearing. If they take you away, I won't get a chance to prepare for that hearing. And if I don't get a chance to prepare, *I will not be there.* I *never* go into a court-room unprepared, and I'm not about to make an exception for a jackass *ex-con* like you."

His surprise was so great, his entire body jerked. "What did you just say ... How long have you been holding that—?"

She pointed her finger again to stop him, and her steely eyes never left his as she lowered herself onto the cold metal of the fold-ing chair across from him. "How long have I known? Long enough. Now sit back down," she used her finger to direct his gaze to the chair on the other side of the table, "and listen up."

Finally speechless, he sat.

"We're not going to dwell on your past," Ashley said, "except to acknowledge that it's one of the reasons they think they've got their man. Let's get straight to the point. Did you do anything that they can charge you with?"

"Not a thing!"

"Klaxton—"

"Ashley, I haven't been alone at any time in the last forty-eight hours. You can check. I left the hospital with Angie, we drove to Chateau Élan ... and we can prove we were there! The guest regis-ter lists us, and we had room service ..."

For the first time, Ashley felt he might just be telling the truth. *But ...*

"Tell me what you know," she said, folding her arms and sitting back as far as the chair would permit.

"The trooper—his name was Hightower—told us our house had burned down."

She waited.

"And ... And that a body was found in the basement."

At that moment, the lanky detective came back in. He had a small cardboard tray with two cups of steaming coffee, napkins, cream, sugar and stirrers. He set it down with a smirk, but exited without a word. Angie directed a satisfied smile at his back.

"It's happened again, just like in New York," Klaxton said when the door closed. "Only this time, in my own home. Jesus Christ, I swear on my grandmother's grave, it wasn't me!"

Ashley leaned back and thought about what he'd just said. She still questioned whether she could trust a man who'd cheated on his wife—her best friend—and who might very well be a killer.

"Angie," he said, eyes widening. "Where is she? They separated us. Have you talked to her? Is she all right?"

It had taken this long for him to ask about his wife, and Ashley made a mental note of it before answering. "She's being held in an-other room. I've talked to her. She's all right, *considering*. But if I'm going to help you, we're going to have to talk about *you*. And you're going to have to answer all of my questions ... honestly." She rose and leaned over the table. "I want you to know this: the first time I find that you've lied to me or left anything out, I'm out of here."

"Straight up, I didn't do it." His voice cracked.

She slowly sat back down and waited for him to collect himself, tapping her long nails impatiently on the table. Once he seemed calm enough, she said, "Okay, here's the score. When a dead woman is found in your home burned like a paper bag, you're a suspect. And at this moment, you look as guilty as homemade sin."

Klaxton started to speak, but she stopped him. "One thing you've got to remember: down here, folks believe that if it walks like a duck and quacks like a duck, it's a damn duck. Also, *Bro*, if the duck happens to be black, it's in the soup automatically. You know that. Right now you're the duck, and they are getting ready to cook you for supper."

His head snapped up. "So that's what you think I am, huh? A murderer?"

"That's lame, Klaxton. You're going to have to do better than that on the witness stand. Do *I* think you're a murderer? Okay, let's do a little role-playing here. I'm a juror, hearing your testimony. Let me see...." She tapped her nails on the table, reeling off each of her points with the tap of a fingernail.

"One. I know, because the prosecution has convinced me, that you are one arrogant, lowlife, cheatin'-on-your-woman son of a bitch. Two. There were twelve people in New York who believed you were a murderer. People pretty much like me. A jury of your peers. Three. They believed it enough to send your ass to Elmira State Prison.

"Based on all that, just what am I supposed to think? That the bogeyman sneaked into your house while you were away and killed your hooker girlfriend?"

Klaxton gasped. "Stephanie?"

Until that moment, Klaxton had considered Ashley a major pain in the ass. Now that his worst fears were true—the dead woman was his former mistress—he was terrified. He needed Ashley desperately—just like he knew that if he didn't do every-thing she said, he might land behind bars again.

"Okay, okay, I know it looks bad when you put it like that," he said. "But there was also an appeals court that believed I was innocent. And they made me a free man. I was exonerated."

She nodded. "Lack of evidence? Prosecutorial incompetence? Jury tampering?"

"All of the above. Officially? The lawyer Angie's father got me was able to throw out the first trial. The homicide happened on the ... dead woman's premises. No witnesses. Only reason I was fingered was because I was having an affair with her. The ... dead woman ... *Cheryl* and I had our differences—just like Stephanie and I did—

but they weren't that serious. That's the God's truth, Ashley. Believe me. I wouldn't go out like that."

Ashley had met plenty of shady people, but believed she was getting the truth from Klaxton—or at least as much truth as he was capable of. She knew that seasoned defense attorneys in capital cases stopped short of asking their clients if they were guilty: a technicality that allowed them to represent them without addressing guilt or innocence directly. Her insistence on knowing, yea or nay, was personal. But now, her due diligence had been satisfied—almost.

"Here's something you're damn sure going to tell me," she said. "Keep in mind that I'm your attorney, and our conversations are privileged. I could be disbarred if I ever reveal anything you tell me—even to Angie. But remember this, too: if I catch you in a lie, I'm dropping you like that." She snapped her fingers.

Digging a small notepad and a pen from her purse, she handed them to Klaxton. "Write down names and contact information for every woman you've screwed other than your wife since you've been in Atlanta. No wait … make that every woman you've even *thought* about screwing. We'll start there."

Klaxton froze. He knew how close Angie and Ashley were. Was that friendship more important than an oath? He hoped not.

Slowly, he picked up the pen.

Ashley felt something crawling up her leg and brushed at it. "They must have lice in here or something. I can't leave here until you finish. So don't take all day."

He slid the pad back to her. When she saw the two names on it, she shivered in disgust, knowing she'd been right about Vickie Renfroe all along.

"You haven't been formally charged yet, right?"

He shook his head. "Don't think so. I asked, and *kept* asking what the charge was, but they keep changing their story. The local fuzz just mostly chatted about the weather. That detective had only been here a few minutes before you got here."

A thoughtful frown appeared on her face, causing her brow to furrow. "Okay, that's good. Usually a person isn't locked up without being read his rights, *and* letting him know what he's being charged with. But they can hold you for seventy-two hours just for the hell of it. Okay, let's roll with that. If they want to play hardball, I'll give them something to swing at."

She thought a moment more, then looked pointedly at him. "After I find out the charges, I'll have to find out what agencies are involved." To his questioning look, she said, "If it's murder, the locals are in charge. For other stuff, like arson—or drugs, or cross-ing over state lines—they call in the GBI. Maybe even the FBI."

He nodded, his face clearly showing how overwhelmed he was by that thought. And that was exactly where she needed him to be.

"If you're charged with murder, we're going to need money for bail," she said. "Lots of it, because of your past."

"But I was innocent—"

"Doesn't matter that you were found innocent the second time. They'll consider you a flight risk, especially since you left New York so soon after your second trial."

He fixed his eyes on the tabletop between them. "Money's not a problem. You know that, Ash."

She thought but didn't voice her suspicion that money wasn't a problem because her best friend worked around the clock, while Klaxton seemed to have more free time than any doctor she knew. But *that* could wait until she could kick the ass of a free man, instead of someone behind bars. "You're still in street clothes," she mused, pondering the meaning of that. Her brow furrowed again. "But that's not right. Something's slowing them up."

"What do you mean?"

"You should've been in an orange jumpsuit before you saw me. Something's not clicking here. What is it?"

She shook her head, stood, and began pacing. Her heels tapped on the tiles as she tried to figure out what was wrong with that … and a few other things.

Something told her he wasn't cold-blooded enough to be a killer. But real life, plus the history of the justice system, taught even the most casual observer how deceiving looks could be that way. While Klaxton was no Hannibal Lecter or Ted Bundy, he was smooth and intelligent, just as those killers had been.

Was he stupid enough—or cocky enough—to have a fling in his own home? *Probably*. But was he stupid enough to kill a defenseless woman in his own home, and then set a fire to cover it up? The only answer she could come up with was, *Probably not*.

Even so, he was her client now, and she had promised to defend him. She stopped pacing and looked at him. "Let's work on getting you out of here. If they haven't taken you through the booking process yet, something's wrong. Try to keep your mouth shut while I try to find out what it is."

She walked to the house phone beside the door and yanked the handset off its hook. "This is Dr. Staples' attorney. I need to speak to Detective Crowley."

"I'll send him in," a disembodied voice drawled.

In short order, the door lock clicked, and Crowley ambled into the room.

"What are the charges against my client?"

"I thought you knew," he said amiably.

"No, I *don't* know," Ashley said. "And neither does my client. Care to inform me? Care to inform *anyone*?" She slapped her hand on the table in mock surprise. "Wait, I think I know. I've heard this kind of bullshit before. What is it? The good old 'driving while black'?"

She knew her missile had hit its target when the slow-talking detective's face turned red. "You should be asking your client that, don't you think Miss ... what is it? ... Miss Hart?"

"It's Heath. H - E - A - T - H. 'Heath' with two H's and no R's. And since my client hasn't been charged, not only are you looking at holding him against his will—that's a crime, even here —you're also looking at a civil suit."

She pierced him with a look, and he finally answered her.

"Well, Ms. *Heath*, as far as I know, Dr. Staples is only being held for questioning. No charges from me. I only needed to ask him a few questions about the victim found dead on his property. The death has been ruled a homicide." With a glance toward Klaxton, he lowered his voice and added, "We *do* think we have a motive, though."

"Care to share *that* with me?" Ashley snapped.

"You asshole," Klaxton said from the other side of the table. "You lied to me. You led me to believe I was under arrest. Cracker, you don't know who you're messing with. I'll—"

Ashley had several rowdy hardcore rappers as clients, and had practiced her "shut up" look many times. As soon as she finished laying the look on Klaxton, she turned around to deal with the other asshole, who was saying, "It's the folks in New York who wanted me to talk with him. Something about a warrant. But New York just called and said he was free to go. Free as a bird." He glared at Klaxton. "Just don't let him fly too far."

Crowley pushed open the beige-painted steel door and left, and Ashley glanced down at the discarded gum wrappers on the room's dingy floor and knew it was far from over.

Twenty-six

Three days later, Klaxton leaned back in his office chair, phone to his ear, as Ashley's voice yammered on and on. Simultaneously, perhaps a little too loud, Tupac's "Me Against the World" was playing on the office sound system. It was a perfect choice for the mood he was in, and a welcome distraction from what his attorney was telling him. Despite the fact that the relationship had gone sour, he had shared a bed with Stephanie. It was hard enough dealing with her death. But knowing she'd been murdered was a reality he wished he could escape.

"... going to have to find representation for Angie, in the event ..."

Klaxton tuned the voice back out; he couldn't deal with all of this. He was trying to forget about it, in fact.

Taking advantage of a pause in her ranting, he asked, "How's the entertainment law biz going, Ash? Everybody's into rap these days. I got your boy's latest CD. That title cut—'Holiday Hoes'? That's my jam."

Silence on the other end.

The music changed, and Klaxton reached out to turn up the stereo's volume. "Congratulations, Ashley. Your other boy, Kid Dog, just came on V-103! Me and the girls up front were just talking about him! How 'bout that?"

On the other end, Ashley rolled her eyes and glanced down, shaking her head at the pile of papers the case had already generated. Papers that had to be scrutinized, analyzed and transformed into a credible defense if the worst happened.

"Look, Klaxton," she said, "I don't have time for small talk. You and Angie are still under a cloud of suspicion in this arson-homicide, and I need your full attention. One of you could be charged any time, and Angie's acting a little weird on me. I need you to *concentrate*."

Kid Dog's music went away, and Klaxton's next words were, "Okay, okay, I'm listening."

"Good. First of all: I've spent the last half hour convincing my partners they should let me represent you if you *are* charged with murder." She sighed. "And you're welcome."

"Uh, thank you."

"It wasn't easy," she told him. That was an understatement. Robert Johnson's exact words had been, "Miss Heath, you have such an admirable standing in the entertainment industry, we don't want to send a mixed signal. We feel that you are truly more valuable to us in handling our *entertainment* clients."

Ashley had no trouble believing that. In fact, she had to suppress a grin at the picture of the dour old lawyer trying to advise Kid Dog, or any of the other brilliant-but-young millionaire performers she managed.

"I had to remind them about the $10 million I raked in on that tobacco case," she told Klaxton. "That's when they started seeing it my way. But I'm telling you all this for one reason, and one reason only. And that is: you have to understand that I'm putting my reputation on the line for you. My career, my earning potential, my name and credibility. So you need to *stay* straight and *say* it straight every single second."

"Ashley, thank y—"

"Save it. Don't bother. I'm not doing this for *you*. I'm doing it for Angie."

Klaxton felt a headache coming on. "By the way, what's up with you and Joe?" he asked. "I noticed when we moved into his guest room the other night how *comfortably* you sashayed around that house. And that puppy knows you pretty well, it looks like."

"Joe and I have become good friends," she said, fighting for a level tone. "And, with all that's on *your* plate, it's nothing you need to concern yourself about."

"I know you can handle your own *affairs*. Just warning you to look around before you jump, girl. You've seen all that weird voodoo stuff he has laying around: those funky-looking candles, eerie pictures up on the walls, all those jars of different-colored *something* on the mantle in the living room. That housekeeper of his is some kind of voodoo queen, and I think he's mixed up in it, too. Also for Angie's sake," his voice turned ironic, "I'm just reminding you what you told me the other day: If it looks and walks like duck, don't be surprised if it quacks and lays an egg."

Ashley kept silent. Of course she'd seen the strange carvings and masks, and a lot more.

Klaxton took her silence as resistance. "Ashley, we had to fire that crazy-ass woman because Angie found salt in her office that she'd left there."

"How do you know Mrs. Caldwell left the salt? She leave you a note?"

"Look, I'm not making this up. I caught her trying to hang a string of beads behind the file cabinet. That woman's nuts. And I think Joe's just like her! Even if he's not, it's obvious he has no control over her."

Although Ashley had promised herself she'd hold her tongue, it was impossible. "Thanks for the warning," she spat, "but *I don't need it.* If you're looking to be somebody's daddy, look elsewhere. All the raising I'm going to get has already been done."

There was no rebuttal, and she didn't expect one. "Now that we've got *that* out of the way, let's get back to the real issue. No matter how that woman got in your basement, we're talking murder, and you're the prime suspect. Now that I know who she is, or was, it's pretty obvious to me that you're the most likely candidate, and your dear wife *and my best friend* is Number Two. You're the only two with the obvious means and opportunity. As to motive, remember that night at the housewarming? A fool could've seen that you had dumped her and she was looking for revenge. That's *your* motive, son. And Angie's is that you were sleeping with that woman all this time behind her back."

Ashley took a deep breath to calm herself, but it did little good. "Klaxton, Angie's my friend, but I guarantee you, if you were *my* man—and thank God you're not—that would be motive enough for me to turn on you. And if you don't think those white boys on this case aren't thinking the same way, think again."

Klaxon picked up a file on his desk and flipped through it nervously. "That may be, Ashley, but I distinctly remember hearing Johnny Redneck back at the jail say there weren't any charges against me or Angie. If they had anything on us, wouldn't they have moved by now?"

Ashley took another deep breath and ran her fingers through her short hair, not believing he was acting this dense. And remembering the NFL middle linebacker from Baltimore who escaped trial in a homicide in which he was clearly implicated. "Are you really as stupid as I think you are, Klaxton? Fool, they're just messing with your head. After the Ray Lewis case, everybody in law enforcement and criminal justice in Metro Atlanta learned a big lesson. Nowadays, if there's not enough to make the charges stick, they don't make an arrest. They play the waiting game, giving the suspect—that's *you,* in this case—just enough rope to hang himself. What they should have done with Ray Lewis."

Klaxton sputtered, "For what it's worth, a lot of people—me included—believe Ray Lewis got a bad rap. Another case of the crab syndrome—one brother trying to earn a rep at the expense of another while pulling our whole race down."

This time, she didn't roll her eyes; instead, she put a weary hand over them. "Can we discuss the politics of being black another time?"

"All right," he muttered. "O-*kay.*"

"Klaxton, *think.* Who could have done this besides you or Angie? And I know it wasn't my girl. Do any other scenarios pop into that thick skull?"

"Burglary?"

"Klaxton."

"All right, all right, here's one." Klaxton hit the power button on the sound system. "Crack addicts looking for stuff to pawn broke in and caught Stephanie, oh, I don't know ... maybe leaving a message about our affair for Angie. To keep her quiet, and because they were still half-crazed on drugs, they killed her—"

"—and then set fire to the house to disguise the homicide," she finished. "Sure, and God didn't make little green apples, either."

"Okay.... How about this? Stephanie flew into a rage and broke into the house. She didn't know we were gone. She was going to force me to tell Angie everything. Or she was going to tell Angie herself. When she couldn't find either one of us, she took an overdose of pills—Vicodin, Oxycontin, some kind of painkiller—and then set the fire. You know, committed suicide to frame us."

Ashley considered this. "The coroner's report hasn't come back yet. But if this crime tracks the one in New York—if the *perpetrator* is one and the same—it will show a toxic amount of drugs in her system. Or it could be simple smoke inhalation. Her revenge is a long way to go for an alibi, but it isn't all together out of the question." She sighed. "The only other theory I can come up with pertains to the name of the *other* woman on your cheat list from the other night."

All she heard was silence on Klaxton's end.

"Is it possible, Klaxton—I'm not going to say her name—but could *she* have staged this whole thing to set you up?"

He sat up straight. *Could Vickie be capable of something like this?* He'd taken care to be respectful to her, but Vickie was, in a sense, a woman scorned. He shook the cobwebs from his head, struggling to remember if Vickie had ever said anything about Stephanie. Ashley, sure—Vickie had *plenty* to say about Ashley. But Ashley was still living and breathing just fine. Frustration crossed his face when his memory came up zero. To his knowledge, Vickie didn't even know Stephanie.

And if what Vickie *did* know Stephanie? It made no sense that she would lure Stephanie to their home, kill her, and then torch the house. Framing him still wouldn't get her what she wanted. To have him, she'd have to kill Angie. *And*, he thought, *she's smart enough to know that.*

"No, I don't believe she had anything to do with it," he said at last. "That was a one-time thing. She seduced me, and as soon as I realized it, I put a stop to it before ... *before* anything happened. And you swore if I wrote those names down you'd honor my confidence!"

"I have, and I will, Klaxton," Ashley said. "I'm just trying to make sense of this. But really, it doesn't add up. One thing I learned in law school, though: once you have all the pieces, every puzzle has a solution."

"Ash, Stephanie was a hooker. Probably been with thousands of men since she followed us here. All those men have something or other to hide, and some of them are shady operators. Suppose she was blackmailing one of her clients and threatening to tell his wife about Hubby's extracurricular activities?"

"Then why would *Hubby* end up in *your* basement to kill Stephanie?"

Klaxton thought a moment. "Okay, here it is. Say he was stalking her, and she went there to have it out with me, or with Angie, or hell, with both of us. Stephanie wasn't the brightest light in the universe. It would have been easy to follow her without her noticing, and then trap her. Or maybe it was a pimp. Hell, I don't know if she had one or not. But, if so, and she was holding back money, that's all the motive a real player would need."

It was Ashley's turn to be silent. What he was saying sounded almost credible. The next thing was to get a private investigator on the case, look harder at Stephanie's background, and let the chips fall. "Okay, a stalker's possible," she acknowledged. "I'm going to do a little checking on my end. And if any of those detectives contact you, page me immediately. Just go about your business, act normal and be careful. No boulevardin' around town on the make—"

He snorted.

"You heard me. Keep your nose clean, and everything else, too. Don't talk to Crowley or anybody else without me there."

"Right, I know that. Just remember, I'm innocent. And Angie is too."

Ashley hesitated, "Okay, and *you* remember this: they're in touch with the NYPD and Manhattan DA's office. What one of 'em knows, they all know. So you need to be upfront with me at all times. Got that?"

"I got it!" Klaxton's voice went up a decibel.

"There's something else you need to know, too."

"What is it? How much worse could it get?"

"I don't think they're interested in Angie, but they've probably got a man on you as we speak. Maybe the DA doesn't have any evidence. But believe me, they're digging ... which means it will probably be just as easy for them to walk up on you and Vickie as it was for me. We don't need that right now." She paused. "And Klaxton, for what it's worth, I knew you were screwing her from Day One."

Klaxton's mouth opened, but he closed it just as fast. Denying it was useless, and antagonizing Ashley anymore was dangerous.

"Why Angie's still with you, only God in Heaven knows," she went on. "They say every woman has her limit, and I guess she just hasn't reached hers. But I'm going to keep my personal feelings out of this and just say that, as your attorney, I'm advising you to cease all contact with Vickie ... *and any of your other pets.*"

He made no response, fearing he'd only provoke her into breaking her vow of confidentiality and telling Angie the whole story. That was the last thing he needed.

He heard Ashley sigh. "Okay, Klaxton, gotta run. I have to line up the PI and examine the autopsy report as soon as it comes in. And oh, there's nothing in the media about your involvement in the case—yet. And we've got to keep it that way as long as we can. So keep a low profile. As soon as I can get some things lined up, I'll get you and Angie over here to take your depositions. In the meantime, go to work.... *Stay away from Joe's office....* and go home together and mind your business."

"Ashley, please keep them away from Angie." The anguish in his voice reverberated through the phone.

"You know I have no control over that, Klaxton—except to get your statements and alibis ASAP. Like it or not, if the DA can't get to *you*, they'll try to get to you through her. If I know the DA, that will come." She glanced down at her notes. "We're going to need the names of anyone you talked to at the resort. Chateau Élan, wasn't it?"

"Yeah. We got there pretty late on Friday night, so we only talked to the hotel clerk, the room service man, and the manager. But we talked to the manager again the next morning."

"Good. And we'll have the names and times from your receipts. They'll let us establish your whereabouts for that period. That's going to be critical. So I'll need your debit or credit card receipts."

Klaxton's moan wasn't what she wanted to hear. "Ashley, I didn't use a card, I used cash. We paid for everything with cash. And I didn't get any receipts." He tried to laugh, but the attempt failed. "Guess I've always been a cash-and-carry kind of man."

She sighed. "Well, we'll deal with that later. Transfer me to Angie's extension. I want to see how she's holding up."

"Angie's not here," Klaxton said, his words painted with concern. "She's at Joe's house. When she saw the house, she … she hasn't been able to do much of anything this week. I got a doctor from the agency to cover for her at the office, and the Coleman Group's picking up all of her deliveries at the hospital."

"Yeah, I can only imagine what she must have thought when she saw the house," Ashley said. "Is there anyone at Joe's with her? She probably doesn't need to be alone. Besides, you both need to account for every minute of every day."

"Yeah, I know. That crazy woman Caldwell's there with her. I begged her to come with me to the hotel last night, but she said no."

"What? What hotel?" The soft skin between Ashley's eyebrows wrinkled in confusion.

"Ah ... Angie and I got into a pretty heated argument last night. It was her dad's fault. You know there's no love lost between me and Angie's dad."

Ashley sighed. "What could her daddy possibly have to do with anything?"

He sighed. "Do we have to get into this?"

She slipped out of her high-heeled pumps, reached down and over, pulled open her lower right-hand desk drawer, leaned back in her chair and propped her feet on a stack of files in the drawer. "Now is *not* the time for you and Angie to be apart. And you sure don't need to be seen checking into a hotel in the middle of the night! So yes, we *do* have to get into this."

In a voice that sounded as weary as she felt, he said, "If you must know, she called her dad last night. He's coming to town on some business, and Angie wanted to ask Joe if he could stay with us at his place. I told her that her father could get a room."

"I don't see the problem. Joe's got plenty of space."

"Because I know my father-in-law's going to be an asshole the whole time. He was when ... when I had the trouble in New York. Always sticking his nose in my business. And the last time I checked the guest list for my business, his name was nowhere on it."

Klaxton hoped this answer would appease Ashley. What his male ego wouldn't allow him to admit was the *real* reason he'd left Joe's house. It wasn't because of the argument, but because he was scared. When they got into bed, the lamp on his side of the bed kept turning on and off. Angie had laughed, dismissing it as a quirk in the wiring, told him to unplug it. But being under the same roof with Mrs. Caldwell, who had been caught in the act of trying to cast spells or some other nonsense on Angie, Klaxton was already uncomfortable.

Even after he finally got the light to turn off for good by unscrewing the light bulb, he couldn't get over the feeling that someone was watching him. The feeling became so strong that he eventually got up, got dressed and woke Angie. She refused to leave with him. Her father's name came up in the discussion, and that gave him enough of an excuse to get out of there without admitting he was scared.

He didn't tell Ashley any of this, but he didn't have to. She was pissed enough.

"That's not good, not good at all, Klaxton," she said. "Look, when I talk to her, I'll tell Angie exactly what I'm telling you. You guys have to be united, if only for appearances' sake. *Especially* for appearances' sake."

He bit his lip, realizing that she was being a lot kinder than she usually was … maybe kinder than he deserved. "I know I come across a little raw sometimes, but I appreciate what you're doing for us. When you talk to Angie, please tell her I love her, and I'll come see her tonight."

A knock came at his office door. After a quick goodbye to Ashley, he said, "Come in," and placed the receiver back into the cradle. He looked up to find Vickie standing there, a medical file in her hand. Realizing that she'd managed to walk into his office without being announced annoyed him.

"Sorry to hear about your house," she said.

When he frowned and didn't answer, Vickie entered the room and sat down, crossing her legs at the ankles.

"I'm not able to chat with you at the moment," he said. "Got some pressing business I need to handle."

The edge in his voice startled her. Without moving, she said, "Klaxton, who was Stephanie Rogers, and what was she to you?"

He blew out a long breath of air. It was turning into another long, long day.

Twenty-seven

The hot water sluicing from the showerhead usually transported Joe from the petty frustrations of daily life. But not tonight. In the days following the fire, he'd barely slept a full night through, and his thoughts kept returning to the body in Klaxton's basement.

Even more disturbing, he couldn't shake his questions about Ashley's role in the whole affair. Since Courtney's death, he had looked to her memory and presence, still very real, in times of crisis. Before the fire, he believed his wife was urging him to move on. Today, he wasn't so sure. Perhaps she was warning him instead. Most of all, since the day he recognized the body lying in the morgue as the angry, drunken woman he'd bumped into at the Staples' front door months earlier, he hadn't been able to get the connection out of his mind.

He'd gone to Klaxton the Monday after the fire. Klaxton admitted that he and Stephanie were lovers, but he'd broken things off just before she barged in on the housewarming party. "But," he insisted, "that was my home, man. I wouldn't torch my own place just to get rid of an ex-lover, and I could never take a human life."

Joe had been reassured—then. But now, knowing about the similar case in New York made that assurance evaporate. If appearances proved accurate, his status as landlord was about to be history as well, his newfound financial stability gone with the wind.

He definitely wished Ashley weren't so involved with the Staples. Was she capable of defending a man she knew to be a killer? Joe sighed. He had no room to point fingers: Who, at this very moment, was sleeping in his guest bedroom? The supposed murderer's wronged wife! For fear of upsetting Angie, his houseguest, Joe kept quiet about his suspicions. But in his mind, the almost identical deaths of two of Klaxton's lovers couldn't be coincidental. *No way. No how.*

Yet Joe had seen stranger things before ... some of them right here in his own house. In spite of the heat and steam enveloping him in the shower, he was chilled by the thought that something evil might have happened the same night he and Ashley went to Dante's. If he'd given in to his desires ... Now, he was glad he waited to invite her into his bed.

In spite of his trepidation, Joe smiled as he stepped out of the shower, remembering how much they had laughed that night. He wanted to believe that was the real Ashley—smart, sophisticated, but with a simple, pure side she didn't often reveal.

As he was drying off, he heard the doorbell. It had to be someone Solly knew; the puppy's incessant barking didn't begin until after the first ring. Joe looked at the clock, noting it was 8:30 p.m. on the dot. His date was on time, and he was not. Not only was Ashley beautiful, she was also punctual. He wondered briefly if his own lateness was a sign of his growing ambivalence about her.

He stuck his head out the bedroom door and saw Angie down the stairs, greeting Ashley. Solly, who'd been yipping excitedly, sat watching, his tail motionless for once.

As they hugged, Joe noticed that the women were a study in contrasts: Ashley looked splendid in a robin's egg-blue cashmere sweater set and smartly fitted navy silk boot-cut pants. Angie was still tousle-haired and wearing her nightgown and slippers. He tried to remember how long it had been since he saw his houseguest up and fully dressed, but couldn't.

"You two ladies go in the living room," he called down the stairs. "I'll be down in a few."

Both women waved and smiled, and as Ashley grabbed Angie's arm and walked her into the living room, he went to dress.

∞

"Angie, what happened to you today?" Ashley said as they settled onto the sofa. "I thought for sure you'd be at Trease's. I left three messages with your service. I was worried!"

Angie fixed her gaze on a small gold figurine on the room's fireplace mantle. "Things have been so crazy lately, with the fire and everything, you know? I ... I'm just so afraid they're going to take Klaxton away from me." Her eyes traveled to her lap and stayed there.

Ashley noticed that Angie's face looked thinner, almost gaunt. Her eyes were puffy, and even at 8:30 at night, she had the demeanor of someone not yet fully awake after a long, deep sleep.

Ashley had never suffered from depression, but she knew it when she saw it. "It's going to be okay, sweetie," she said gently, placing her hand over Angie's. "I know it's a rough time, but neglecting your appearance is only going to hurt, not help. Hold your head up and *show* 'em they're wrong."

Angie still didn't look up; her hands remained in her lap, motionless.

Ashley had to break her friend's malaise. "Angie," she whispered, "did you know Joe was married before?"

That got Angie's attention, and she looked up. "No. Who told you that?"

"He did, silly. His wife died three years ago. From cancer."

"I ... I'm sorry, I didn't know."

Ashley shrugged. "No biggie. I just wondered if you did." She continued, "And girl, you don't need to miss another week at the beauty shop. Your eyes are swollen, and you're dragging around like a zombie." She put up a manicured hand to forestall Angie's rebuttal. "I realize you love your man, but you should love yourself a little bit more. Ain't no man on God's earth worth neglecting yourself for. You think they sit around and pine about *us*?"

"But—"

"I don't want to hear it," Ashley said. "For example, where is he now? At the first sign of trouble, he runs off to some hotel."

The words hung in the silence between them. Finally, Angie said, "I ... I didn't know how to tell you he'd left—"

"It's all right about that. But I'm not going to sit around and let you do this to yourself. I want to see that strong woman I know. You have to get yourself together—and if I have to kick your butt to get you to do it, I will."

After another silence, she said, "Why don't you come with us tonight? We're just going to dinner. You probably haven't eaten anything all day ... have you?"

Angie shook her head. "I'm not hungry, and ... I'm really tired, Ashley. I ... I have a lot of things I need to deal with, and I need time alone to think. Besides, I don't want to butt in on you and Joe. Maybe next week?"

Ashley nodded, satisfied. "Maybe I'll send you back a dessert, especially if we go to Brio. I know how you love the tiramisu there."

This time, Angie attempted a smile.

"And I'll definitely see you at the salon next Friday, okay?"

"After what you just told me," Angie replied, "do I have a choice?" She reached up and pulled a loose strand of hair forward. "You've got a point about the hair."

Smiling, Ashley reached out to hug her friend.

Joe entered the room, saying cheerily, "If you girls can tear yourselves apart, we need to get going. Angie, why don't you come with us?"

Ashley, catching his eye out of Angie's line of vision, gave him a barely perceptible shake of the head.

"Joe, thanks," Angie said, and rose from the sofa. "Ashley invited me, too. But I'm still tired, so I'll sit this one out. You two go on and have a good time."

With a wave of her hand, Angie moved like a sleepwalker toward the stairs. Joe turned out the lamp by the door, then heard Solly whimpering.

"Don't be scared," he said. "You're the baddest bear in the woods." After a final pat, he nuzzled the little guy before pulling the door tightly shut.

Twenty-eight

As Ashley had feared it would, Klaxton's case picked up steam. No arrests, no charges, and not even an actual allegation, but in less than two weeks, the buzzards of the media were circling.

She reached into a file and pulled out a newspaper clipping from the Metro section of the previous day's *Atlanta Journal-Constitution*. The headline read, "Body Found in Fire Identified." Below it was a grainy black-and-white halftone of a woman wearing a low-cut bustier that revealed a lot of cleavage and left little doubt as to her line of work.

The accompanying article was brief: *"The body found in a fire at an affluent Dunwoody home has been identified as that of Stephanie Rogers, 27, of Atlanta, DeKalb police said. Initial reports indicated the cause of the fire as arson, and police are questioning the homeowners, Atlanta physicians Klaxton Staples and Angie Bowen-Staples, who were reportedly out of town when the blaze broke out."*

Ashley sighed. "Girl, you knew this was coming. The *AJC's* on it now. And the minute the media finds out what happened in New York . . ."

She couldn't finish. Didn't need to. From representing enter-tainers, she also knew exactly how the news would proliferate: from hard news on the printed page to a talkfest on news radio, with listeners calling in to denounce everything from racism to extra-marital affairs. Next, TV news vans would camp out at the crime scene, or anywhere else they thought they could get a tidbit to report on. Continuing print coverage would keep the story alive for weeks. Ultimately, the story would gain eternal life in cyberspace, through newspaper-spawned chatroom sessions and linkage to Internet search engines.

Sighing again, she clicked on her PC's screensaver and went to the newspaper's Web site. Scrolling down to the "Metro" link and clicking on it, she found the latest piece of bad news: "Dunwoody Doc Being Questioned in Arson/Homicide."

"Oh, boy," she whispered, seeing the first mention of the word "homicide." To top it all off, the New York connection was already there: the prior conviction, the similar circumstances, the prison term, and the mysterious circumstances surrounding the death of Stephanie, who was referred to as a "high-class call girl" by an unnamed police source.

Ashley knew the source of the latest info—the detectives work-ing the case. "Yep, just like I thought. They're playing hardball—pitching us a couple of strikes to see if we swing." Although the reporter had mentioned that Klaxton's New York conviction was overturned, she knew *that* part of the story would get little attention.

No, Crowley and Company were counting on pressure from the publicity to smoke Klaxton out—either to force a confession, or prompt him to try to flee a la′ O.J. Simpson. Now that the New York case had been blown open, the depositions she'd taken would be little help.

Her brain already mapping strategic next steps, Ashley began mentally drafting her next conversation with her client. She needed to get to him ASAP. But it would be better if he came to her, not vice versa, to remind him who was in charge. With all he had going against him, the biggest single thing was his own egocentric, prideful attitude. But even if he'd read the paper this morning, she knew it was her who'd have to rein him in—and especially after what Joe had told her the last time they talked.

She hit the intercom button. "Mary, get me Dr. Klaxton Staples on the phone ... please."

∞

After a long expense-account lunch at Mumbo Jumbo with a feisty new client in the music field, Ashley felt reenergized for her most difficult appointment of the day. It arrived right on time, with Mary buzzing her: "Ms. Heath, Dr. Staples is here."

"Give me just a few moments," she replied, although her desk was clear. After two minutes had elapsed according to the second hand on her watch, she hit the intercom. "Please show Dr. Staples in, Mary."

When she looked up, he was standing in the doorway.

Surprise Number One: he was on time. Surprise Number Two was his compliant mood. Yes, he was dressed impeccably; ecru Armani blazer over a starched paler ecru shirt of Egyptian cotton, open collar with no tie. Chocolate-brown flannel trousers and dark brown tasseled Bruno Maglis completed the understated outfit. But his usual smirk was gone.

"Hi, Ashley. How are you?" he said quietly as he walked in.

She nodded. "I know you're busy and so am I, so let's get right to it. Have a seat."

The minute he lowered himself into the visitor's chair, she said, "First, let me say I regret that the two of us got off to a bad start on a personal level."

He nodded.

"I respect the dedication you show your patients. As your attorney, I intend to show you that same deference. I expect you to reciprocate by following my advice to the letter." She took a breath. "I've advised you to limit your contact with certain people, and to be careful of every step you take. I'm still advising that."

Klaxton wriggled like a schoolboy in his chair. "I ... Ashley, we're talking straight here, right?"

It was her turn to nod.

"If you're hinting that I should move back in with Angie over at Joe's house to show some kind of united front ... well, that's not going to happen."

She had already decided, considering Angie's emotionally fragile condition, not to continue encouraging that. But his arrogance annoyed her. "That's not what I'm talking about. I'm referring to your relationship with Vickie Renfroe. She's been seen with you lately."

She could have slapped him, and he wouldn't have been more surprised. "Come on, Ash! Joe sent her up to my office one day last week with some notes on a case we're consulting on together. That all! I've done everything you told me to do."

"That's funny. I didn't know she'd been to your office. Thank you for admitting that without me having to dig it out of you. But, yesterday, y'all were seen together in the parking lot of your office building." She leaned forward and placed her hands on the desk. "Klaxton, that's suicide for someone in your position."

His face turned wary. "Who said that?"

"Who told me isn't the issue here. What you need to know is that you *are* being watched. The media's on this, you have *got* to handle your business better. One slipup, and you could be back in custody in a New York minute! Is that what you want?"

"Ha ha," he said, yet his voice was free of mirth. "I've done time before. But like a prison buddy of mine used to say, 'Time will go on whether I'm in jail or out.' The same goes for me."

He leaned toward her, elbows on knees. "Ashley, some things you've got to understand about me. I spent three years of my life in the joint listening to some prison psychologist telling me to vent to get rid of my anger. He used to say I was in denial, too. But he was wrong. Anger has nothing to do with how I choose to live my life. I'm a grown-ass man and I make my own decisions. Sure I've made some mistakes. We all have. But I also graduated summa cum laude from Hampton and magna cum laude from Howard University School of Medicine because I earned it, *not* because it was given to me.

"Yet—what happened in New York taught me one thing. It doesn't matter that I'm a doctor and can afford ... rather, that I *choose* to wear a two-thousand-dollar suit. In them white folk's minds, I'm still a nigger."

He leaned back in the chair, waiting for Ashley's rebuttal. When it didn't come, he continued. "Ashley, we were born into all of this bullshit, but we sure as hell don't have to stay there. Society expects a black woman to be some kind of rock that never moves. And that same society expects a black man to break down every time his life gets turbulent. Do I look like I'm about get down on my knees? No. And you won't ever see that. And I'm not asking for anyone's pity. I might not beat this case, but I'm not going to bow down, either."

His words were delivered quietly, without bluster. She was impressed. "Klaxton, I have to ask you something. I'm saying this next thing to you not as Angie's friend, but as your attorney. For the record ... although technically, it's irrelevant ... try as I might, I don't see you as a cold-blooded killer."

He opened his mouth, but her red-tipped finger flew up. "Egotistical? You bet. Guilty of indiscretion? Oh my gracious, yes. Capable of murder? No. But I have to prove that to the rest of the world. To do that, I'm going to have to hear a whole lot of truth from you. What you just said is a start. But I need more than that to defend you. When we finish our investigation, we might know who the real killer is. But that takes time, and I don't think we have a lot of time."

She picked up a piece of paper from her desk and waved it gently in front of him. "Things like this worry me. This is the arson investigator's report. Kerosene was used to start the fire. There were no prints on the can, or on the gun found in Stephanie's car. But the gun was registered to you. And," she leaned forward again, *"the arson report is public record.* That means the media has a connection between New York and this case. Do you see why I need you to start talking?"

He looked at the report, then back at her, and nodded. "She ... must have stolen the gun out of my house. I kept it in the nightstand drawer next to the bed."

"Okay, let's stick to that. Back at the jail, you listed Stephanie as one of the women you'd been intimate with since moving to Atlanta. How long was the relationship?"

He thought a moment. "As just friends? Five, maybe six years. Cheryl and I used to hang out with Stephanie after they got off work. The other thing? Since right before Angie and I moved to Atlanta."

Ashley nodded. "Go on."

"After Cheryl's ... death, Stephanie was just about the only one besides Angie who believed I was innocent. She wrote me once or twice a week. Even came to see me in prison. After I got out, we ... hooked up. When Angie and I moved to Atlanta, she followed. I tried to get her to go back, but she wouldn't." He sighed. "The truth was, I needed her friendship. We picked up where we left off in New York, saw each other ever since ... until a few days before the housewarming."

She covered her eyes. "Two years as lovers, and five or six years as friends?" She pulled one hand away. "Does Angie know any of this?"

He shook his head. "I ... didn't think she'd ever have to. I'd broken up with Stephanie at that point."

"So what happened after that?"

Suddenly, Ashley saw the tortured eyes of a man who'd been stalked. "She never stopped calling me. I changed all my numbers, but she always had the work number.... I *am* a doctor, and my office number's in the Yellow Pages. And somehow, she got my home number. The week before our housewarming, I finally put it to her in no uncertain terms." He smiled sadly.

Ashley didn't reply, and Klaxton added, "But I only saw her once after then, and that was at the hospital. She was trying to salvage things between us. But I told her for the last time it was over." He looked away. "Unfortunately, Angie saw Stephanie at the hospital. I told her it was a coincidence, and she never mentioned it again."

Ashley's jaw dropped. *Uh, uh. No woman in her right mind would believe that!*

Now, she understood Angie's slow deterioration over the last few months. And her heart broke for her friend.

"There's more," Klaxton said before she could speak. "Vickie came to my office to tell me that Stephanie had confronted her at the club where she sings. To ... warn her about me."

"Oh my God," Ashley said, shaking her head. "Klaxton, this woman was obsessed with you. The night of the housewarming, she came to your home to tell Angie about you two." She didn't finish the thought; several scenarios, all unpleasant, were filling her head.

"There's one more thing I guess you need to know."

She looked at him. "More than this? Isn't this bad enough?"

He shook his head. "At the hospital ... Stephanie tried to blackmail me. For $50,000. Said if I didn't pay it, she'd tell everybody about us."

"Fifty what?"

"Fifty—"

"Never mind. I think I'm getting the picture. Well, I asked for it, didn't I?" She made a wry face and picked up a legal pad with hands she willed not to tremble. "Okay. Your whereabouts are covered on the night of the murder. But the fire could have been set earlier. I'll need a more detailed accounting of that entire day, and any documentation you can get to go with it. And sooner rather than later. So plan on—"

"I love her, Ash."

Startled, she looked up, and saw the agony filling his eyes.

"I don't care what you or anyone else thinks. Angie's the only woman I've ever loved. Chateau Élan was going to be like a new start for us. It ... didn't turn out that way. Even before we got stopped by the trooper. Man, this is crazy." He pressed his hands to his eyes.

"Stay with me, Klaxton," Ashley urged. "We're finally starting to get somewhere. You've got to keep a clear head. What if it was one of Cheryl's and Stephanie's friends who did this? Or a family member? Or one of their old boyfriends? What ... What if whoever did this is coming for you next? Or Angie?"

Though harsh, her words seemed to redirect him. He lowered his hands to his lap and visibly relaxed.

"Okay," she said. "You need to get back to the office, and I have to be in court in an hour. We'll talk soon. I need some time to catch up with the PI I hired. Just keep your mouth shut, and for the last time, *stay away from that little heifer in Joe's office.* Don't talk to the media, and call me the minute you hear anything from the police. You got that?"

He looked up with eyes that were reddened, but free of tears. "I won't let you down this time. And I'm counting on you, too. Angie and I both are."

The door closed behind him, and Ashley kicked off her pumps and laid her head on the cool marble of the desktop, thinking the unthinkable. Klaxton and Angie's lives were so intertwined with the victim's. How could she ever prove Klaxton's innocence to a jury?

Twenty-nine

Joe wasn't ready to admit the doubts that had been plaguing him to Ashley. So he came up with the perfect place to take her: Dave & Buster's. The entertainment-themed restaurant's arcade reverberated with the sounds of "Don't Worry, Be Happy" as they entered, and Joe tried to put that advice into action.

At the arcade, he easily lost himself in attempting to combine skill and luck at the pinball machines, while Ashley ran circles around him on the racecar-driving video game. At midnight, they were still going full force at laser tag, when he recalled he had an early appointment the next morning and reluctantly called it quits. Despite the late hour, they laughed at their competitive one-upmanship all the way home, delaying any serious discussions for at least another day.

But this morning, his mood was in stark contrast to the previous night's. He sat at the kitchen table, still in his robe, wondering what was bothering Mrs. Caldwell. Since she admitted to being the one who put salt in Angie's office, and then a string of beads, his housekeeper had been quiet. But her silence in the past few days was turgid, like water stored behind a dam, poised to surge forward at the floodgate's release. Joe hadn't been angry with her; in a way, he understood why she felt compelled to do what she did. No, it was something else causing her to behave this way.

Knowing she wouldn't talk until she was good and ready, he did his best to ignore her as he grumpily awaited his first cup of coffee. The smell of just-ground Costa Rican dark roast made his nose open when she poured the steaming coffee into his cup. He noted that her lips were pulled tight, like a lady's purse with the strings drawn. Watching from behind his newspaper, he sensed that the bursting of the floodgate was at hand.

While he sipped from his cup, she walked to the stove, her back to him, and resumed stirring a pot of grits cooked with ham hocks, just the way he loved them. When she shut off the gas burner and turned to refill his cup, he couldn't help smiling at how much she resembled the women in the painting that hung on the kitchen wall to her right: a print of three gray-haired black women decked out in their finest churchgoing attire, including gloves and hats and multiple strands of paste pearls. Their demeanor clearly said, "Look here. I'm somebody's mother, and don't you go trying to mess with me." This was the exact look on his housekeeper's face at this moment.

As if she'd read his mind, she scowled at him and said, "Dr. Joe, did you remember to call your mother?"

Without answering, he watched her walk to the refrigerator and remove a note from beneath a magnetic replica of a Heinz pickle jar. She handed the note to him and placed her left hand on her hip, giving him a hard gaze. He'd seen the stance before, and knew he'd better read fast, think fast, and answer promptly.

"I left this message, along with several others, on your desk," she said. "They are all from your mother. Did you not see them?"

"Mrs. Caldwell, you must be psychic," he answered with a stab at cheerfulness. "Planned to call her this weekend, 'matter of fact. Is that what's been bothering you?"

Her next words caught him off-guard. "Dr. Joe," she said, and took a deep breath, "it is *not right* for you to have that woman staying here in this house. It is *just not right!*"

"Y-You mean Ashley?" he stammered, confused.

She shook her head. "No, not Miss Heath. You know that I am very fond of her. I am talking about Dr. Angie. It is just not right for her to be here in this house. She is causing nothing but turmoil!"

"How could you say that, Mrs. Caldwell? I hardly even know she's here most of the time."

"It is not that she makes any noise. It is her *presence*. There is something wrong with her. Her spirit is disturbed."

As gently as he could, he said, "I don't understand. Has something happened that I don't know about?"

To his surprise, she didn't say anything else; instead, she strode to the stove and started dishing grits into a bowl.

Her drift had him truly stumped, to the point that he didn't even know what to ask next.

She placed the steaming bowl in front of him—a rainbow of aromas, textures and colors in a palette that ranged from pale ivory to butter yellow to the deep rose of ham hocks. Seconds later, a small plate with a pillow of steaming biscuit and a glob of strawberry jam appeared next to it.

"Thank you," he breathed. No matter how frustrated he might be with their conversation, he could never resist her cooking, so he stirred the melting butter into his grits while Mrs. Caldwell stood beside him, wiping her hands on her apron. A small smear of the jam stood out on the otherwise snow-white garment.

"Look, why don't you fix a plate and sit down, too?" he said. "I'm sure you made enough for two. You always do. That'll give us a chance to talk."

He'd made the offer before, but she rarely accepted. Today, sighing, she did, bringing her own plate to the place on his right.

Folding her arms in front of her, she fixed him with another of her gazes. "I am not going to take long to say this, because I don't know how much time we have to be alone. I am just going to be as truthful as possible."

Her voice still held irritation, so Joe didn't push; he simply took a bite of his biscuit.

"Dr. Angie's father came by the other day when you were at the office."

Joe's mouth was full, so he could only raise his eyebrows.

"They went upstairs to her room and had a shouting match."

"About what?" Joe mumbled, and took a quick sip of coffee.

"He wanted her to pack her things and move back to New York. He told her she needed to start taking her medication again."

Joe placed the cup back into the saucer so hard, it clattered. "Medication?"

"I knew those two were going to be a problem the minute I laid eyes on them," she said, putting a dab of jam on her own biscuit. "The moment I laid *eyes* on them, I smelled trouble. A *shady* kind of trouble. I tried to shoo them clear of you, but they kept going until they befriended you."

Now, even her ham and grits couldn't compete for his attention. He looked at her, fork in mid-air. "By 'shooing away,' I guess you mean the items you put in their office."

The answer came in her small nod and cutting-eye glance.

"I still don't understand why you felt the need to do that."

"Him in his expensive suits, and her pretending to be help-less," she muttered. "They knew I was onto them. That is why they did not want me cleaning their office space anymore." She looked at Joe and added, "And out of the blue, you go and invite them into your home. You don't even know them!"

Joe bit back his instinctive reply: that she really didn't know them either. "Mrs. Caldwell, it would've been rude if I hadn't offered them a place to stay. For God's sake, they lost everything when their home burned down. They're starting from scratch. My invitation didn't come from the wild blue yonder.... It came from my heart. It never occurred to me that you'd have a problem with it."

She smiled and briefly touched his hand. "Dr. Joe, you know how highly I think of you."

He nodded.

"Well, that is partly because you are a kind person. Unfortu-nately, your kindness is the weakest part of you. Most people appreciate kindness, and return it. But some people take advan-tage of kindness. Those 'some people' are the Staples. I learned many ways to figure out what is wrong with a person, where their evil side is coming from ... yet I still cannot figure out what is wrong with those two. Especially Dr. Angie."

She looked at him, desperation in her eyes. "I swear to you ... something is very wrong. I am afraid that whatever it is will affect you in some way. Who is going to pay their rent if he goes to jail? Surely she will not continue renting the office if her husband goes to prison."

"I'm not worried about that," Joe lied. "And I still don't see why you say something's wrong. They both put in as much time in the office as I do. If they didn't care about people, they wouldn't do as much as they do for their patients. I think they'll manage to work through their problems. They've just had a run of bad luck."

Like the women in the picture on the kitchen wall, Mrs. Caldwell gave him that look. "I am not the only one who thinks something is wrong," she said. "Did you know that the police are watching this house?"

"Where did you get that from?" Joe said, astounded.

"The day after they came to stay here, the police came, and they have been watching the house ever since. All times of the day and night. I write it all down." She drew a small notebook from her apron pocket and opened it. The pages were covered with lines of neat writing. "They switch cars. A lot. One day they were here in one of those ... those conversion vans. It was made to look old, but I do not think it was. It just needed painting."

"May I see that?"

She surrendered the book reluctantly, sitting quietly while he read the neat list of times and types of vehicles she'd noted. When he looked up again, she was standing.

"Come, I will show you."

Joe rose to follow her to the window, and she pulled the curtain aside and pointed.

Parked about fifty feet down from his driveway was a Ford Excursion. It was black with black painted rims. The windows were also tinted black.

"Looks like a drug car to me," she said.

He shot her a sardonic look.

She smiled. "With the windows all tinted like that? Must be a drug car."

Mrs. Caldwell loved her police dramas a little too much, but she was also right. "I can't believe I haven't noticed it," he said, then dropped the curtain back into place and stood upright, rubbing his chin.

"Well, you have had so much on your mind," she said, relieved that she finally was being heard.

"You're probably right about being watched, but if police are watching the house, I should've noticed."

"Dr. Joe, how could you have known with your busy schedule? And, they are very good. But I know something they do not. I know who lives in this neighborhood, and what kind of cars they drive. So I knew right away that van was not from around here.

"But," she added conspiratorially, "they are not here to watch you or me. They are here watching Dr. Angie, I am sure of it.... When you were the only one here, there were not any strange cars. Now that *she* is here, there is always one."

Joe walked to the table and began clearing the dishes. "I hope you don't mind if I share some of what we talked about with Ashley," he said to Mrs. Caldwell's back.

She whirled around, saw what he was doing and walked toward him. "Do you think she will understand? About the evil?"

"I don't know," Joe said carefully. "I don't know."

He dreaded what Ashley's reaction might be to hearing his housekeeper's assessment of her best friend. Or worse—that because he'd shared a building with Klaxton, he'd be painted with the same brush as Klaxton was being smeared with. The thought made his stomach tense. He'd worked so hard to establish his own practice, to earn the respect and trust of his patients and the community. Despite wanting to be loyal, Joe's faith in Klaxton was waning. As Mrs. Caldwell's words sank in, he felt more convinced than ever.

And Ashley. As difficult as it was to admit it, she had become too important to him, and too quickly. Undoubtedly, some distance was in order, at least until the woman's murder was resolved. Maybe he shouldn't even tell her what Mrs. Caldwell had just told him. How could he be certain at this point whom he could trust?

Thirty

Klaxton pulled back the shade and peered through the grimy window of his hotel room to the street, seven floors below. It was only a little after 10:30, but with an unseasonably cold night and a prediction of sleet or snow, Peachtree Street was devoid of cars and pedestrians. The silence seemed to hold an ominous, unseen presence. He couldn't sleep, and he couldn't concentrate well enough to read. He was too stressed even to get in bed and just lie there. Since Ashley's last warning, it felt as though hidden eyes were watching his every move.

He and Angie had just hung up from a long, intense and pointless telephone conversation, and her tearful accusations that he was running around on her again still rang in his ears.

"Baby, I haven't," he pleaded.

"Then why are you staying in a hotel instead of here with me, where you belong?"

Klaxton could hear her father's influence in the question. As if they didn't have enough to sort out together without him butting in. The idea of his frequent presence at the Fry household was more than Klaxton could take. But he knew better than to say that to Angie right now.

"So why don't I come back?" he answered. "That Mrs. Caldwell gives me the creeps. I have to keep my blood pressure down, and she makes it go up.

"Look, honey," he finally said, "let's be strong for one another. We're both under constant scrutiny, and if we're not careful, the Man will split us apart. Divide and conquer. We have to stick together or we're screwed."

From the other end of the line came only the sound of muffled sobs and sniffs—sounds that made him want to go through the phone line and shake her. It was her father, he knew. Dr. Bowen had reduced his educated, sophisticated, responsible adult daughter to a simpering child. Klaxton thought briefly about what he'd like to do to the old man if he ever got the chance. Wondered again how one old man could have such a tight hold over his grown daughter. He murmured softly to Angie until she was calmer, then ended the conversation and proceeded to pace—walking to the window every few laps around the cramped room.

They were watching him. Even if he couldn't see them doing so, he knew. He'd been burned once before. No doubt that redheaded cracker, William Crowley, was responsible. That's how cops acted if they thought they had the goods on you. They didn't care if you were innocent. As long as the DA thought a conviction was possible, all they cared about was clearing cases, not catching actual criminals. It had been that way five years ago, and it was that way now. And even though the force had plenty of brothers on it these days, it was still Whitey that ran the show, even more so in the Deep South.

Since Day One, Klaxton had pegged Crowley as the kind of creep who took pleasure in putting an educated niggah like himself where he thought that niggah should be—locked behind bars taking orders from some dumb-ass. They especially disliked the ones who were better dressed and better looking than they were, worrying that the niggahs were going to take away their white women. He was probably lucky that it was a black woman and not a white one, like Cheryl, whose body had been found in the fire.

The pacing didn't help, and the quickie in their suite at Château Elan was the last time he and Angie made love. He couldn't even leave the hotel without the unseen eyes of the Man watching him.

There was no chance of sleep anytime soon. It wasn't the fault of his accommodations. Although they felt confining compared to the spaciousness he'd been used to in his ruined home, the room was clean and nicely appointed. Not the Ritz-Carlton, but comfortable enough to afford a good night's sleep. Under other circumstances.

He paced again, watching himself in the bureau mirror—a worried man with half a hard-on and half a mind to turn tail and run. But he knew it was useless to leave. In these times, it was impossible for someone to disappear on a tropical island with a big stash of cash. In addition, he was half-sick with grief and guilt. The headaches were virtually nonstop now, and his worries were wearing a hole in his stomach; he could hardly eat for the heartburn. True, he'd wanted to break it off with Stephanie, but even in his wildest dreams, he didn't think it would come to this. He'd wanted her out of his life, not dead.

Bad thoughts for a lonely winter night. His heart was pumping more adrenalin than his body could absorb, and even though the heat in the room was turned off, he was popping a sweat. So he decided to do something he hadn't done in years.

Dropping the shade, he walked to the bed, knelt and pulled out a soft Italian leather suitcase from underneath, grunting a little with the effort. It was bulging with Egyptian cotton shirts still in their laundry wrappers, and Armani sweaters he hadn't bothered to hang up since he checked in.

Bunched into one corner was his old black medical bag. Had he not made the impulsive decision to take it with him on the trip, it would have been destroyed by the fire, too. Lucky that state trooper hadn't had reason to search his car. Until today, he hadn't remembered what was in there.

One tug of the silver-colored metal buckle opened it, and he reached in and pulled out a small cellophane bag of weed. He'd purchased it on a whim during a club crawl in upscale Buckhead, where Atlanta's yuppies and buppies partied with professional athletes, players, dealers and women looking for sugar daddies. It was a world he felt very far away from tonight.

He took a paper from the bag and rolled a joint, surprised at how easily the technique came back to him. Seconds later, he pulled in the smoke and let it settle in his lungs. He doubted it would work quickly, so he took a bottle of Amstel Light from the honor bar to take the edge off while he waited for his high.

By the time it came, though, he barely noticed, immersed as he was in his darkening thoughts.

Stephanie. There *had* been times ... but, really, he didn't wish her dead. She was an enthusiastic sex partner and a faithful companion, someone there when he needed her, without questions ... until toward the end. *Why is it that women, however educated or beautiful or well-cared-for, all want the same thing in the long run?* he wondered, noting the sudden heaviness of his eyelids. *Respectability, affluence, family. It doesn't matter how they get it, they want it. What ever happened to women's lib?*

The marijuana was fogging his brain so much he could no longer focus. Yet instead of easing his tension, it made him more anxious.

"Why did she have to fall in love with me?" he asked the room. "Why do bad things happen to everyone I ever care about?" He took a swig of his beer, nearly missing the nightstand when he set it down again.

"Well? Why? Answer me," he demanded. But there was no answer, and never would be an answer.

Was it all a bad dream? Or had he blacked out and actually killed Stephanie without remembering? Or Cheryl? Maybe he *was* crazy. Maybe he deserved to go to jail. After all, two women were dead. Two women and a little boy, or girl. Cheryl had been carrying his child. Surely he deserved punishment for that. If not for Cheryl, for the child.

"Maybe I *did* kill her," he whispered, and felt tears spring to his reddened eyes.

He sat on the bed, meaning to only stay there for a second, but his pounding head started to swirl and he fell back on the pillows.

What came next was like a dream. He saw Stephanie, Cheryl and his unborn child screaming for his help. They were at the edge of a fiery, swirling pit, being sucked closer to the abyss as they tried to flee. The unborn child took on the form of his lost sister, Charlotte, who was holding out her arms to him, and then Joe Fry's housekeeper, scowling and shaking her fist at him. Her screams echoed as she was pulled toward the pit.

He struggled to move, but his feet were leaden. Helplessly, he watched as they sank and disappeared. He still tried to move toward them, but he was tied up, and someone was placing fifty-pound weights on his chest, one at a time, until his whole chest was caving in and he was suffocating and his eyes were swollen shut.

He smelled the cutting odor of burning flesh, smoke streamed into his lungs, and he began coughing uncontrollably. It was like there was a fire in his throat, a searing pain that made him cry out.

Gasping, he awoke and sat straight up, rocked by the sudden memory that he'd been having this same dream almost every night since the fire. Stuck in that state midway between REM sleep and consciousness, he struggled to go back to the dream. He had to know how it ended. Had to *know*!

"All this is my fault," he babbled, feeling the singeing pain in his burned throat. "I've got to get to Angie ... before she falls in! I can't let her go into the fire!"

He blinked, then glanced around the room in astonishment. It looked like a tornado had ripped through it. Clothes and newspapers were scattered everywhere, and a linen-draped room service cart was stacked with dirty dishes and the nauseating-looking remnants of what appeared to have been a cheeseburger plate and an ice cream sundae. At some point, he must have ordered from room service, tipped the bellman and devoured the meal—but he remembered none of it.

As he surveyed the room, he got a few more surprises. The navy Armani blazer he'd worn to the meeting with Ashley lay crumpled on the floor. His laptop, which he remembered logging off and shutting down, was booted up, the screen ablaze in lurid reds and purples. On closer inspection, he realized that the site was an adult chat room. His credit card lay next to the computer.

His panic increased. Either somebody was playing a cruel trick on him, or he was in the midst of another nightmare. "Who am I?" he wondered. "What the hell is happening to me?"

A surge of anger roared through him like a wave on Waikiki. It wasn't him. It was *them* ... the ones who were watching him. They hadn't stopped, and wouldn't. They wanted to break him.

With new energy flowing through him, he sprang from the bed. *They want to see pressure? Fine.* He'd give it to them, and a little taste of what he was feeling to boot. And he no longer cared about the consequences of doing so.

He rooted through the suitcase, still open on the floor, and threw on the first clothes he put his hands on. Minutes later, he walked out of the hotel's front entrance, taking in a full breath of the fresh, cold midnight air. The earlier snow flurries had turned into misting rain, clearing his head a little.

In the car, he fired up the engine and headed up the ramp onto 285, then to I-75 South toward downtown. A rimmed-up Lexus honked at him as he shot past the slower-moving car.

"That's what I hate about these niggahs in Atlanta," he chuckled, enjoying the moment. "They can jack up a nice car, but they don't know how to drive it."

The Lexus overtook him and shot past, going at least ninety. Klaxton pressed the accelerator and gained on it. But he soon tired of the chase and slowed to hop onto I-20 East just past Grady Hospital. Flooring the accelerator, he whizzed by Turner Field on his right, and continued until he reached the Panola Road exit, where he got off, zipped down to Covington Highway and turned left.

When he stopped at the red light on South Hairston, he checked his rearview mirror. No cops in sight. But it wouldn't have mattered if they were parked right next to him; he no longer cared about anything except the freedom he was feeling.

Jubilant at this temporary respite, he pulled into the parking lot of the club where Vickie worked on the weekends.

∞

By the time he climbed onto a barstool near the stage, his anger had evaporated. "That's what I'm talking about! Damn, she's fine," he muttered, still buzzing as he watched her move in the tight red dress she wore. "I could use a little bit of that tonight." He waved as she turned and caught sight of him. Still singing, her response was a confused smile.

After the set, she joined him at the bar, where he was nursing a glass of Riesling. She turned to Mark and ordered a margarita, then faced Klaxton. "I've got to say it: What's a nice guy like you doing in a place like this?"

Mark's eyes narrowed at the man who already looked like he'd had a little too much to drink, but he delivered Vickie's margarita and walked to the other end of the bar. Klaxton kept his focus on Vickie.

"Klaxton, really, what's up? I've barely seen you since the fire, and tonight you show up here looking half in the bag?"

"Watching out, being watched," Klaxton replied, slurring his words.

Vickie put her hands on her hips, looking like a Sunday school teacher. "Man, pick your head up and look at me!" When Klaxton complied, she relaxed. "That's better. You keep your head up, Klaxton, you hear me? I know you've been under a lot of pressure, but you have a lot of people on your side. Act like you know it."

"Thanks, Vickie. I needed to hear that. In times like this, you need a woman who'll stand by you." He paused for a moment, then added, "I'm really sorry about ... you know. That I dragged you into this mess."

She put up a hand. "You know I have feelings for you. But I don't want to compound your problems. I may not like your attorney, but she's giving you good advice. Anyway, who knows?" She sighed. "Maybe someday things'll be different."

His good mood faded a bit. "Yeah. You never know what tomorrow will bring."

"True enough," she replied, and looked him straight in the eye. "But I know one thing. People like you and me have had our share of knocks, but we haven't let them drag us back to where we came from. Remember that."

The saxophonist hit a few warm-up notes and Vickie nodded to him, then turned back to Klaxton. "Gotta go. Don't get yourself into trouble, but ... call me if you need me."

After draining the contents of his wine glass, Klaxton walked to a table in that exaggeratedly slow pace used by inebriated people who think walking slow will disguise the fact.

Vickie knew the set by heart, and let her mind roam back to Klaxton and his odd behavior. When he told her that he had to stay away from her, and why, she understood. And she knew he wasn't capable of the crimes he'd been accused of. But clearly, the stress was getting to him. The fact that he'd shown up here was proof.

She would have loved to ask him a few questions about the woman from the housewarming. The one whose body was found in the fire. The woman who had come up behind her right here in this very club and tried to warn her off him. She was a discarded girlfriend, that was obvious. And a prostitute, according to the newspaper. But so much had happened after Stephanie paid her the visit, Vickie never had a chance to tell him about it. It had to have been the night before the fire. Since the news of the woman's death, Vickie had revisited their brief conversation over and over in her mind. What if she had listened, been more sympathetic? Would Stephanie be alive? Where had she gone when she left the club?

Vickie let her voice drop to a whisper as she ended the song she was singing. After a moment of hushed silence at the shocker ending to the Nancy Wilson standard about a woman who glimpses her man kissing another woman, the crowd burst into applause and whistles, and Vickie bowed deeply from the waist. Something about her conversation with Stephanie was still eluding her. But what?

∞

As soon as the applause faded and she could leave the stage, she headed straight for Klaxton. "Look, Klaxton ... I understand the restrictions you're under, but I need to talk to you. Away from here. Can we go out to the parking lot for a few minutes?"

Her eyes were sympathetic, which was exactly what he needed. Minutes later, they were sitting in her car, Vickie at the wheel.

"Do you want to go for a ride while we talk?" she asked.

"Let's ride. Will my car be okay parked up front?"

"Yeah. The bouncer spends as much time there as he does inside the building. He keeps an eye out."

Surprising to both of them, they didn't talk of what happened between them. "Joe's been riding me at work," she said quietly. "He all but threatened to make me take a leave of absence if he saw you and me together again. *Unpaid* leave."

Klaxton sighed. "I guess that's my fault. Or at least Ashley's. She probably talked to him."

"Well," she replied with a nod, "I don't know if you want Joe Fry to be babysitting you—or me. I think the world of him, but he's a strange one."

Reminded of the night he spent in Joe's house, Klaxton's head whipped toward her. "Why do you say that?"

She shrugged. "I told you about the way he acts about his artwork."

Klaxton nodded. "Go on."

"And he's terrified of spiders. Absolutely terrified. And you should have seen how ballistic he went when he found salt in the break room. I told him I spilled it while I was eating my lunch, but … you would've thought he was trying to sweep the tile off the floor, he was sweeping so hard!"

In spite of how creepy he felt, Klaxton had to laugh at the image of his dignified associate grabbing a broom. But then the conversation turned to his trepidation about Angie. "The fight Angie and I had about her father coming down to Atlanta is over, the old man has come and gone, but she still insists on staying at Joe's house. To tell the truth, I think Ashley has something to do with that."

"Well, I know Ashley Heath's a bitch," Vickie said. She ignored Klaxton's sharp intake of breath and continued. "And that might have something to do with everything. That woman is sweet on you, I just know she is! That's the way with some women. They hide their feelings."

"Look, I don't agree with you," he replied, wisely choosing to leave out exactly *why* he disagreed. "Anyway, she's my attorney. What am I supposed to do?"

"Hey, I know she's a good attorney." She gave him a sly smile. "After we had a little ... encounter in the office, I checked her out. But I think you should get someone else to handle your case. Remember, your wife's her best friend, and I don't care what she might have said to you, you're nothing to her 'cause she can't have you."

"Tell you what ... I'll think about it."

"Good enough." She stopped at the intersection and turned to him. "While we're out, why don't I swing you by my apartment and have a drink or something."

Considering his alternatives—to go back to a lonely hotel room, or back to Joe's house and Angie's anger—her offer sounded good. And what was the risk? It was late, and he was sure he'd shaken any tail he might have had.

Soon, she was using her key to let them into her apartment.

"Nice place you got here," he said, taking a seat in an over-stuffed chair. "Comfortable. Got everything you need ... sofa, loveseat, some picture of some celebrity and you on the wall."

He heard her laugh. She was still laughing when she returned from the kitchen with two beers in her hand. "Yeah, that's Kid Dog. One of my idols. My boss at the club got me backstage passes to one of his shows. "

She pulled up an ottoman and lowered herself onto it, then handed the cold bottle to Klaxton. "Drink that, and you'll feel better in a second."

He did so, then leaned his head back and closed his eyes, thinking that this was the first time he felt safe enough to relax in a long time.

When she heard him snoring, Vickie got up from the ottoman and raised his feet to rest there, then covered him with a blanket. Quietly so she wouldn't wake him, she called James to tell him she wouldn't be back for her last set. As she hung up the phone she thought she heard Klaxton speak, saying something like, "Angie ... No! Angie, no more!"

She walked back to make sure he was all right. His eyes were open, but she didn't think he was awake ... at least until he said, "Vickie, I want you to promise me one thing. No matter what happens, you've got to believe I never killed anyone. I'm a lot of things, but I'm not a murderer. I ... I think I lied to Ashley the other day."

"About what?" Vickie asked, her heart breaking to hear the sadness in his voice.

"I told her I was going to beat this rap. I just don't think that's going to happen. I think I'm going to have to do some time.... But that's the way things are sometimes. If you love someone ... I mean, *really* love someone ... you should stand up for them."

With that, his eyes closed, and he began snoring softly again. Vickie walked to her room to get ready for bed, allowing herself only a brief moment of regret.

Thirty-one

He woke to the rich aroma of coffee, and recognized another pleasant and familiar fragrance—perfume. It seemed to ease his nerves. Then, he remembered where he was. He opened his eyes and sat up, fighting the thick mind-fog that obscured his vision. *Oh, my God! How did I end up here?*

Vickie appeared before he had the chance to ponder the question. Even in such a befuddled state, he couldn't stop himself from admiring her. The lavender silk robe, tied loosely at the waist with a corded silk belt, was loose and flowing, and it was obvious from the firmness of her nipples that she wasn't wearing a bra. He could only stare at her in awe and pull the blanket higher in his embarrassment.

He struggled to find words that wouldn't offend her. It would've helped if he could remember what actually happened the night before. At that moment, he wasn't sure if he should be thanking Vickie for a night of passionate lovemaking, or apologizing for not coming on to her. Which would she find less insulting, he wondered. Assuming they must have been intimate simply because he woke up in her house? Or, if he hadn't made a move, apologizing for not finding her attractive?

He chose a neutral course instead. "Nice place you have here," he said, his bleary eyes taking in the sand-colored walls. The warmth coming from the fireplace felt good to him.

"I hope you slept better after I woke you up long enough to move you to the sofa," Vickie said, her expression cautious. "I was afraid you'd get a crick in your neck if you stayed in the chair. Oh, and thanks again for the compliment. I kind of like this little place."

Klaxton gave her a puzzled look. "What do you mean by 'thanks again'?"

She moved to the sofa to sit beside him. "You don't remember?"

Even though she sat several inches away, hands tucked neatly in her lap, he was still overwhelmed by her perfume and beauty, and felt even more uncomfortable.

She didn't seem to notice. "You said the same thing last night, when you first came in. That's when you first noticed the room." She smiled. "Do you remember making that silly comment about my picture of Kid Dog?"

Klaxton swiveled around to look at the picture behind the sofa. "Oh, yeah. I remember. Guess I *was* kind of out of it." He gave her a sheepish smile.

Vickie returned his smile. "I guess it just slipped your memory."

He finally asked the question he'd been dreading. "So, ah ... did anything else happen I should know about?"

"What do you mean?" Unaware she was doing so, she rested her hand on his thigh.

Her touch seeped through the blanket and warmed him in a familiar way. Taken aback, he stirred and moved slightly away.

She noticed. "No, we didn't make love, if that's what you're talking about. But I wanted to." A brief smile crossed her face. "You were a perfect gentleman. Don't think I could've gotten you up even if I'd given you a lap dance. You were so tired, you fell asleep while I was talking to you."

He nodded toward the crackling blaze in the fireplace. "Really nice. Thanks for that, too."

She said, smiling again, "I started some breakfast. Oh, that reminds me ..." She gave him a quick tap on the leg as she stood. "I'll be right back."

He heard kitchen noises, got up to peek through the window's Venetian blinds. He was relieved to find no suspicious-looking vehicles in sight.

It was only then he remembered leaving his car parked in the club's parking lot the night before. The car was nowhere near the top of his worry-list. He was a man with a clouded mind and a troubled marriage, and had spent the night at another woman's house. And that last worry was akin to playing right into the investigator's hands. Yet there were Vickie's feelings to consider. She didn't deserve for him to just up and leave.

He threw the blanket aside and headed for the small kitchen. When he approached, he heard her singing in the way many women sing while performing mundane chores. "You have a lovely voice," he said in admiration. "You're a woman of many talents."

Vickie didn't seem startled, even though he thought she might be. Familiar with the normal sounds of her living space, she probably heard him coming. "Thank you," she replied simply, her brown skin unable to conceal her blush. "Did you find everything okay?"

"Yes, fine. But don't stop singing. I was enjoying it."

She blushed even harder. "Oh, stop! After the set at the club last night, I'm surprised I can carry a tune today."

"Yeah, I remember that spin you put on Miss Nancy Wilson. Tore that number up, didn't you? I'm surprised your time hasn't already come."

She smiled, pleased that he remembered her ambitions. "I have some irons in the fire, and they *are* looking pretty good. James ... that's my boss at the club ... he has a friend who's trying to hook me up with an agent who might be able to get me to open for R. Kelley when he comes to Atlanta next month. I've been working on a demo, too ... in case that comes through. But if it happens, this concert will be the biggest thing I've ever done."

With the last sentence, her eyes met Klaxton's, and he could hear the passion in her voice. He regretted prejudging her when he first met her, labeling her as an opportunist looking for a man at any cost. He fought it, but the earlier discomfort between them was becoming something more.

Apparently, she had felt the change, too. "Ah, breakfast is almost ready," she muttered, not looking at him. "Go ahead and have a seat."

Klaxton complied, but he suddenly realized he was losing the fight—not to hunger, but for the gorgeous woman next to him. As she put their plates on the table and took the chair right next to him, that hunger became an ache.

"You really love her, don't you, Klaxton?" she said, her look as direct and forthright as her voice. "I heard you call her in your sleep last night."

Her words made him freeze. It was as though she'd heard his lustful thoughts about her, and was trying to use guilt to deflect them by mentioning Angie. Carefully, he said, "Yes, I really love her. We've been through a lot of stormy weather together. I'd lay down my life for her. I really would."

When he looked up from his plate, he saw that her dark eyes were flashing. His gut tightened.

"Do you think she feels the same about you? I just see you two as an odd couple. She's always got that serious playing-the-doctor attitude at the office, and talks about how she never takes a break. And you? Why, I bet you don't even have your pager with you."

"I do have a bad habit of leaving it in the glove compartment of my car," Klaxton replied, upset to hear his words trip over themselves. "Since I'm in family medicine, I don't get a lot of emergencies. But Angie's an OB-GYN, and you know how that can be. She's always on call. So it's our work ... not our personalities ... that makes us seem so different." He glanced down, away from her probing eyes. "And yes, I do love her."

"Well, it didn't sound like love last night," Vickie said. "More like pain."

"It may have been," he admitted. "I've been on a merry-go-round lately. Last week I was busy as hell at the office, healing the sick, solving other people's problems. When I wasn't at the office, I was at my lawyer's office. And last night I was out on 285 in a jam-up race with some thugs in a jacked-up Lexus. I think I can safely say I was a little stressed last night."

"I think you're still a little stressed."

Her tone caused Klaxton to realize how he'd been running on. "Sorry about that," he said, abashed. "I guess my stress is running out my mouth, huh?"

She chuckled, but then her voice became quiet. "That's okay, Klaxton. You've got a right to run on, and I don't mind."

The doorbell rang, causing them both to jump a little.

"Bet it's the paperboy," Vickie said, glancing at the clock on the wall. "Most of the people in my building just buy a paper at the corner store, but I still subscribe. I know this kid's family, and I know they need the money. Today's his day to collect. He's just a little early."

The bell rang again, and she rose from her chair. "It'll only take a sec. Go ahead and eat before the food gets cold, okay?"

Klaxton had just enough time to take one bite of sausage before he heard Vickie exclaim, "Hey, you can't come in here!"

He jumped up, wondering if Vickie knew her paperboy as well as she thought, but stopped when he heard someone say, "I'm looking for Dr. Klaxton Staples."

Forgetting that he wasn't supposed to be here at all, he ran into the living room. Standing there was Detective William Crowley.

"Well, well, what do we have here, Dr. Staples?" Crowley said, stepping past Vickie. He pulled a piece of official-looking paper from his jacket pocket.

But not only had the detective found him, the media had, too. Just as he opened his arms in a pleading gesture to try to reason with Crowley, a photographer—who'd been standing unnoticed in the doorway—flashed a picture.

The next morning Klaxton, appearing that he was being crucified, was on the front page of the *Atlanta Journal-Constitution*. The headline read:

Dr. Klaxton Staples Arrested for Murder
of Atlanta Call Girl.
Murder Suspect Has Secret Life?

Thirty-two

When the alarm clock went off at 6:30 a.m., Ashley turned over and slapped the button to stop the annoying beeping, then muttered, "It's going to be a blue, blue Monday. No doubt about that."

During the long night, she had tossed in her bed while thinking about Angie, Klaxton and Joe. Ironically, the least worrisome of the three was Klaxton, who contacted her as soon as he was finally formally charged on Sunday morning. After she chewed him out for being caught in Vickie's apartment, she consoled herself with one important fact: Now that the arrest had actually been made, she could move forward with her plan of action.

Although now, I might have to change my plan, try for a Guilty by Reason of Stupidity verdict.

Chuckling at that, she rolled out of bed and stood. She'd reamed him out again when she saw the picture of him in the *AJC*, then again at the jail. The night before, she'd been up after midnight comparing what she extracted from Klaxton with the private investigator's report: the kind of challenge the litigator in her loved.

More worrying was her inability to get in touch with Angie. It had been nearly twenty-four hours since Klaxton's arrest, and

Angie still hadn't responded to her many phone calls and e-mails. Bail had been denied—routine in homicides—but Angie would have no way of knowing that. And the current awkwardness between Ashley and Joe kept her from going over and banging on his front door until she could get to Angie, try to fathom what was going on with her. Joe's sudden coolness bothered her more than she wanted to think about right now. But she couldn't help thinking about it. When she had to cancel their date after learning of Klaxton's arrest, she sensed that Joe was ... relieved. And actually, ever since the fire, he'd been distant toward her. Sure, the fire was disturbing, but why would something like that have affected a relationship they both seemed so happy about?

Or maybe it was because of what I said about Mrs. Caldwell. She thought back to their conversation about his housekeeper's superstitions. How Joe told her about the police watching his house, and Mrs. Caldwell's suspicions why. Ashley had scoffed, "Roots and voodoo again? Joe, that's ridiculous! All this talk of restless spirits reminds me of a vampire-film spoof."

But maybe the old woman's onto something, after all, Ashley thought as she headed to the phone to try Angie again. Angie was so depressed the last time she'd seen her. And it wasn't like Angie to not return her calls and pages.

Angie's voice mail picked up again, and she wondered if she should bug the answering service again. But no. She had other priorities right now. She'd keep working on Klaxton's case. Surely she would hear from Angie soon.

∞

Impeccable in a black cashmere Ralph Lauren pantsuit and ivory silk blouse, Ashley stepped smartly toward the DeKalb County Courthouse. Apart from a single panel truck with satellite dish displaying the local ABC Network affiliate's logo, she saw no signs of media. Even the veniremen and jurors who frequently lounged in front of the courthouse on breaks were absent. *Good. One less worry.*

Not that there weren't plenty of others. On the way to the courthouse, she'd called Angie's office several times, had paged her, too—but every time, was told that "Dr. Bowen-Staples" was out of the office indefinitely. The Staples' answering service hadn't heard from her since yesterday. Rather than leaving yet another message, Ashley reluctantly rang off and slipped her cell phone into her briefcase.

No reporters accosted her as she passed through security and hurried up the stairs to the second-floor conference room. She stepped into the room to find Detective Crowley and the DA, an older, gray-haired brother named Ira Hutchins, seated at a long, county-issue mahogany table. "Glad you could make it, Ms. Heath," Hutchins said, shooting the gold cufflinks on his shirt as he stood. "You've met Detective Crowley?"

"I have," Ashley replied, shaking Hutchins' hand. "How are you, Detective?"

"Fine," Crowley said, nodding but not standing while Ashley took a chair across the table from the two men.

Hutchins said, "It seems that your client has quite a history."

"I don't know what your definition of *history* is, Mr. Hutchins," Ashley replied, keeping her voice level, "but Dr. Staples' criminal history is restricted to one case five years ago ... one in which my client was wrongfully convicted *and* wrongfully incarcerated. He was exonerated by a jury of his peers. There's no evidence linking him to this murder, either. And I'll move to suppress any evidence you plan to use that relates to my client's wrongful incarceration ... *if* this case even comes to trial."

Ashley glanced at Crowley, who was busy examining his hands, which were splayed on the conference table.

Hutchins responded. "I'll cut right to the chase, Ms. Heath. We're prepared to make your client an offer. One that it would behoove him to take."

Ashley was sure what that meant—they didn't have enough evidence to go to trial. She exulted inwardly, but kept her expression bland as she reached for the pitcher at the middle of the table and poured herself a glass of water.

"Let's save the taxpayers some money and the courts some time," Hutchins continued. "I'm going to offer this one time, and one time only: manslaughter two, fifteen to twenty."

Ashley took a sip of water and leaned back in her chair. "With all due respect, Mr. Hutchins, why do you think we'd entertain such a ridiculous idea? As I've told you, my client is innocent."

"It's a good offer," he said. "If Staples stays out of trouble, he'll have a chance at parole in seven years. The victim's body was found in your client's home. We have knowledge that he was also having an affair with the woman—"

"Furthermore," Crowley jumped in, "we got the toxicology report back Saturday. Excessive amounts of hydrocodone and acetaminophen in the victim's bloodstream, consistent with ingredients found in Lortab. The same drug that was found in the New York victim. Your client's gun was found in the Atlanta victim's car. We intend to use the gun to connect him to the crime scene."

The gun wasn't a surprise. The drugs were. Her PI found them in the New York case, but she didn't expect them here.

Though she hid her reaction quickly, Crowley noticed, and smiled. "Dr. Staples has access to this drug, which was also the cause of Stephanie Rogers' death. In addition, Dr. Staples was seen with the victim at one of the hospitals where he works shortly before she was found dead. We have a witness who's prepared to testify to overhearing a very heated exchange between Dr. Staples and Ms. Rogers on that occasion." He glanced at his notes. "A Ms. Baker. The mother of a pediatric patient at the hospital."

Ashley was silent, and Crowley smiled. "There's more. We impounded Dr. Staples' car. In it we found traces of marijuana, and marijuana was found in his hotel room."

"So you plan to convict my client because he had an affair?" she said, turning cold eyes on Hutchins. "More than half the male population would be in jail if that were grounds for arrest."

"Ms. Heath, I—"

"Or is this because he smoked a joint? Dr. Staples isn't perfect, but you haven't given me anything to make me believe you can convince a jury he's guilty of murder. All of your so-called 'evidence' is circumstantial at best."

She stood, hiked her briefcase over her shoulder. "I guess we'll see you in court for a very short trial."

"I'll give you time to reconsider," Hutchins said, standing.

Looking at Hutchins, she allowed her glare to soften a bit. Whatever problems she had with Crowley, Ashley at least felt comfortable that this DA was doing his job as he felt the evidence directed him to. "Thank you, Mr. Hutchins. I'll take your offer to my client. But I have to warn you, I'll strongly advise him against it. And I believe he'll take my advice."

She gave Crowley a cutting look. "And Detective, if you have any more pieces of so-called evidence, I'll expect that you'll make sure my office receives them immediately. Right?"

"He will," Hutchins said, and opened the door for her.

∞

Her head swirled as she exited the courthouse, retrieved her car from the parking deck and headed back to her office. Only once she was behind the wheel did she let her face collapse. *Possession of illegal drugs, maybe with intent to sell. And the big ones, murder and arson. And this victim had the same drugs in her system as the New York one did.* Ashley allowed herself a moment of panic.

∞

Ashley's instincts had been on target. Joe *was* relieved she had to cancel their date—but his relief was based on a far more complex scenario than she imagined. He was still shaking from the phone call he'd gotten at 3:15 a.m. on Sunday morning from a drunken and tearful Vickie Renfroe. Unfortunately, the ringing phone awakened the whole household, including Solly, who set up a loud series of warning barks. Mrs. Caldwell went thumping down the stairs in her housecoat to calm him. Angie remained in her room, but Joe had heard her moving around.

At first, Joe could barely make out what his receptionist was saying, she was sobbing so hard. "I can't understand you," he finally said. "Calm down and slow down." And, like a small child taking quick, sipping breaths to stop the tears, she did.

"I ... found out something," she hiccoughed. "I'm not sure, but ... you need to know it."

"Okay," he said as patiently as he could. "What is it?"

"I can't tell you over the phone. I just can't! It's too creepy! You need to come here. Or meet me somewhere."

The idea struck him as bizarre. Then, he remembered her behavior the night of Klaxton and Angie's party, and how very young and high-strung she was. "Vickie, it sounds like you've had a few too many tonight. Am I right?"

"I only had a couple of drinks at the club—"

He sighed. "Look, you don't need to be out driving around at this hour intoxicated. Can't this wait a few hours?"

"No!"

"Is anyone bleeding? Is anything on fire?"

After a small silence, she whispered, "No."

"Then whatever it is can wait till daylight. Take some deep breaths and one or two Advils, and try to get some sleep. Call me tomorrow when you wake up, and we'll take care of whatever it is. Okay?"

"Okay. Okay."

Her voice still held tears, but less panic when they ended the call. Had he been a betting man, Joe would have been certain that was the end of it. But at 7:21, she called back, and this time he was able to persuade her to tell a little of her story to him over the telephone. What he heard had him out of the bed and yanking jeans and a shirt from his closet.

"I'll meet you at the Waffle House on Piedmont Road," he promised.

As he was racing to get dressed and leave, Ashley called and cancelled their afternoon date. Later, he hoped he hadn't been rude to her in his hurry to get off the phone and out the door. But with his mental conflicts about her since the fire, it wouldn't have been wise to tell Ashley what Vickie had just told him. Not until he was sure. Or maybe, not even then.

∞

The delay gave Vickie a head start; she was already in a booth and stirring half-and-half into her coffee when he got there. She looked haggard, but it would do no good to tell her so.

"Tell me everything," he said, waving away the menu the waitress offered.

Thirty-three

While she sat in the jail's waiting area, Angie concentrated on keeping her breathing under control. Klaxton had asked her to visit right away, but she couldn't. Seeing Klaxton in jail again wasn't going to be easy. She needed to be strong—and she hadn't been for a long time.

Her father, with twice her years as a physician, saw the signs of it right away and called her on it. "Daddy, I have to get through the next few weeks, and I can do it alone," she told him, flashing her eyes. Reminded of the guilt he bore from her childhood, knowing better than to say more, he left the next day for home.

She willed the return of her composure while she leafed through an ancient copy of *Field & Stream,* yet felt tears already forming. She couldn't afford to be weak, and that knowledge was how she got the courage to go off the pills Daddy had been feeding her for years. Yes, she needed them sometimes; the pains in her abdomen waxed and waned. But her father insisted that she not suffer, and had pushed various pills on her since her teen years. Some of the pills were for pain, some for much more. Till lately, she'd seen no reason to refuse any of them.

The hardest thing about giving up the Oxycontin was not being able to sleep. After a restless night, she'd tried again to sleep that afternoon. She'd finally risen after four p.m., moving around the borrowed guest suite like an automaton, showering, fixing her hair as best she could and trying to disguise her puffy eyes with makeup, dressing carefully—the first time in days she'd worn anything but nightclothes. Bypassing the kitchen to avoid Mrs. Caldwell's suspicious eyes, she slipped out the front door. The rest was pretty much a blur until she got here.

After what seemed an eternity, she heard a clanking noise and looked up to see Klaxton being brought in by a burly uniformed officer. The chains around his ankles forced his steps to be choppy, and his face appeared sallow against the fluorescent orange of the prison jumpsuit. He was unshaven, and his hair was unkempt.

"Don't cry, baby, I'm doing fine," Klaxton said, sliding into the wobbly plastic chair opposite her and shifting his weight to avoid falling. "How's the office going?"

"Things are taken care of," Angie said, drying her face with a tissue she took from her pocket. "I called in the temp service to cover both our caseloads for a while. Daddy left yesterday. I told him to keep his room at the Ramada. I'm going to stay there for a few days." To Klaxton's surprised expression, she said, "I'm wearing out my welcome at Joe's. Or at least, with Mrs. Caldwell."

Klaxton nodded. "Okay, baby. Ashley's been trying to get in touch with you. Have you talked with her yet?"

She shook her head. "I'm going to call her."

"You're a strong woman, Angie."

The words brought fresh tears to her eyes. *Strong?* Right now, she couldn't even face her one and only friend, couldn't bear to return Ashley's calls. The shame that Ashley had been right about her marriage was too deep.

She crossed her legs and pushed her hair behind her ears, forcing deep breaths to slow her heart. He waited, never taking his eyes off her face.

"Look, Klaxton," she finally said, "I don't know how we're going to get through this. I'm exhausted. Can't even think straight. I ... I don't know if I can help you like I did last time."

His eyes widened. "Do you believe I did this?"

She shook her head, then passed a hand across her face. "You're innocent. I know that. No doubt."

"Don't worry, baby." He raised his handcuffed arms in supplication. "Ashley's doin' her thing. She's got a PI on the trail, and she's filing a new motion or something every day, seems like. She's going to get us out of this."

"I ... I don't deserve a friend like her."

"Yes, you do! And *I* need you. I couldn't have done it without you before, and I need you now, too."

She dabbed at her eyes with a crumpled tissue. "This is all my fault. My jealousy's getting in the way of our happiness. I know that. But you're to blame, too. If you'd just stopped—"

"Baby, I *have* stopped. Nothing happened at Vickie's place. I told you what happened on the phone. And there's nobody else. Never will be again. Honest."

She kept her eyes down.

Even though there was no heat in the cramped, airless room, Klaxton felt his face flush. "Letting Stephanie stay here in Atlanta was a mistake," he whispered. "I admit that. But I ... I needed someone. You had changed. In your heart, you know that. You were always 'on call,' and never had time for me. I needed somebody to talk to."

He caught himself, realized that he was falling back into a pattern he'd sworn to give up. "But I knew it was wrong. And as soon as I could ... what went on between me and Stephanie ... I ended it. It was never about her."

Her eyes met his, and they held rage. *"It was never about her?* Now, let me see. Where have I heard *that* before? Maybe in New York?"

Klaxton gasped. "How can you say a thing like that to me at a time like this? I know you're angry with me, but I've never loved any woman but you. I'm guilty of some indiscretions, yes. I'm also guilty of being at the wrong place at the wrong time." He smiled bitterly. "I guess every man in here's singing that song. But one thing's for sure—I never killed anyone. Remember? You met me at the hospital, and we left from there. No matter how you feel, you know that's the truth. And ... if it comes to a trial, I know you'll tell the truth."

She said, more softly, "I know you're not a killer. But if the police aren't looking for anyone else, they're not going to find any-one else. And Daddy told me ... he doesn't want anything to do with it this time. I'll do everything I can to get you out of here, but it's going to take some time."

She looked at him, new resolve in her eyes. "So don't worry, Klaxton. I'm ready to talk to Ashley now, and I have a plan that just might work." Without another word, she stood and left the room.

∞

This late in the year, it got dark before six o'clock, so Angie walked cautiously to the poorly lit parking lot a block from the jail entrance. Pulling onto the highway, she suddenly realized she was famished—a feeling she hadn't experienced in weeks. A blue and orange neon sign on the other side advertised the presence of a Gladys Knight Chicken & Waffles restaurant, and she made a quick left turn at the median, then a right into its parking lot. She fairly jumped out of the car, almost dizzy with hunger.

After enjoying her first substantial meal in two weeks and several cups of coffee, she headed toward downtown. She would go into the office and catch up on the mail and her patient files. *No,* she thought suddenly. The food and caffeine had given her an energy surge, and she meant to take advantage of it. Now, she could carry out her plan.

A wave of nausea formed in her throat, and she pulled in a breath to suppress it. *There is,* she reflected, *no time like the present.*

She veered onto 285, reaching for her cell phone.

∞

Vickie rarely made it to bed before dawn after her Saturday-night set at the club, so she often napped on her sofa on Sunday afternoons. But this Sunday was different.

She pushed her pillows around her and put her feet up, then clicked the remote until she found a movie she wanted to watch. *Big Momma's House,* on HBO Comedy, was mindless enough, she decided, and settled back with the Sunday crossword, telling herself it was going to be okay.

Usually, this ritual had her snoozing within half an hour. Today, her mind kept going back to that morning's Waffle House conversation with her boss.

"Whatever you do, don't breathe a word of this to anyone," Joe had told her. "If you see or hear from her, contact me immediately."

She nodded, but he wasn't satisfied. "Immediately. You hear?"

"Yes, Dr. Fry. I hear you. So you think it's true?"

"We can't afford to think otherwise," he replied, frowning

"But don't you think we should call the police?" she asked him.

He shook his head. "That was my first thought. But think about it. Klaxton's already in trouble. If this turns out to be nothing, it'll only cause more trouble for them, and you and I will look like interfering fools." He smiled. "And I don't think either of us wants that." *And I sure don't want to lose both my tenants unless I have to.*

"No, I don't want that, either," Vickie had replied, and told Joe about Klaxton's heartfelt advice and honorable behavior the night she got drunk and stupid. "I *know* Klaxton's a good person," she said when she finished. "And I don't think he's guilty of doing what they're saying he did. I don't want to cause him any more trouble."

Joe nodded. "Neither do I. And from what you told me, I really think we can handle it ourselves. At least until she tries to contact you again. I'll contact the police. And, I'll call Ashley as soon as I'm sure she's awake. Meanwhile, don't initiate any contact with anyone. Do whatever you usually do, which is ...?"

She shrugged. "Veg out on the couch all day like a mashed potato."

Grinning, he said, "Fine, do that. Let the answering machine pick up your calls. Do you have Caller ID?"

She shook her head, and he chuckled. "Me neither. Guess we both need to get into this century." He thought a moment. "If I need to call you, I'll let it ring twice, then hang up and call right back so you'll know it's me. If we don't talk by tonight, I'll come by in the morning and pick you up and take you to work."

Despite her protests that she could take care of herself, he'd been adamant. *No use taking risks*, he said firmly. *Better safe than sorry.*

"Meanwhile," he had added, "don't go out, even to take out the garbage. Sit tight and get your rest while I find out what our next steps should be."

Remembering that reassurance, it wasn't long before she could finally concentrate on the movie.

∞

Angie had to try every key on her ring before she found the master that opened the building's back entrance. She found herself cursing the darkness and had to laugh at the irony, since one of the things she was looking for was the box of extra candles she'd stashed in her desk after a post-Thanksgiving shopping splurge one lunch hour. "Curse the darkness, light a candle," she whispered, and chuckled.

She had intended to telephone Vickie from the car, but realized she didn't know her number, and would have to wait and look it up in the building directory when she got to the office. Finally, she found the right key, and after fumbling for the light switch in the dark back hallway, made her way to the second-floor offices, unlocked the room where the medicines were stored and retrieved what she needed, then dug the candles out of her bottom desk drawer.

Now, for the telephone call. She was breathing fast, but that was good. Her rapid breathing would lend credence to what she was about to say.

Angie found the number she needed and dialed, but wondered, after two rings, if she'd misdialed. Panting, she hung up and started over.

"Little missy's gonna get a great big surprise," she muttered when the phone started to ring again.

Thirty-four

Whenever he was nervous, Joe paced. With his long stride, it only took him eleven and a half steps to lap the living room, a fact he knew from long experience. But he'd been so distracted since he got home from the early morning meeting with Vickie, he forgot to count paces or laps. He looked down at the cordless phone in his hand, as if doing so would cause it to ring. Why hadn't Ashley picked up her cell or her home phone, or at least replied to the messages he'd left in the past few hours?

Hearing a beep, Joe reached into his pocket for his cell phone, checked the Nokia's LED display: 6:37 p.m. No wonder his stomach was rumbling; it was past time for supper. All these noises were making him antsy—even more than usual. And the butterflies in his stomach ... were they from appetite, or anxiety?

He didn't hear Mrs. Caldwell moving around the kitchen. Regardless, there was an enticing aroma emanating from there, one he couldn't quite place. Gravy? Hash browns? His stomach was so fluttery that he must be either starving, or about to throw up. He hit redial for Ashley's cell number, and it was ringing. *Pick up!* he thought, his frustration growing. *It's important!*

But she didn't, and he didn't want to leave another message, so he hung up and headed for the kitchen. Even if Mrs. Caldwell was at some church function, she'd probably left him something to eat. She always did.

∞

Angie hung up the phone and tiptoed around the darkened offices. She could almost smell the slut's cheap perfume in Klaxton's office. The other one, Stephanie, had gone into great detail about how she'd seen Vickie and her husband exiting this very building together late one evening. How many times had he betrayed her with this bitch, in the very place they worked ... for all the others to see—the receptionists and nurses, even the janitorial service they'd hired to replace that nosey Mrs. Caldwell?

On top of the pain was humiliation. *Public* humiliation. It wasn't Klaxton's fault if these women came on to him. He was a walking target for the greedy whores who pranced around looking for a good lay and, beyond that, a steady income to buy them respectability.

She was too angry to cry. And that, for a change, was a welcomed thing. Action was the answer, not despair. She had to act swiftly, and this time, had to vary her method to avert suspicion. She hadn't thought about that before. Back then, her rage had kept her from thinking—the anger, plus the pills her father handed out like candy to keep her quiet.

Once more, she reconsidered the candles. To have candles at three different crime scenes would be too much of a coincidence. But after a moment, she shook her head. So long ago, the candles had helped keep her sane after what her father had done to her. After that, they helped quell her feelings of worthlessness. Then, they helped suppress some of the ache after Mother—her only protector—had died. She didn't want to use them this time, knew it was risky, but ... she *needed* their light. Their warmth. Needed the strength they gave her. It was worth the risk. She stopped suddenly and giggled. "Third time's a charm." *Haha.*

She moved swiftly around the darkened suite, lighting candles, humming softly.

∞

Vickie almost hung up when she realized it wasn't Dr. Fry, but Klaxton's wife on the other end. Now, she was glad she hadn't. Her employer's instincts had been on target. She willed herself to sound calm and low-key as she said, "Sure, Dr. Staples. You know I'll do whatever I can to help your husband's case. I'll be there as soon as I can."

"Thanks, Vickie," Angie had replied. "You're an angel for coming back here to the office to meet me. I want to record your answers to my questions, and I left my tape recorder here." She forced a chuckle. "And I guess you know I'm staying at Joe's. There's more privacy here, too. I'll leave the back door unlocked."

They ended the call, and Vickie picked up the phone to call Dr. Fry. As she did, she wished she'd asked if Ashley Heath would be there, too. Were she and Dr. Staples in cahoots? Yet there was also something going on between Ashley and Dr. Fry. Which side was the woman on?

But guessing did no good. The key was to let Dr. Staples believe she was buying her flimsy story, and then alert Joe. Then he could call the police so they'd have the place staked out before she got there.

Vickie clicked off, took a deep breath, and began dialing.

∞

Joe rang off Vickie's call and dialed 911, knowing that his worst fears were realized. But with Vickie's help, they could at least avert another tragedy.

He repeated the office building's address to the emergency operator and said, "Tell them to hurry. It's a life-and-death situation!" He then tried Ashley's cell phone again. In the middle of the first sentence of his message, she picked up.

"Look, I don't have time to explain," he snapped. "Angie's gone off the deep end, and if what I suspect is true, she's going to need you worse than Klaxton does.... No, I don't have time to explain. Just meet me at the office building."

He threw the phone down without waiting for a response and finished dressing.

He paused at Mrs. Caldwell's room on the way to his, but heard no sounds. *She's probably still at church,* he thought. *Just as well.* With luck, all would be resolved by the time she showed up.

Knowing he'd be late getting back, he flipped the porch light on his way out. Nothing happened. *Damn! It's out again.* He dead-bolted the front door and raced for his car.

∞

The office building was dark when Vickie drove into the parking lot, giving her an even creepier feeling. Where was Joe? He'd practically hung up on her, and she'd tried his number several times on the drive to the office. Each time, she got a busy signal.

She pulled into a spot several spaces away from the showy putty-colored Mercedes she knew belonged to Dr. Staples. The only other car in the lot, Mrs. Caldwell's old brown Subaru, was parked in the corner on the back row.

She turned off her headlights and sat for a moment in the car, remembering the night Stephanie had walked up to her at the bar of the supper club. She had tried to warn Vickie about—what? At the time, she'd thought the woman was just trying to get her away from Klaxton for selfish reasons, and she shrugged off the woman's appeals and rushed off to do her second set. By the middle of her first song, Stephanie was headed out the door. Nobody saw her alive again—except the killer.

The memory made Vickie shudder, and she looked around the parking lot. *Where's Dr. Fry? Where are the police?*

When she realized the answer to her questions, she almost laughed out loud. *Well, they'd hardly be dumb enough to reveal themselves at this point, would they? Yeah, I can just see them and Dr. Fry pulling up, lights flashing, and wandering around the parking lot. One look out the window, and Dr. Staples would know exactly what was coming*

Knowing the time had come for her to be braver than she'd ever been before, she straightened her shoulders and got out of her car.

At the building's back entrance, she saw a sliver of light at the bottom of the door. As promised, Dr. Staples had propped it open for her. She made her way down the wide hallway, passing up the elevator to take the narrow stairs up to the Staples' second-floor suite. The elevator had never stalled that she knew of, but if it did tonight, she didn't want to be in it.

The door to the Dr. Staples' office was unlocked, too; it only took slight pressure from her hand to make the French doors glide inward.

Vickie glanced around the dim room. No sign of anyone. Even so, she was suddenly overcome by the eerie, half-lit stillness and the smell of candlewax. She'd never fired a gun, never even held one in her hand. But she wished she had one now.

Maybe I should I have waited in the car for a while, she thought suddenly. *Made sure Dr. Fry and the police were really there.*

With a small shake of her head, she decided it was too late to worry about that now. *Of course they're out there, silly*, she chided herself. *This is important!*

She proceeded to the door next to the reception desk. Oddly, this door was locked.

"Dr. Staples, it's me," she said softly, tapping on the door.

A moment passed, but there was no answer. She knocked harder. "Dr. Staples? Are you there?"

Again, no one answered. She repeated the knock. "It's me, Vickie," she called, much louder this time.

She was trying to decide whether to knock again when she heard a soft voice behind her. "Looking for me, slut?"

Vickie felt a sharp pinch on her neck. Seconds later, her legs grew limp and she collapsed into darkness.

∞

Joe cursed as he tried to maneuver his SUV into the emergency lane. Other cars kept looming up behind him, also attempting to escape the unmoving line of backed-up cars on 85-North. Fuming, he pulled out sharply, floored the accelerator and generated a series of angry honks from a Ford truck looming large in his rearview mirror.

It had taken him an eternity to get this far, and best case, he still had a good ten minutes to go. *Where are the damn police?*

Another question followed, one he didn't want to face: *Why didn't I tell them what I knew before now?* That was a pointless question; he already knew why. Fear and testosterone had taken hold of his better judgment. *And the money. Always the money.* The fear of losing everything he had because he'd made a stupid decision in renting to Klaxton and Angie without a background or reference check. That's what had kept him silent for far too long.

It was too late for second-guessing, or self-blame. He tried Ashley's number again. Busy. He tried Vickie's cell number several times with no success. He dialed 911 again, and was told by the exasperated operator, "Sir, the police are on their way! Please stop tying up the lines. There's nothing more I can do until they get there."

He hit the off-button and lost all caution, veering to the right and into the exit-only lane for Piedmont Road. Let the cops stop him. He prayed they would.

Thirty-five

Ashley kept her eye on the speedometer as she drove to Joe's office. The BMW's powerful engine and deluxe shocks made ninety miles an hour seem like fifty. But getting stopped for speeding would only delay her, and she didn't want that risk. She had to get where she was headed quickly. Something was wrong. Angie was in trouble. That much she knew—and little else.

She hadn't returned Joe's calls or messages. Hadn't even listened to the messages at first because she was—what? Angry? Hurt? *A little of each*, she decided. *But mainly confused.* The attraction between them, so swift and strong, collapsed just as suddenly as it appeared. And the relief in his voice when she called that morning to cancel their plans? She'd played it off at the time, but the memory felt like a knife slicing through her. So when her phone rang and the Caller ID showed Joe's number, she let it ring and busied herself tidying the condo, sifting through armfuls of accumulated mail and designating most of it for the wastebasket.

Throughout the day, his messages grew progressively more emphatic. But, until the last one, she had no sense there was real trouble. She didn't completely understand what Joe had said, just that his voice sounded tense. If Angie was in trouble, why in the hell was she at the office? Yet Angie had been acting so strange since the fire....

From then on, time had seemed to speed up.

At least he cared enough to call me for help, she thought, and pushed the accelerator as hard as she dared. The red BMW sped into darkness.

When she pulled into the building's rear parking lot, her heart jittered at what she saw. "Damn," she muttered, and rushed to park the car in the nearest available spot.

From outside the two-story white brick structure, there was little evidence of a fire; she could see no flames or smoke from any of the building's many windows, and no structural damage. But the circle of bright red trucks in the parking lot, their headlights creating a nimbus of smoky light showing men in slickers swarming like bees, confirmed what she already knew from the smoke-smell.

She scanned the small crowd for Joe and saw him almost immediately in the floodlights, standing near his SUV about twenty yards away. She walked toward him, searching the scene as she did. In the back of the lot, past the fire trucks, she saw two cars. One was a red Volkswagen. The other, Mrs. Caldwell's battered brown car. Like the Volkswagen, it was parked behind the barricade.

Ashley wasn't worried about the housekeeper's car being there. Once, Joe had laughingly told her that Mrs. Caldwell often parked it there, and why. The memory brought a smile. And she was sure she'd seen the red Volkswagen here before, just couldn't remember who—

"No." The word came from her mouth when she saw the third vehicle, but she wasn't aware of saying it. She was too busy running toward Joe, cursing her high heels for slowing her down. *No, it can't be ...*

She raced up to Joe, who wordlessly held out his arms.

Her panic wouldn't allow her to accept his embrace, or the terror on his face "Where's Angie?" she panted. "Her car's in the parking lot. Over there in the shadows! I—I didn't see it at first."

"I … I know." Joe glanced at the red Volkswagen. "Vickie's car is over there too."

Ashley looked at all three cars, then her head whipped back to meet Joe's eyes. "But why …?"

"I wasn't able to … get to her soon enough. And I forgot Mrs. Caldwell might be here. Didn't think to warn her—"

"What? Warn who? About what? What are you talking about?"

His gut clenched like he'd been punched in the stomach. How could he tell her what he suspected about Angie? And how could he tell her what a stupid thing he'd done? That he'd set this whole thing up and promised to be there for Vickie—and that very promise had given Vickie the courage to go in alone? He put her in harm's way, and then failed her. And if Mrs. Caldwell was in there, he'd failed her too.

A female firefighter came rushing up. "Dr. Fry, I'm Lieutenant Strait. We found your receptionist. Come with me."

∞

"How is she?" Joe said, bending over the stretcher to get a closer look at Vickie's smudged face under the oxygen mask.

The lieutenant gave a reassuring smile and eased her heavy respirator off her shoulder. "I know it looks bad, but she should be okay. Smoke inhalation can do funny things to a person."

When Joe looked at Vickie again, he agreed; she did look bad. A scorched smell came from her long hair, which had partly burned off, and her face and arms showed blackened smudges. Her soot-stained clothes looked even worse. The lack of consciousness troubled him, but at least she was alive, and he saw no obvious burns.

He reached down and lifted one eyelid, then the other, instinctively took her pulse. As he had dreaded, her pupils were wide. But she was breathing all right, if slowly. She moaned when he touched her.

"She's a little out of it," Strait said. "Well, more than a little. And more than I'd expect. This whole thing is strange."

Joe swiveled his head up at her, and she explained. "It's funny ... the part you said was Dr. *Angie* Staple's office was pretty burned up. But on her husband's side, there was no fire damage at all. Everything was just trashed. Big piles of broken glass, like someone took a hatchet to a bunch of pictures and stuff. And there was nothing on any of the walls. You think there's been a burglary, too?"

"I ... I don't think so," Joe said. "Any sign of Angie Staples?"

The lieutenant shook her head. "We've gone over most of the building. If she *was* in there, she's probably not now."

With the speed of a rocket through her heart, it all came clear to Ashley. Angie's distance. The odd behavior. The candles, *so many candles!* And the fire. No, *fires.* One in New York, the recent one at the Staples home, and now here ...

"Noooooooo!"

When he saw Ashley's face, Joe bolted upright to take hold of her, but she slipped out of his grasp and took several awkward steps toward the building before collapsing to her knees.

She tried to maintain her reason by pretending that her queasy stomach had caused her knees to buckle. It didn't work. She felt Joe's strong arms lifting her, and one look into his eyes told her he already knew.

"Joe, this can't be happening," she cried out. "Where is she?"

"I don't know," he said, feeling his own tears start. "But we'll find her. We'll find her."

He held her as she grieved for her best friend.

∞

Joe saw the paramedics roll Vickie to the back of the ambulance and called to one of them, "Hey, man, a favor. When you get to the hospital, ask them to do a tox screen on her, okay?"

"Are you her doctor?"

"Ah ... yeah. Yes." Without mentioning Angie's name, Joe told him enough of his suspicions for the man to nod before he closed the ambulance door.

"Aren't you going with her?" Ashley asked. She'd stepped away so Joe could examine Vickie. Her sobs had finally abated but she was still trembling.

"No," he said, reaching out to hold her. "These people are better-equipped than I am for emergencies. She'll be fine."

"Joe ... Angie's not fine."

"I know. I know, honey."

"Drugs. Joe ... Angie mentioned she'd been taking something to help her sleep. I thought it was sleeping pills, but ... Ever since the fire, she's been acting so strange. Do you ... Do you think she'd use them to ... ?" She waved a shaking hand at the ambulance, now waiting to pull into traffic.

Joe reached out and she leaned into his arms, and another silence fell.

So much needed to be said, but not now. He couldn't face it. A barrage of conflicting feelings assailed him—relief, guilt, gratitude and sadness. Worming in and around those was the realization that his dream of financial security was gone—again. And he had let his desperate desire to protect his practice get in the way of protecting Vickie. It would be a long time and many prayers before God would forgive him. That much, he knew.

But the main thing, he told himself ... No, the *only* thing ... was to find Mrs. Caldwell, to make sure she was all right.

Still holding Ashley, Joe freed one hand and reached for his cell phone. As he did, he saw Lieutenant Strait motioning to the driver of the ambulance, now turning onto the street. The ambulance stopped, the driver rolled down the window and the lieutenant, running toward it, yelled, "Hold up! Two more inside the building. One's conscious, the elderly woman isn't."

He heard Ashley gasp, and this time, it was her arms that supported him.

When he'd seen her ancient Subaru, he allowed himself to feel relief. Made himself believe that she'd come to clean the offices, then hitched a ride with some friends to play bingo, like she often did. But now, his unimaginable fear had become truth.

∞

An unmarked vehicle screeched into the parking lot, narrowly missing two plainclothes detectives who gave it the finger as it sped by. The vehicle squealed to a stop inches from the barricade, and Detective Crowley emerged. His face held a familiar smirk. Entering the building, he brushed past the firefighter guarding the door with one terse word: "Police."

He found Joe and Ashley in a small medical lab area untouched by fire, bending over a woman crouched in the fetal position and making keening sounds. He recognized the woman, but didn't approach. As brave as he pretended to be, a crying woman made his knees quake.

"Angie?" he heard Joe say in between the high-pitched wails, "can you hear me?"

"She ... She doesn't even sound human," Ashley sobbed, kneeling by Angie and stroking her clammy forehead.

In truth, Angie looked little like the woman Ashley and Joe knew. Her hair was matted and her cheeks appeared sunken. The smoke and her crying had caused her eyes to swell almost shut.

Finally, Angie looked up at them. She didn't seem to recognize Ashley at first, but soon her eyes sparked with recognition. "I killed them, Ashley! I killed them!" As she spoke, she reached up and smacked her forehead repeatedly, then looked back to Ashley and said defiantly, "I got rid of all of *them*. Cheryl, Stephanie, and Vickie!"

When Ashley saw Crowley stride toward them with handcuffs, beaming, she knew he'd heard Angie's confession, too. She gave a shuddering sigh.

She couldn't blame the irritating smoke for the tears that poured from her eyes. She was supposed to be able to make sense of this. But everything was happening too fast for her mind to keep pace. So she did the only thing she could—she took her friend into her arms and rocked her gently. "I'm here, Angie. Don't say anything else. It's going to be okay."

Angie stared at her with drowning eyes. "They were evil, Ashley. *Evil*—"

"Angie, stop—!"

"You don't understand! I *had* to kill them. They tried to take Klaxton away from me. I couldn't let them—"

She began to wail again. When her sobs eased a bit, Crowley hovered above the two women, flashed his badge and addressed Angie. "You have the right to remain silent. Anything you say can and will be held against you...."

Thirty-six

Ashley sat shaking her head over the cup of coffee Joe had just poured for her. With every shake, another tear hit the table's surface.

They were sitting in the breakfast nook of Joe's house, which seemed strangely silent and empty without Mrs. Caldwell's presence. It was the first time they'd been alone together since Angie's arrest. When Ashley made a split-second decision to represent her friend, Joe stood by her while Crowley read Angie her rights and led her away.

"Joe, this is going to be tough," Ashley whispered, wiping another tear.

"I know," he said, and reached out to stroke her hair. Next, he picked up his spoon and tapped his cup before stirring sugar into his coffee.

Ashley tried to smile, remembering that day in his office. But Angie's arrest had shaken something loose inside of her. Like a rain-swollen stream enduring another deluge, the water welled up in her eyes and started to flood back into her throat. She could taste vomit rising, but pushed it back. She was strong; she *had* to be if she were going to help Angie. And she had to stop crying!

She forced a chuckle that sounded more like a croak. "I cried like this the day my father left. After that, I told everybody he was dead. I cried like this when the other kids teased me for being half-white. I swore I'd never tell anybody my mother was a white woman. But … I can't do that this time. I can't hide anymore. I have to help her. Wh-Why couldn't I help her before!"

After a moment, she felt his hand on her shoulder, but she couldn't stop the tears from rolling. "I … I can't remember the last time I called my mother, told her I love her. I always blamed her for Daddy leaving, so I only saw her when I had to, or when she begged me to come see her. Why do I *do* that to people? Am I really so weak that I'm not comfortable in my own skin?"

And what is it inside me, what part of my soul, makes me cut people out of my life rather than love them, flaws and all? Has my whole life been a lie? Was the strong persona I prided myself on just some sort of candy-coated hoax?

Another headshake, another tear splattering the table. "Angie's the *last* person I could've imagined doing something like this." She looked at him, her tear-stained eyes begging for understanding. "She's my best friend, and she needs me, and I don't think I can even be in the room with her!"

He looked at her untouched coffee, her trembling hands, then reached out, placed two heaping spoons of sugar and some half-and-half into the cup. She couldn't pick up the cup, so he guided it to her mouth and refused to take the cup away until she sipped from it.

She made a terrible face, but after a moment, her hands stopped trembling and her eyes seemed a bit clearer. "Thanks. I-I didn't realize how much I needed that."

"I know," he said. "I figured a little sugar wasn't a bad idea."

She nodded, but waved his hand away when he reached for the cup again. This time, she was able to pick it up herself.

"I ... I don't know what to do next. I ... I need to go see Angie, but I don't know if I—"

"Angie will be all right till you get there. Right now, you've got to take care of yourself. Get back that powerhouse attorney attitude. I've always liked that, you know."

For an instant, he saw her smile. Too soon, it disappeared.

"I know she's done some terrible things but ... She was ... She *is* my best friend. So what's the matter with me? Why am I not barging in and taking over like I always do?"

When the tears started again, his heart lurched. To keep his own tears from showing, he leaned down to pet Solly, who was napping in his doggie-bed. "I kind of know what you mean," he said. "My brain's reeling, too. But if you feel like talking, I'm here."

"How ... How did you know it was her?"

He looked away, wondering if she was ready for all he had to say. But, he had promised to help her. "Look, I know I've already talked to the police, but I kept a few things from them until I could talk to you. I got a call from Vickie in the middle of the night last night...."

Joe recounted Vickie's revelation—that Stephanie Rogers had paid her a visit at the supper club to warn her off Klaxton. And then the mysterious call from the woman who refused to identify herself but told Vickie her time was up. That Vickie thought she recognized the voice, but couldn't be sure. He told Ashley of Vickie's second call—that she was on her way to meet Angie—and that she hung up before he could tell her to stay put. With difficulty, he told her of his involvement—and then, about his failure in judgment that almost cost Vickie and Mrs. Caldwell their lives.

"It's been all over the media about the similarities in the cases," he told Ashley. "While I was waiting to hear from Vickie, I went on the Internet and pulled up some articles about the case in New York. The victim in that case had drugs in her system, and kerosene was used to start the fire. And ... candles had been used to light the kerosene."

Ashley nodded. Her PI had found out the same things.

"Suddenly, I saw it all like Technicolor," he said. "Two women Klaxton was fooling around with ... drugs ... candles ... fires. It all fit. Stephanie was on her way to confront Angie. Next thing we know, Stephanie's dead. That was the missing piece to the whole puzzle."

He looked at Ashley. "I didn't want to say anything about Angie until I was sure. I'm sorry. I ... I should have told you sooner."

"It's all right." Ashley pushed the coffee cup away. "I knew she was irrational about Klaxton, but what woman in love *isn't* about her man?" She raised her head. "Joe ... Angie and I were so alike! But I would have never done something like that. So how could the Angie I know kill two people and try to kill two others?"

Joe considered her question and gave her the best answer he could. "I guess it's like you said ... People aren't as rational when it comes to love. And security. And all the motherhood-and-apple pie stuff. Most of us go off, get mad, but don't do anything else. And others? Well, they have a different way of dealing with things."

Her nod was slow, still disbelieving. "It's one of the all-time biggest clichés, but ... it's like you said. You can't judge a book by its cover. I mean, Angie had it all—the best. Maids, private schools, not even a student loan to repay. But ... But she must have been a wreck inside, enduring all that, and never feeling like she could talk about it.

"And Klaxton." She shuddered, and fresh tears appeared in her eyes. "Do you think he's known all along that Angie did it?"

"I don't know," Joe replied, searching his memory. "I don't know what Klaxton knew, or didn't. If he did know, he went to prison rather than implicate her. But there's one thing I *do* know."

She looked up at him, expectant.

"Regardless of his infidelities, he loves her. The first day I met him ... you should have seen the way his face lit up when he talked about her."

Ashley thought a moment. "Klaxton once said to me that he was a strong black man. I didn't understand. All I could see was his womanizing." She looked away. "And maybe I was reacting to my own situation, too. To my father. To what he did to our family. I didn't want to hear the words 'strong black man' from anybody. But now ... I think I understand what Klaxton meant. I mean, he did his share of griping about being put in prison. But ... I never once saw him giving up, like my father did when he left us. I ... I've given him a really bad rap, haven't I?"

Joe reached out to pat her hand, not sure if her last statment was about Klaxton, or her father. "Like you said, we don't know everything yet." He smiled. "Talk about books and covers. Look at Mrs. Caldwell. She's an odd-looking old bird, but she probably saved Vickie's life just by delaying things until the police got there. No way could anybody have predicted that!"

She turned to him, new confusion in her face. "Does Mrs. Caldwell work at the office every night?"

Joe shook his head. "She deep-cleans twice a week—Saturday and Wednesday nights. But I forgot that sometimes, she goes in on Sunday nights instead of Saturday." He smiled. "Mrs. Caldwell's hooked on thirty or forty different TV shows, and sometimes they switch the schedule around. When she doesn't go to church, she's in front of the tube."

His face fell. "She kept warning me about Angie. Even admitted to sprinkling salt in her office to keep away the evil spirits. But I thought she was just being her usual stubborn, superstitious self. I don't know who got to the building first, Angie or Mrs. Caldwell. Probably Angie, or she would have noticed Mrs. Caldwell's car in the parking lot."

"Maybe not," Ashley said. "She was focused on setting the place up for ... for when Vickie got there."

He felt relief that Ashley had stopped crying and started thinking. "Good point. Anyway, Mrs. Caldwell heard voices upstairs, and went up there to find Angie standing over Vickie with a hypodermic in her hand. Mrs. Caldwell," he smiled, "I'd love to have seen this ... threw herself on top of Angie, knocked her out, and then called 911. The fire was already started, but the fire trucks got there before it spread too far."

Another smile, this one bigger. "So Vickie owes her life, in a funny kind of way, to my little old housekeeper."

"Who nearly died herself in the attempt," Ashley pointed out, and reached for her coffee cup with steady hands. This time, she drained it.

"Right," he sighed. "I feel guilty about that. I knew she had high blood pressure, and I fuss at her constantly about the way she eats. Do you know she still goes down to the Municipal Market and buys fatback and chitterlings? She puts 'em away. And ham hocks, and all that other delicious stuff that's so bad for you ...." He gave Ashley a grin. "Well, I make an exception for the ham hocks. But I should've known she was at risk for a stroke, and watched out better for her."

She laid her hand over his. "Hey, it's not every day she comes across a homicide in action in a burning building. What did the doctor tell you?"

"If she continues to do well, they'll move her out of ICU tomorrow. Thank God."

"Amen," Ashley agreed. She looked away, then back at him. "I have a lot more questions, but we're both so tired. I'm going to head home, and you have to promise me you'll try to get some rest." She stood, and he followed suit.

"Are you okay to drive?" he asked.

She nodded. "Yeah. It's not far."

She got her coat off the sofa where she had tossed it when they came in, then turned back to him. "One more thing."

He gave her a questioning look.

"Sometimes you *can* judge a book by its cover. Like you. You look too good to be true—but you really *are* a good man. I thank God every day for sending me you."

With a wicked smile, she put her arms around him, coat and all. When she released her embrace, he opened his mouth to say more. But she put her finger to her lips, stopping him, and left without another word.

Thirty-seven

"Stop this!" Mrs. Caldwell said when Joe opened the passenger door for her. "I can do for myself. Dr. Parsons told me I will be good as new as long as I stay away from the fatty foods." She sniffed. "However, doctors do not know everything. Good common sense is the best medicine of all."

Joe grinned at Ashley, who was removing the overnight bag from the SUV, and pushed the aluminum walker up to Mrs. Caldwell as she wedged herself out of the cab. Over her continued protests, he helped her to the front door. He looked up and noticed that the porch light was on. In broad daylight.

He resolved to have the whole porch rewired once his life returned to normal. Then he smiled, remembering. *Not that it will change a thing. Or maybe it's God's way of saying* I *need to make a change.* Get back in control of his destiny, bury the past, and let Courtney rest in peace … this time for good.

Yeah, maybe that's for the best. Looking at the past, then letting go of it had worked for Vickie. She and Mark, the bartender at the supper club who'd been mooning over her for years, had gone away together to Barbados for the weekend. Joe glanced at Ashley.

Yes, I've been looking at the past too long. Definitely need to turn around and look ahead.

He helped Mrs. Caldwell into the foyer and got her seated on the sofa. Ashley followed with the overnight bag.

"Listen to me, Mrs. Caldwell," he said, "speaking as your doctor—"

Before he could finish the sentence, she was on her feet, unwrapping herself from her vast navy all-weather coat and dropping it on the arm of the sofa.

"Excuse me, Dr. Joe," she said, and began maneuvering the walker around him toward the kitchen. "You both look like you could use a fresh cup of coffee. I would like one myself."

With that, Mrs. Caldwell was back in business.

∞

In late spring of the new year, Angie's trial started. At first, Ashley didn't think she could defend someone so close to her. But, knowing that no other attorney could champion Angie better than she could, she gained the firm's permission. Now that she was a full partner, she had more sway. They agreed, as long as another partner assisted her.

Ashley defended her client like a tiger defending its young, reasoning that Angie's crimes were the result of a mental illness. She engaged not one, but two forensic psychologists to testify in Angie's defense. Both stated that Angie suffered from dissociative identity disorder. Unable to fight back against what tormented her—first a controlling, sexually abusive father, then a cheating, deceptive husband—Angie's hidden personalities took charge.

The second doctor offered a simple explanation: "Dissociative identity disorder used to be known as irresistible impulse," he told the jury. "People with this aren't in control of their actions. Instead, they act, as the name implies, on impulse. The action can be as simple as tapping on a coffee cup to relieve stress, or biting one's nails before an exam to ease tension. Unfortunately, in this case, the impulse was far more serious.

"It is not my opinion that Dr. Staples' actions were deliberate," he continued. "Instead, they were an attempt, however tragic, to relieve her immense pain over her failing marriage and a sexually abusive childhood. Her explosive behavior brought her release." The doctor smiled at the jury. "Around here, it might be what some people call 'spells' or 'fits'."

The jury responded warmly, and Ashley felt relief.

DA Hutchins poked holes in her defense at every turn. He even argued that Angie showed intent by planting Klaxton's gun in Stephanie's car to frame him. And that because of that intent, Angie couldn't have been mentally ill. Ashley rebutted that leaving the gun behind was even more evidence of Angie's skewed mental state. In spite of his fervent prosecution, Ashley held no ill will against Hutchins. This was an expensive and high-profile case, and the DA had a job to do.

Because Stephanie was drinking heavily, she was easy prey. In one of Angie's lucid moments, she described how she'd met Stephanie at the hospital that night and forced her, at gunpoint, to drive while she sat in the backseat of Stephanie's Honda. When they arrived at Angie's house, she forced Stephanie into the basement, drugged her, then packed for the weekend trip with Klaxton. She would meet him at St. Joseph's Hospital after his rounds.

Before leaving to drive Stephanie's car back to Crawford Long Hospital and pick up her own car, she lit candles to start a slowly timed fire, the same as she'd done in New York. She had learned the trick during a chat with one of her patients' husbands—a New

York City firefighter. That chance conversation, Angie proclaimed, was fated, because the candles had always helped her burn away the pain every time her father violated her, and later, healed the imperfections in her marriage. In her skewed mind, what better method to help rid herself of the women who tried to destroy her marriage?

However horrendous it seemed, hearing these things gave Ashley some odd comfort—and a strategy to use to defend her friend.

Sometimes, Ashley wished her heart didn't ache every time she had a moment to think. But whether she wanted it or not, Angie's case was in her hands. Perhaps that was fated, too. Because of the statue of limitations, Angie's father would probably never face charges. By helping Angie now, Ashley could help her gain some small justice for what had been done to her as a child.

She was pleasantly surprised at Klaxton's loyalty. Before, she'd been appalled at his insensitivity toward his wife. Now, she seemed his only priority. There would always be things about Klaxton and Angie's relationship Ashley couldn't understand. Still, his unswerving devotion now seemed genuine.

This morning, after months of battling in and out of the courtroom, the fight was over. Before long, the jury would be back with their verdict, and the press could move to the next high-profile case. Until the jury came back, there was nothing else to do but wait.

Ashley and Klaxton took turns pacing outside the courtroom.

"What do you think her chances are, Ashley?" Klaxton said. "If they find her guilty—"

Ashley continued pacing. "Klaxton, you have to stay positive. If they find her guilty, we'll ask for the most humane outcome during the sentencing phase. They'll have to listen to us. She's sick."

That was true enough. Since her arrest, Angie kept slipping in and out of the other, murderous personalities. If it weren't for the high levels of medication the doctors prescribed, she wouldn't be in court at all.

"Even when somebody's craz … sick like Angie, they put them in prison," Klaxton said, his voice a moan. "I saw plenty of 'em at Elmira. Hell, I still can't believe the judge ruled her competent to stand trial!" His eyes welled up at the thought of his beautiful, gentle wife locked behind bars. "I've been down that road. She won't make it!"

"Klaxton, dammit, you gotta think positive!"

He calmed a bit, but his sad eyes kept their desolation, and the tears that had been building began to fall. The once youthful-looking, gregarious physician had aged markedly. His shoulders, muscular and straight before, sagged a bit now. "I should have seen it coming! I never realized she was so sick—that *we* were so sick. I … never realized how much I hurt her. I'll never forgive myself."

Ashley stopped pacing at last. "Yes, you will! You *have* to! Now that we know what's wrong, you and Angie can get help and heal together." *Unless they send her to prison, that is.*

She took a breath to forestall her own tears, then added, "Let's pray that when the jury comes in, the verdict will be in our favor."

Klaxton nodded, wiped his eyes with the back of his hand, and whispered, "May God have mercy on my baby. And give just a little of whatever He has left to me."

Thirty-eight

At mid-morning the next day, Ashley's cell phone rang; the jury was in. Now, she and Angie sat behind their heavy maplewood table and watched the jury file into their box. Klaxton was right behind them, in the front row of the spectators' section. Joe sat in the back row. As soon as he'd heard, he rushed to the courthouse, hoping that God had listened to his prayers.

After the courtroom was seated, the judge asked the jury for their verdict. Hearing that, Joe held his breath. The seconds it took for the bailiff to hand the judge the paper, him to look it over, and have it returned to the foreman seemed an eternity.

The judge turned in Angie's direction. "Will the defendant please rise?"

Angie and Ashley both rose to stand, accompanied by Ashley's partner from Johnson and Browne.

The judge addressed the jury next. "On the two counts of arson in the first degree, how do you find?"

"We, the jury, find the defendant guilty."

Dear God, Ashley thought, devastated. *Not 'guilty but mentally ill.' Just plain old 'guilty.'* Even though she'd tried to prepare for this, she felt suddenly numb from the knees down, and had to grab the edge of the table. Angie didn't react in any way.

And then, the rest of the verdicts came. For trying to murder Vickie and Mrs. Caldwell: guilty. For the murder of Stephanie Rogers: guilty.

Ashley glanced back toward Klaxton and saw the unstoppable flow of tears coming down his cheeks. Still, Angie's face showed nothing.

The judge thanked the jury for their service and released them from the courtroom. Then he instructed the officer to return Angie to custody until sentencing.

Angie's eyes were daggers as she placed her hands behind her back and the officer cuffed them. By the time she was led out of the courtroom, her face once again held no expression at all.

∞

Joe made his way to Ashley, thinking to offer any consolation he could. As he did, two officers approached her and handed her a document.

"Oh, dear God," Ashley moaned, and the papers slithered out of her hands.

Klaxton reached her in time to grab them before they hit the floor. He scanned them. Then, with a muttered oath, he handed them to Joe.

When Joe comprehended the information he'd just read—that the New York DA's Office was requesting Angie's extradition to stand trial for the murder of Cheryl Jaworski—he turned his head away. There was no need for words. They all knew Angie would be gone for a long time.

Ashley gave Klaxton's arm a squeeze and led him to a nearby chair. She talked to him for a while, then straightened up and saw

Joe looking at her. She bit her bottom lip and dropped her head. When she looked up again, her eyes met his. The need in her eyes was clear, the urgency palpable. And for the first time in years, Joe felt his heart lift.

It was all so easy to see now. Joe had pushed her away so easily before. At the time he'd been selfish, thinking only of his real-estate investment and reputation as a physician. At one point, he had even imagined that Ashley was helping to cover up Stephanie Rogers' murder.

I was wrong. Oh, God, thank You so very much for letting me be wrong!

He made his way toward her. At first, he simply stood beside her, unsure of what to do next. Then she reached out her arms. They fell into a hungry embrace, each silently vowing never to be apart again.

Epilogue

Ashley rolled up the SUV's window as the car sped toward Joe's birthplace, Fort Valley, Georgia, 130 miles south of Atlanta. Her hair, newly coiffed the night before courtesy of Trease, lifted her spirits. But she still felt anxiety at the prospect of meeting Joe's mother. After all, his mom had known Courtney from childhood. *Well, she must be wonderful if she raised this man,* Ashley reassured herself, and turned to Joe just as a yelp came from the backseat.

Joe smiled. "Sounds like Solly's as nervous as you're acting. But you don't have to be. You'll like my mom. And I can't wait to meet yours."

She returned his grin. "I'm not sure you deserve that. My mom's got a lot of baggage."

"Don't we all?" he said. "But maybe your mother's already learned what you and I have. That the key to overcoming our adversities is to just keep moving forward."

Smiling, she reached out to touch his shoulder. "Amen, brother. You can preach that anytime."

He pressed the accelerator harder, and the SUV sped faster under the bright Georgia sun.

∞

About the Author of

Irresistible Impulse

∞

Joe Lester grew up on a farm in Pulaski County, Georgia. He earned his Bachelor of Science degree from Fort Valley State University and his dental degree from Meharry Medical College School of Dentistry.

Today, Dr. Lester owns and operates a busy private dental practice near Atlanta, and renders dental treatment to troubled youth detained in the Georgia Department of Juvenile Services, where he interweaves dental services with guidance, insight and hope.

He and his wife, Kimberly, have three grown daughters and reside in Lithonia, Georgia. He speaks at various events, and both he and Kimberly are active in their church. An outdoor person who loves hunting and fishing, he spends much of his free time with his favorite and dearest diversions, his two young grandchildren. Currently, he is also working on his next novel.